SHE had closed the door and was coming slowly towards him across the book-filled room, a graceful girl in a riding-dress of apricot-colored velvet. Her head was bare, and the thick waves and curls of her dark hair showed glints of reddish-bronze where the light touched them; her eyes were of a clear amber-gold, fringed with long lashes and set beneath straight, dark brows. An unusual face, not beautiful by ordinary standards, but striking in its contrast between broad, serene forehead and the warm vitality of eyes and lips.

That was his first thought, and then his attention was caught by a brooch fastened in the creamy lace beneath her chin, and a sharp sense of shock drove everything else from his mind.

"Who are you?" he demanded, and his voice was husky and unsteady. "In God's name, tell me who you are!"

She halted before him. "You have already begun to guess, I think," she said in a whisper. "I am Elinor—your wife!"

BELOVED REBEL

✿ ✿ ✿

Sylvia Thorpe

A FAWCETT CREST BOOK • NEW YORK

BELOVED REBEL

Published by Fawcett Crest Books, CBS Publications, the
Consumer Publishing Division of CBS Inc., by arrange-
ment with the Hutchinson Publishing Group

Copyright © 1959 by J. S. Thimblethorpe

ISBN: 0-449-23607-2

Printed in the United States of America

10 9 8 7 6 5 4 3 2 1

BELOVED
REBEL

❖ ❖ ❖

THE PROLOGUE

September, 1680

THE marriage-ceremony had taken place in the beautiful private chapel which was all that remained of the original buildings of Fairwood Priory, and when it was over, the bridal party walked back through the formal gardens and across the wide lawns to the handsome Tudor mansion where the wedding-feast awaited them. Since the chapel was small, only the immediate family of bride and groom, and a few very important guests, had witnessed the actual ceremony, but the great hall of the mansion itself could scarcely accommodate all those who had been bidden to the banquet, for this was the wedding of the heir of Fairwood, and must be celebrated with suitable magnificence.

Seated between her newly-made husband and Sir William Ashbourne, his grandfather, the bride moved wearily in her chair and stifled a sigh. The sumptuous meal seemed interminable, and she felt overpowered by her surroundings and cut off from all that was comfortable and familiar. She wished with all her heart that the wedding could have taken place, according to custom, at her own home, but her father's house in Taunton was twenty miles away, and Sir William's age and infirmity prevented him from leaving the Priory. Nor would he have considered, even for a moment, any suggestion that he need not be present at the marriage of his heir.

Elinor stole a timid upward glance at him as he sat beside her. She was secretly terrified of the gaunt old man with his stern, bearded hawk-face, his one fierce blue eye and the black patch which covered the empty socket of the other, lost nearly forty years before at the battle of Edgehill. She could only be thankful that she was at present seated on his blind side and so safe from his cold, piercing regard. Reassured of this, she turned her own gaze to her bridegroom.

Gervase Ashbourne was in his twenty-third year, a tall, lean young man in whose aquiline features could already be traced a close resemblance to his redoubtable grandfather. His rich bridal attire became him well, and he bore himself with the quiet assurance befitting a soldier and a courtier. Although negotiations for their marriage had been in train for nearly a year, this was Elinor's first meeting with him, and, dazzled and fascinated though she was, it was inevitable that he should seem a somewhat awe-inspiring personage to a bride whose thirteenth birthday was barely six weeks behind her.

He sat now with one hand supporting his chin and the other toying idly with the stem of a glass, staring straight before him and totally oblivious of the little girl who watched him with such wistful, wondering eyes. Elinor sighed again. No doubt he was sadly disappointed in her, for she knew that she was small for her age and not particularly pretty, so that the magnificent wedding-gown made her look and feel like a stiff little doll incongruously decked in silks and laces and pearls. If only, she thought enviously, she were more like Priscilla Ashbourne, Sir William's ward, who had been the chief of her bridesmaidens, and who was blue-eyed and golden-haired like a princess in a fairy-tale. Priscilla was only distantly related to the Somerset Ashbournes, but Sir William had taken her in when the great plague swept away the rest of her family, and for fifteen of her sixteen years she had lived at the Priory.

The banquet was over at last, and the guests rising to their feet. Hubert Ashbourne, Gervase's younger brother, hastened dutifully to his grandfather's side, and the bridegroom became aware of his bride at last. With grave courtesy he bowed and offered her his arm, she set a timid hand upon it, and together they passed through the smiling crowd and out on to the terrace on the south-west side of the house. Sir William followed slowly, leaning on Hubert's shoulder and pausing now and then to speak to one or other of his guests, and by degrees the rest of the company drifted after him. There would be dancing presently in the hall, when the scurrying servants had cleared the tables and the remains of the feast from the great apartment, but for the moment most of those present were content to stroll quietly on the terrace, or to gather in laughing, chattering groups, enjoying the warm September sunshine.

Elinor found herself in a group composed of Gervase, his grandfather, her own father, and several more middle-aged or elderly gentlemen, and looked wistfully along the terrace to where Priscilla was the centre of a gay cluster of young people. She would have liked very much to join her, but could not summon up the courage to do so alone, and Gervase appeared to be absorbed in the conversation of his elders. It might not be considered proper, she reflected dubiously, for her to leave the bridegroom's side, no matter how dull the company he had chosen, and on this day of all days it was of supreme importance not to deviate by a fraction from correct behaviour. She must remember that she was no longer merely Nell Dane, daughter of the richest merchant in Taunton, but Elinor Ashbourne, with all that that implied of dignity and tradition.

The conversation of the men about her had turned to politics, and to the visit to the West Country that summer of the Duke of Monmouth, the King's eldest son. Elinor felt a faint stirring of interest. She had had the good fortune to be presented to the Duke, and had thought him the most fascinating person she had ever met—until she was introduced for the first time to her husband.

"How much truth, I wonder, is there in the rumour that the Duke sees himself as successor to His Majesty?" one of the gentlemen remarked, and Sir William gave a short, contemptuous laugh.

"More truth, my friend, than there is in the tale of a secret marriage between his mother and the King," he said bluntly. "This talk of a black box and the documents it is supposed to contain is no more than a clumsy attempt to convince the common people that Monmouth is His Majesty's lawful son. The King himself has exposed that plot for what it is worth."

"Maybe, Sir William, but better a Protestant, say I, be he bastard or no, than a Papist who will bring us under the heel of Rome!" It was Thomas Dane who spoke, the sturdy merchant who, in spite of the ambition which had prompted him to ally his family with that of the staunchly Royalist Ashbournes, could not, even on his daughter's wedding-day, refrain from voicing the opinions which were held by so many of his class. "The people have heard too much of damnable Popish plots to accept calmly the prospect of a Catholic king."

There was a general murmur of agreement. It was two years now since Titus Oates had launched his first wild disclosures of a plot to kill King Charles, massacre Protestants wholesale, and convert the kingdom to the Romish faith, but the tide of terror had not yet subsided. Conceived and fostered by those who sought to exclude the Catholic Duke of York from the throne, it had swept through the country with the irresistible force of a forest fire, spreading from a small and improbable beginning to menace the highest in the land, costing many lives, discrediting the Lord Treasurer, the Earl of Danby, and threatening even the Queen herself. In the minds of most people, fear of the Catholics was inextricably bound up with fear of France, England's old enemy who was now waxing increasingly powerful, and beneath the goad of that double threat, fear had swelled to panic which expressed itself in a blind, destructive hatred.

"The Duke of York is the lawful heir," Sir William said stubbornly, "and the King is firm in support of his brother. As long as His Majesty remains adamant, all attempts to exclude the Duke from the succession must surely fail."

"Yet 'tis said that His Majesty's love for Monmouth is very great," the first speaker replied, and another added dubiously:

"It is also said that in his heart the King himself

leans towards the Catholic faith. In truth, so many and conflicting are the rumours we hear that a man knows not what to believe!"

"One thing, Sir John, you may believe, and that is the ruthless greed of Louis of France," Dane retorted explosively, "for that stands proven before all the world! France is a Catholic nation and the traditional enemy of England. Was not my Lord Danby found guilty of taking bribes from King Louis, and is not the King's chief mistress both a Frenchwoman and a Catholic? By God, sir! this country has sore need of a Protestant champion."

"No one denies that, my friend, but I doubt if 'twill find him in the Duke of Monmouth," Sir William replied dryly. "What right, after all, has he to the throne? No more, save that he is the elder, than a son of that same Frenchwoman, the Duchess of Portsmouth, or of the Duchess of Cleveland, or even of Madam Gwynne, the actress? No, no! England has not yet come to the pass where she must offer her crown to one whose claim to it is so slight!"

Elinor looked anxiously at her father. He was becoming heated, his always florid complexion deepening to crimson and his jaw thrusting itself aggressively forward as he glared up from his lesser height at Ashbourne's sardonic, high-bred countenance.

"The time may come, Sir William, when England will realize that a man's religion is of more importance than his birth!" he declared truculently. "Aye, when she is writhing under all the horrors of Popery, which, as my Lord Shaftesbury has so truly said, goes ever hand in hand with slavery!"

"If that day comes, sir, I have no doubt that she will

look for her salvation to one who has not only shown himself a staunch and able champion of Protestantism, but who has a legitimate claim to the throne. I refer, of course, to William of Orange, nephew of the King and husband of the Princess Mary."

Mr. Dane brushed William of Orange aside with a scornful wave of his hand. "A stranger, sir, a foreigner! Englishmen will demand an English king." Another murmur from those about him approved the declaration, and the stout merchant nodded portentously. "One thing at least is certain. If His Grace of Monmouth looks to Somerset for support, he will not look in vain."

"His Grace, I am sure, would be gratified to hear it," Ashbourne replied ironically, "since there is small doubt that his late progress through the West was made to try the temper of the people. The fact remains, however, that in spite of Monmouth's popularity, and the love His Majesty bears him, the Duke of York is still the lawful heir, and after him, unless the Duchess bears a son, comes his daughter, the Princess of Orange."

Thomas Dane shrugged his broad shoulders. "There are those who would like to see Monmouth on the throne when his father dies, and there are those whose hopes centre on Prince William," he said ponderously, "but both parties are at one in abhorrence of Popery and in wishing to see the Duke of York excluded from the succession. God grant that wish be fulfilled, say I!" He turned suddenly to Gervase. "You are silent, lad, yet you have closer knowledge of these matters than we who dwell so far from London! What say you?"

There was a brief, significant pause. Gervase was by

far the youngest man in the group, yet all waited eagerly to hear his reply. He was something of an unknown quantity to most of them, for Sir William had taken him to London at the age of fifteen to establish him at Court, and since that time his visits to Somerset had been few and fleeting. He had frequented Whitehall, and served with Monmouth in the Low Countries and in Scotland, so it was to be supposed that he could speak with some authority on the subject now under discussion.

Yet for a moment he seemed reluctant to do so. Until Dane's question had been flung at him point-blank he had taken no part in the conversation, and now, before he replied, he shot a swift glance at his grandfather. The look which Sir William gave him in return was unreadable, and after a few seconds Gervase said quietly: "It is true, sir, that His Majesty loves the Duke of Monmouth very dearly, and it is equally true that there is a considerable faction which would like to see Monmouth named as the lawful heir, but who can tell whether or not that wish will be fulfilled? As for the Duke himself, I know him for a brave man and an able soldier, but what hopes for the future he may or may not harbour, I am not sufficiently honoured with his confidence to say."

Some of the gentlemen looked disappointed, for this told them no more than they already knew, but a smile of grim approval touched Sir William's lips.

"You have learned a measure of diplomacy, if nothing else, in the years you have been away," he said sardonically, "and you remind us that such talk as we have been indulging in is indiscreet, and may even be dangerous. Come, gentlemen, let us turn to homelier matters! These weighty subjects have no place at a wedding, and it is an ill thing when our children must needs teach us discretion. Gervase, take your bride in search of sprightlier company. I'll warrant she has had a surfeit of old men's talk."

This was pleasantly said, with a kindly glance at Elinor, but it was none the less a command. Once again Gervase offered his arm, and as they moved away along the terrace, Elinor, who had listened intently to the conversation, said shyly: "I have seen the Duke of Monmouth, and spoken with him, too. My father took me to the great assembly at Hinton St. George, and when I made my curtsy to the Duke, someone told him that I was betrothed to you. He said that you and he were old comrades-in-arms and asked when we were to be married. I told him September, and he kissed me and wished us well, and said that he would have liked to dance at our wedding."

"Aye, and so he would, had affairs not demanded his return to London," Gervase replied carelessly. "That would have pleased you, would it not?"

"Oh, yes, indeed, for he was so kind and handsome and gay. Besides, it would be pleasant, in years to come, to be able to say that the King's son was a guest at my wedding."

The artless words drew a faint smile from him, but did not dispel the air of preoccupation he had worn all day. He said lightly: "I see that I must regard His Grace as a rival, and how can I hope to prevail against him? He wins hearts wherever he goes."

Elinor's cheeks burned and she hung her head, for if she had lost her childish heart it was not to the Duke of Monmouth, King's son though he was, and she dreaded that Gervase might guess that fact. She was spared the necessity of a reply, however, for at that moment they reached the crowd of young people at the end of the terrace, who welcomed them with jests and laughter.

"In truth, Gervase, we were about to come and carry the bride off by main force," Hubert declared cheerfully, "for I swear the company you had chosen was not to her taste! Why, man, this is a time for gaiety, and not for grave discussions with your elders!"

Elinor smiled gratefully at him, for she liked Hubert immensely. Ever since her arrival at the Priory two days before he had spared no effort to make her feel at home, for he seemed to understand how lost and frightened she felt amid all this unaccustomed grandeur. In looks he bore little resemblance to his grandfather and brother, for he was slightly built and only moderately tall, with a sensitive face, and brown eyes instead of piercing blue. He was not strong, and this was generally accepted as the cause of his remaining at Fairwood instead of endeavouring to make his own way in the world as his brother had done.

Priscilla was regarding her new kinswoman with a decidedly critical eye, and Elinor felt, not for the first time, that Miss Ashbourne disliked her. This was disappointing, for, lacking brothers and sisters of her own, Elinor had looked forward to acquiring, through marriage, relatives of her own generation. Priscilla, it seemed, found the prospect less enchanting.

"How hot your cheeks are, Elinor," she said unkindly now, and glanced up archly at Gervase. "What can you have been saying to the child, cousin, so to put her to the blush?"

The attention of everyone within earshot having been thus drawn to her confusion, Elinor blushed more hotly than before and looked imploringly at Gervase. He was frowning slightly, but he made no reply, and for an instant there was an indefinable tension in the atmosphere. As though aware of it, Hubert said easily: "Whatever the cause, 'tis vastly becoming. You should endeavour to cultivate so pretty an accomplishment yourself, Priscilla."

There was more laughter, and one or two teasing remarks at Miss Ashbourne's expense, and the momentary awkwardness passed so swiftly that it might never have been. Priscilla directed one flashing glance at Hubert and then turned her back upon him, but her cousin was so accustomed to her tantrums that he was impervious to them, and paid no heed whatsoever.

After a while, music sounded from the hall, and Gervase led his bride in to open the dance. Elinor loved dancing and she had been well taught, and once her initial nervousness had passed she was able to enjoy herself wholeheartedly for the first time that day. Now the revels began in earnest, and though Sir William and the elder members of the company were content to be mere onlookers, everyone else flung themselves joyously into the dancing. Sunset was succeeded by dusk and then by darkness, but in the candle-lighted hall the celebrations continued with unabated jollity, the musicians in their gallery playing tirelessly while the gaily-clad throng below laughed and danced and flirted in time-honoured fashion.

As the evening advanced and the wine continued to flow freely, the gaiety became a trifle boisterous, and Elinor, retiring breathless from the dance, discovered

that the costly lace on her gown was torn. She looked
about her for Priscilla, intending to ask her help in pin-
ning up the torn flounce, and discovered her on the
other side of the room. She started towards her, but
was delayed by the necessity of skirting the throng of
dancers, and before she could reach Priscilla the other
girl had turned away and disappeared through a doorway close by. There was something almost furtive
about that unobtrusive withdrawal, and Elinor hesitated for a moment or two; but since the lace must be
pinned if it were not to be damaged beyond repair, and
she was too shy to seek the aid of any of the other
ladies, she quietly followed Priscilla through the doorway.

The room beyond was empty, and she paused in
perplexity for a few seconds before discovering a second door, half hidden by a curtain of heavy tapestry.
She slipped through it, and found herself in a corridor
where the sound of music penetrated but faintly, and
the only light came from a half-open door at the farther end. Elinor was halfway to it when she realized
that the sound of weeping was coming from the room
beyond.

She halted in dismay, wondering whether to turn
back, but then it occurred to her that Priscilla, if
indeed it were she who wept so bitterly, might be in
need of help, and she tiptoed resolutely forward. She
had almost reached the door when a man's voice spoke
within the room to halt her again in shocked, incredulous surprise.

"My love, my dearest love, don't cry!" There was
pain as well as entreaty in the low, urgent tone. "Your

courage has been so great thus far. Do not let it fail you now!"

"I cannot go on pretending!" Priscilla's voice was despairing, broken with sobs. "Oh, Gervase, why? What have we done that we should suffer so?"

"When did suffering ever demand a reason?" Gervase said bitterly. "This marriage had to be—you know that! It was all settled before ever I returned from Scotland. My wishes were not even consulted."

"You could have refused," Priscilla retorted tearfully. "Oh, why did you not, when we found that we loved one another? You are a grown man, and Sir William could not have forced you to it."

Elinor heard Gervase sigh, deeply and wearily, as though this was but repetition of arguments used before.

"But you are still his ward, sweetheart, and he would never have given his consent to our marriage. If 'twere not Elinor, it would be some other heiress, for I must have wealth if Fairwood is to survive."

"Fairwood!" There was a vicious undertone now in Priscilla's voice. "That is the only thing Sir William cares for in this world, and sometimes I think that you are as besotted as he. What is Fairwood, after all, but land and houses, earth and wood and stone? Why should our happiness be sacrificed to these cold, lifeless things? If he is in need of money, let him sell some part of the estate."

"That he will never do," Gervase replied sternly. "Nor, God aiding me, will I! For six generations our family has held this land, nor suffered a single acre of it to pass into other hands, save only during the Commonwealth when a damned Parliamentarian sat in my grandfather's place. God's light, Priscilla! how can you have lived here all your life and yet not understand the ties which bind us to this place? Think how they fought for it throughout the late wars, my grandfather and his sons! Then when the King came into his own at last there was another struggle before Fairwood was ours again, and ever since there has been a fight of yet another kind to save it from slow decay. The wars, and years of neglect by strangers, have drained our fortune to the dregs. Money is the very life-blood of an estate, and money Thomas Dane has in plenty. I could not refuse his daughter's hand! I am the heir, and I have a duty to my inheritance."

"Sir William has trained you well, has he not?" Priscilla was no longer weeping, and her voice was sullen. "Duty, and Fairwood—that is all that matters! But these things mean nothing to me. I only know I love you, and that though you say you love me, you have let our hope of happiness slip by."

"There was no hope, Priscilla. Happiness was beyond our reach even before we realized where it lay."

"It is all Sir William's doing," Priscilla said drearily. "He suspects the truth, I am sure, but he does not care what pain we suffer as long as his plans go smoothly. I begged him not to make me act as bridesmaiden today, but he would not listen. It was a cruel thing to do, to make me dance attendance on the woman who has taken you from me." Her voice sharpened with sudden spitefulness. "Woman, did I say? No, an awkward, tongue-tied brat more fitted to marry one of her father's apprentices than an Ashbourne of Fairwood!"

"Elinor is not to be blamed for our plight," Gervase said quietly. "She, poor child, is more to be pitied than anyone. Our need, and her father's ambition, have between them placed her whole future in pawn. God grant she does not come too bitterly to regret this day!"

"What of our future?" Priscilla asked petulantly. "What regret can she know to match with ours?" Her voice broke again. "Gervase, I cannot bear it! I cannot go back, and dance and laugh when my heart is near to breaking."

"Sweetheart, you must! If anyone were to guess the truth there would be such a flood of gossip that we should all suffer. Come, let me dry your tears! 'Tis hard, I know, but have courage just a little longer. In a day or two these damned festivities will be over. Elinor will go back to her schoolroom, and I to London, and you will find a measure of peace again."

"To London!" she repeated in a tone of blank dismay. "But when will you return?"

There was a pause. In the darkness outside the door, Elinor stood rigid, her hands clenched tightly on the heavy silken folds of her skirt. She was trembling from head to foot, but a dreadful fascination held her rooted there while every word she heard struck a fresh blow at her world, which had seemed so bright and happy a few short minutes before.

There was movement inside the room, and Gervase came slowly into her range of vision and stood gripping the tall carved back of a chair. In the candle-light his face looked strained and very pale. After what seemed a long time he said in a low, resolute voice: "In two or three years' time, when Elinor is old enough to be my wife in more than name." Priscilla uttered a gasping, inarticulate protest, and he looked up at last. "My love, it is the only way! Do you think I could stay here, in the same house with you, knowing that you are beyond my reach for ever? It would not be possible! However strong our resolve, the time would come when our desire for each other would prove even stronger. I must go, for your sake and for hers." He paused, but she made no reply, and after a moment he added wearily: "Time is a great healer, Priscilla, and life must go on. You, too, will marry, and you will be happy. Try to believe that."

"No, Gervase, no!" With a rustle of silk she stumbled across the space between them and flung herself into his arms, clinging to him desperately. "Take me with you to London! I do not care that you cannot marry me. I want only to be with you." She broke off, gazing up into his face, reading there an unyielding denial of her wild entreaty, and then with a sob of despair buried her own face against his chest.

Elinor could endure no more. She turned and fled back along the corridor, neither knowing nor caring whether or not they heard her. She did not stop until she reached the hall, where, blinded by tears, she ran full tilt into someone who caught her by the shoulders and held her fast.

"Why such haste, little sister?" It was Hubert's voice, bantering at first, then changing to quick concern as he saw her tears. "What is it, child? Why are you weeping?"

Elinor stared up at him, struggling for control, for

some answer to his question, and said the first thing that came into her head. "I have torn my dress."

Hubert's face cleared, and he laughed with undisguised relief. Had she been older and less distressed she might have wondered at the measure of anxiety which for a second or two had darkened his eyes.

"Is that so great a tragedy? We will find someone to set it to rights, and then you must dance with me again." He put an arm about her and led her along the edge of the room, away from the place where his grandfather was seated. "We cannot have tears at a wedding-feast, least of all from the bride herself!"

Sir William, established in his great chair by the hearth, and momentarily deserted by his guests, was watching the dancers while memory carried him back to his own marriage-feast in this same hall more than fifty years before. His bride had been a girl of birth and fortune—no other match would have been permitted—but it was a love-match none the less, and had remained so, through good times and ill, until the day of her death. She had borne him five sons and three daughters, and seen them all precede her to the grave, and died herself just three months before he regained possession of Fairwood after the long years of poverty and exile. Her death, coming at such a time, was a blow from which he had never wholly recovered, and it was a lonely and embittered old man who returned to the Priory with the only surviving members of his once numerous family. These were the widow of his youngest son and her two children, sturdy, three-year-old Gervase, and the frail babe she had borne six weeks after her husband's sudden death.

In these two children, and more particularly in Gervase, all Sir William's hopes and dreams were centred. War and defeat and exile had greatly depleted the Ashbourne fortune, as they had depleted that of so many Royalist families, but where the education of the heir was concerned, no expense was spared. In 1673, despite his age and increasing feebleness, Sir William had made the long and difficult journey to London to establish the boy in the household of a kinsman who held a minor place at Court, and returned to Somerset only when he was certain that Gervase no longer needed his encouragement and support. His hopes of the lad's success were amply fulfilled, but the life of Court and camp was a costly one, and the brilliant marriage Sir William would have liked for his grandson did not materialise.

Nothing daunted, the old man began to look about him nearer home, and so discovered Thomas Dane, with his aspirations to gentility, his motherless only daughter, and his great fortune amassed from the weaving trade which flourished in Taunton Dene. Negotiations were begun, and now, a little more than a year later, Gervase and his child-bride were safely wed, and the financial security of Fairwood was assured.

Looking about him, Sir William saw Elinor being led into the dance by his younger grandson, and studied her with secret approval. He was pleased with the child, though he contrived not to show it. There was intelligence there, and character, and her father's drive and shrewdness tempered by a refinement inherited from her mother, who had come of a good though impoverished family. Some years must necessarily elapse before she could take her place as mistress of Fairwood, but Sir William intended that a good deal of that time should be spent at the Priory; he meant to mould the latent character he sensed in her, and fit her for the place she had been called upon to fill.

From Elinor, his gaze passed to Hubert, and a faint frown creased his brow. Now that the future of Gervase and of Fairwood was secure, he must be thinking of a match for him. Sir William had at one time considered a marriage between Hubert and Priscilla, but lately it had become clear that this would not be satisfactory. The boy was too gentle, too sensitive; Priscilla was foolish and flighty, and needed a stronger hand than her cousin's to curb her wilfulness.

The frown deepened as his thoughts turned to his ward. There was very little that escaped him, and he was well aware of the infatuation which had sprung up between Priscilla and Gervase during the past few weeks. This had been their first meeting for several years, and Sir William was not greatly surprised that Gervase should lose his head over the cousin who had grown to such beauty during his absence. Yet though he might view their infatuation with a slightly contemptuous tolerance, he had no intention of permitting it to interfere with his own careful plans. It was a midsummer madness which would quickly pass; Gervase would be going back to London soon, and his grandfather would see to it that before he returned to Fairwood, Priscilla was safely established in a home of her own.

So Sir William watched the merry wedding-guests, and dwelt with satisfaction upon all he had achieved for the good of his family and the future security of the estate he so greatly loved. But the little bride was dancing with a heart as heavy as her feet were light, while the bridegroom, who had returned unobtrusively to the hall, leaned against one of the carved pillars of the minstrels' gallery and regarded the animated scene before him with sombre, brooding eyes.

1

Rebel-in-Arms

DARKNESS was beginning to fall at last. Sunset was but
a lingering memory of rose and gold in the western
sky, and the first stars glimmered in the deepening blue
above. Gervase could see one shining diamond-bright
through an opening in the leaves which sheltered his
hiding-place, and through weariness and sick despair
realized that an end was coming at last to the longest
day of his life.

He was fortunate in being alive to see that nightfall.
Less than twenty-four hours ago the Duke of Monmouth—King Monmouth, as they had called him since
Ferguson proclaimed him King in Taunton market-
place—had led his rebel army out of Bridgewater in an
attempt to take by surprise the Royal forces under
Feversham, encamped on Sedgemoor. It was a bold
move, and had it succeeded the heir of Fairwood
would not now be a hunted fugitive, but ill-luck and
ill-management, the twin curses which had dogged the
enterprise all along, had between them brought it to
naught. The guide had indeed led them, at about one
in the morning, to the outskirts of Feversham's camp,
but the alarm had been prematurely given, and a wide,
deep ditch, one of several which drained the moor, lay

between the two opposing armies and prevented the sudden, swift onslaught which was the rebels' only hope of prevailing. Against the steadiness of the regular troops, and their overwhelming superiority of weapons and artillery, Monmouth's untrained, inadequately armed peasantry could match nothing but courage and determination. They sold their lives dearly, but morning revealed a scene of carnage from which the shattered remnants of the rebel army were fleeing in all directions, ruthlessly pursued by the victorious soldiers of King James.

Gervase had been one of those—the number was not large—fortunate enough to evade that merciless pursuit. How long his immunity would last he could not tell, nor, for the present, did he greatly care, and if a whole company of Royal troops had suddenly appeared before him he could not have summoned up the strength to defend himself. The night-march, the battle itself, and the day-long flight, first mounted and then on foot, had taxed his endurance to the uttermost. He had had the luck to escape any serious injury, but he had sustained one or two minor hurts, and the combined effect of these had drained his strength yet further.

When defeat became certain, and those who could fled from the stricken battlefield, Gervase had turned instinctively towards Fairwood, the one place which might afford him temporary shelter and the means to attempt escape, but again and again he had been forced to turn aside to avoid capture. Now he had no very clear idea in which direction his home lay. His horse had foundered hours before, and after that he had struggled on on foot, until the approach of evening and his own exhaustion forced him to seek a hiding-place.

He had stumbled upon one by chance. He had been making his way, in the shelter of a hedge, along the edge of a field of standing corn. The sun was setting, its level beams dazzling and blinding him, and the cornfield seemed to stretch on endlessly so that he moved in a kind of nightmare in which the most stupendous efforts failed to carry him any closer to safety. Then suddenly the field ended, and he was looking through a straggling hedge at a narrow, winding lane with a high stone wall beyond it, and above the wall the boughs of thick-clustering trees. It had taken the last of his strength to cross the lane and surmount the wall, and from its summit he caught a glimpse between the branches of a neglected garden and the distant gables of a house. Then he dropped down on its inner side and crawled into a dense patch of undergrowth, where thick foliage and closely entwined branches offered at least an illusion of shelter.

For a while he lay there in a stupor of exhaustion, unaware of the passing of time, and when he again became conscious of his surroundings the light had faded, and the bright eye of a star was looking down at him through the leaves. He lay still, staring at it, and confused thoughts drifted hazily through his mind while his body took the rest it so sorely needed.

The rebellion was over, had ended in disastrous, crushing defeat, and Monmouth was now, like Gervase himself, a hunted fugitive, if, indeed, he had not already been captured. Those of his followers who had survived this day were in like case, and upon those taken, whether of high degree or low, a summary vengeance would be wrought. King James was secure on the throne to which he had succeeded on his brother's death four months ago, and in Holland, William of Orange kept his own counsel and bided his time.

Gervase had few illusions about his own prospect of escape. If he could reach Fairwood undetected there might be a chance, but between him and Priory lay miles of country thick with Royal troops and militia. Nor was it entirely certain that he would be well received at his home even if he succeeded in reaching it, for relations between him and his grandfather had become strained of recent years, and Fairwood had held sternly aloof from the rebellion, contributing neither men nor money to Monmouth's cause. Sir William had never made any secret of his opinion of Monmouth's pretensions, and Gervase's stubborn adherence to the Duke was largely responsible for the rift between them.

Largely, but not entirely. Gervase knew only too well where the real root of the trouble lay, for since his departure from Fairwood at the close of the festivities which marked his marriage to Elinor Dane, he had not returned to Somerset until his arrival there from Holland as a rebel-in-arms. Nor had he, since that time, seen either his wife, or any member of his family.

At first a regular correspondence had passed between them, and from his grandfather's letters, and Hubert's, he was kept informed of events at home. He heard of Priscilla's marriage, some eight months after his own, to Geoffrey Marsham, a neighbouring squire, and knew that the barriers between them were doubled now. Knew, too, as certainly as though he had been there to see it, that her marriage was as much a matter of expediency, and of Sir William's contriving, as his own had been.

A year later had come the news of Thomas Dane's death, and the information that, again at Sir William's command, the house in Taunton had been sold and Elinor brought to live at the Priory. She was now nearly fifteen, and Sir William began to hint that it was time his grandson returned to Somerset. When Gervase ignored the hints, they became suggestions which grew stronger as time passed, and which culminated eventually in an outright command; but by this time it was the spring of 1683, and Gervase, who had been drawn deeper and ever deeper into the political conspiracies of the day, replied respectfully but with finality that it was impossible for him to leave London at present. His grandfather had not written again, and when in June of that year the whole country was thrown into a state of uproar by the discovery of the Rye House plot, Gervase, in common with many other prominent Whigs and known adherents of Monmouth, found it prudent to retreat to Holland. Since that time, no communication of any sort had passed between him and his family.

He had always intended to go back to Fairwood one day, but now it seemed that he might have delayed too long. The thought engendered in his mind a profound regret, for though of late years he had seen little of the place, his childhood there had been a happy one, and his attachment to his grandfather and brother was deep and strong. Now that he was in Somerset again, and within so short a distance of his home, the bonds of family affection were making themselves felt more potently than they had done for years, in spite, or perhaps because of, his present peril.

Nor were these the only voices calling him home. When he had first returned to London after his marriage, he had forced himself not to think of Priscilla, and if this was hard, there were distractions enough at King Charles's Court to teach him forgetfulness. A certain idealistic strain in his character which had saved him then from the grosser follies of his contemporaries had at the same time turned him to intrigues of a political nature, until he became absorbed in the idea of preserving England from Catholic domination, and devoted himself to that end with a single-mindedness which helped him to forget his personal tragedy. Now, however, when the cause he served had gone down in ruin and defeat, the memory of Priscilla again took possession of his mind.

In vain he reminded himself that she had been four years married, and had probably forgotten him in the busy round of caring for her household and her family. The knowledge could no more banish her image from his thoughts than could the remembrance of his own marriage, for Elinor was no more than a name to him, a shadowy, unreal figure whose features, even, he could not recall. Priscilla and Fairwood—that was the only reality! Together they seemed to symbolise all he had ever known of happiness, all that was left of safety and sanity in a shattered world.

He was yielding to an overmastering desire for sleep, and had reached that point where thoughts become confused with dreams. He seemed to be standing again on the terrace at Fairwood, among his wedding-guests, but instead of bridal finery he was clad in the battle-stained habit of a soldier, and when he looked beyond the balustrade he saw, not familiar gardens and parkland, but the stricken field of Sedgemoor. Then the company about him vanished, and in their place were red-coated troopers advancing from all sides to take him. He turned to seek safety in the house, but his way was barred by Priscilla; she looked at him with the cold eyes of a stranger, and he had no power to move her from his path.

He woke with a start, bathed in a cold sweat, and knew a momentary relief at finding himself still safe among the bushes under the darkening sky. For a few seconds he lay motionless, trying to shake off the ugly memory of his dream, and then he became aware of a curious agitation among the foliage to his right. Someone, or something, was forcing its way through the undergrowth towards him.

Dream and weariness alike were overwhelmed by a primitive instinct of self-preservation. He raised himself on one elbow, staring in the direction of the sound, but though the bushes continued to shake and quiver he could see nothing. Very quietly he rose to one knee and drew his sword and so waited, ready for instant action as soon as the mysterious presence disclosed itself.

The leaves gave a final, violent shake and the cause of the disturbance struggled into the more open space where Gervase had concealed himself. It was a little, glossy-coated spaniel, hardly more than a puppy, its soft fur and long, silky ears sprinkled with dead leaves and scraps of twig collected on its hindquarters still hidden in the bushes, bright, inquisitive eyes regarding Gervase, and then it gave vent to its excitement at this remarkable discovery, in high-pitched, frenzied yelping.

Gervase remained where he was, held motionless by dismay yet conscious all the while of the irony of the situation. More than once during the day he had evaded capture by a hair's-breadth, and now, when he had thought himself safe for a few hours, he was betrayed by the antics of a half-grown puppy. The dog was obviously a household pet, and the commotion it was causing was certain to attract the attention of its owners. His sword was still in his hand, but even if he could have brought himself to use it on the little animal, the sudden cessation of its barking would arouse even more suspicion than its continuance.

A moment later his fears were realized. The spaniel fell silent for a few seconds, and in the pause he heard a woman's voice somewhere close at hand, apparently calling to the dog.

"Duchess! Duchess, where are you? Come here to me this instant!"

Duchess showed no inclination to obey, but greeted the summons with an even more hysterical outburst. In the hope of driving her out of the bushes, Gervase waved his free hand vigorously, with the result that she wriggled free of the undergrowth, seized his sleeve in her jaws and shook it energetically, growling all the while.

The woman's voice called again, closer this time and from a different direction, and he realized that she, too, was approaching his hiding-place. Discovery, then, was inevitable, and he would not see Fairwood again. He made no further attempt at concealment or defence, but stayed where he was, looking resignedly down at the innocent cause of his betrayal, still playfully worrying his sleeve.

Apparently the dog's mistress had chosen to enter the clump of bushes at a point where access was easier than at the place he had chosen for his entry. He could hear the rustle of the leaves as she approached, and her voice saying sternly: "Duchess, what ails you this night? What have you found here? If it is—" the words ended in a choking gasp as she parted the last screen of leaves, and saw in the fading light the kneeling man and the faint glimmer of the long sword-blade. He expected her to scream, but after only an instant's pause she said urgently: "Please, please do not hurt my dog! I will make her be silent, but do not harm her!"

Her voice was breathless and shaking, but even so he was astonished at her self-command. Letting fall the sword, he took the little dog by the scruff of its neck and held it out to its owner, saying simply: "I will not harm her, madam, nor have you anything to fear from me. I entered your garden only in search of rest and concealment."

She took the puppy from him, and so for a space they remained, she clasping her pet to her bosom, he kneeling like a suppliant at her feet. It was too dark now for either to see the other clearly, but her voice was the voice of a gentlewoman, and from it, and the slender grace of her figure, he judged her to be young. After a few moments she asked quietly: "Are you one of Monmouth's men?"

He shrugged and nodded. A sense of fatalism had descended upon him, and concealment seemed pointless. "I was one of his officers. Has the news of our defeat spread so far already?"

"We heard only that there had been a battle on

Weston Moor and the rebels scattered. The Duke, so it is said, made his escape."

"God be thanked for that!" Gervase picked up his sword and got to his feet; his voice was hoarse with fatigue, and the effort of rising made his head swim.

As though from a great distance he heard the girl say sharply: "Are you wounded?"

"Naught but a scratch or two!" He brushed the back of his hand across his eyes. " 'Tis but weariness, and I have not eaten these four-and-twenty hours." He looked at the shadowy figure before him, at the pale blur which was all he could see of her face, and at the spaniel, silent now, panting excitedly in her arms. "If of your charity you will refrain from raising the alarm, I will go now, and be for ever in your debt."

"Wait!" Her voice was urgent again, but this time the concern in it was for him. "There is no need for you to go. You are safer here than you would be in the open country, and you are in no case to travel farther. Bide here, and I will fetch you food and drink."

He shook his head. "You must not. I am grateful for your kindness, but it is perilous work aiding a rebel and would bring trouble upon you if it were discovered. Better that I go."

"No one will discover it. My uncle, whose house this is, is a scholar who lives retired from the world with few to serve him. He is a kindly man, and would never deny aid to any in need of it. Wait here! I will not be long."

She turned back the way she had come and the tall bushes hid her from his sight. Gervase sheathed his sword and sank down to a sitting position, clasping his arms about his knees and resting his head upon them.

The girl had spoken truly when she said he was in no case to go on, and if he were to be taken, as well here as anywhere else. So overwhelming was his weariness that he felt he would willingly yield up his freedom if the master of the house would but grant him food and a night's rest.

He had lost all count of time, and when at last the bushes shook and parted, it needed a tremendous effort even to lift his head. A masculine figure, tall and stooping, was looming above him, but he felt neither resentment nor surprise that the spaniel's mistress had not kept faith with him.

"My niece informed me of your presence here," the newcomer announced calmly. "She would have brought food out to you, but it seemed to me that even on a summer night, a clump of bushes was poor hospitality to offer a weary man. You will do better within the house. Come!"

Gervase stared at him. This whole adventure was beginning to savour of a dream, and he could almost believe that he had left the harsh reality of defeat and pursuit behind him when he scaled the wall surrounding this overgrown garden. Somehow he dragged himself to his feet and faced the dim-seen figure before him. "Sir," he said hoarsely, "you do not fully understand. I am a rebel, one of Monmouth's officers. King James's men have been at my heels all day. To aid me is to bring suspicion, or worse, upon yourself."

"No doubt, no doubt," the other man agreed placidly, "but this house is remote, and what few servants I have are completely trustworthy. Nor is it, I trust, against the laws of a Christian country to give food and shelter to a man sorely in need of both. Come, now! Under my roof you will be in no danger."

He turned to lead the way out of the undergrowth, and after a moment's hesitation Gervase followed him. He felt incapable of further argument, nor did it seem likely that this eccentric family would pay any heed to him if he did.

The house to which his mysterious host led him was old and rambling, and seemed to be as neglected as the garden in which it stood. Gervase had a fleeting impression of dark panelling, dust, and a general air of musty decay, and then his guide ushered him into a room which was apparently the one most frequently used. It was full of books—Gervase had never before seen so many in one room; they lined the walls, and were piled on chairs, on the table and even on the floor, but before the hearth, which on this warm July night stood empty, a smaller table and two elbow-chairs were set in a clearer space. The master of the house waved his guest to one of these and Gervase sank wearily down into it, resting his hands on the arms and his head, with closed eyes, against the high back.

His benefactor hastened out of the room again, and when he returned after an absence of several minutes, the younger man was still in the same position, the light from the branch of candles on the little table falling clear and bright across his unconscious figure. The other looked curiously at him, and then with a faint, startled exclamation drew closer, studying the weary face between the tangled curls of the black peri-wig, the aquiline features and the mouth which was imperious even in repose. As his glance left the face and

travelled slowly over the rest of his guest's lean, vigor-
ous person, a gold ring on the little finger of the right
hand caught his eye. He bent closer to examine it, and
when he straightened up again the startled expression
had faded from his eyes, to be replaced by one of extreme thoughtfulness. He retired to the other chair and
remained there until an elderly serving-man entered the
room with a laden tray.

Gervase, roused from the stupor into which he had
fallen, ate the meal set before him in a silence which
neither of his companions attempted to break. When
he had finished, his host bade him a courteous goodnight, and the servant led him out of the room and so
to a bedchamber on the first floor, where he helped
him to remove his battle-stained garments, and tended
the minor hurts he had received during the fighting.
The four-poster bed was large and comfortable, and
the sheets smelled faintly of rosemary. Gervase slid between them with a sigh of thankfulness, and had fallen
into a deep sleep almost before his attendant had left
the room.

He slept for a long time, and when he awoke it was
some moments before he could remember where he
was, but then recollection of the events of the previous
day rushed into his mind. Some kindly destiny must be
watching over him, he thought sleepily, to have
brought him to his present haven, for had he not
stumbled upon this lonely house and its odd inhabi-
tants he would have had small chance of evading capture. He did not even know their names, but they had
undoubtedly saved his life.

He lay there in a pleasant state of drowsiness until at
length the white-haired serving-man came to draw back

the curtains of the bed. The shabby, comfortable room beyond was full of sunlight, warm, golden beams which caused Gervase to inquire with some surprise what time it was.

"Close on five in the afternoon," the servant informed him. "You've had a rare good sleep, sir, and look all the better for it."

"I feel better, my friend," Gervase assured him, stretching luxuriously. "I owe your master a debt I can never repay."

"To my mind, sir, 'tis the young mistress you should thank, her and that dog of hers. But for them you might have laid in them bushes till morning, and none the wiser. Will it please you to rise, sir? Supper will be on the table in an hour or so, and the master would be glad of a word with you first."

Gervase assented at once. Now that he was rested and refreshed, his passive resignation of the night before had passed, and he could face the future with more optimism. If his unknown benefactor would permit him to remain in the house till nightfall, he would make a second and this time, perhaps, a successful attempt to reach the Priory. He hoped it would not be necessary to disclose his identity. Better and safer for all concerned if he remained to this hospitable household merely a nameless stranger to whom they had extended the hand of charity.

When he was ready, the servant led him downstairs to the same book-filled room he had seen the previous night. His host was there, a tall, thin, shabbily-dressed old gentleman with shoulders rounded and eyes dimmed by countless hours spent poring over musty pages, but ready with a courteous greeting and a kindly inquiry concerning his guest's health. On one of the elbow-chairs the little spaniel was curled up asleep, but of her mistress there was no sign. Gervase wondered fleetingly if the lady would appear at the supper table. He would like, he thought, to discover if her looks matched her kindness and her presence of mind.

When courtesies had been exchanged, Gervase turned without delay to the subject of his own immediate future, for it seemed to him that this amiable old gentleman had little comprehension of the danger he courted in succouring a rebel officer. Shut away from the world as he was, and absorbed in his studies, he probably had no idea how thorough and how ruthless would be King James's vengeance upon all who had had a hand, however, remotely, in his nephew's rebellion.

"I am more grateful to you, sir, than I can say, for all your aid," he said firmly, "and, by your leave, I will remain here until darkness falls, so that no one may see me leave your house. Then I will go on my way."

"To be sure!" The elder man looked at him over the spectacles perched on the end of his nose, and it occurred to Gervase that after all those faded eyes were disturbingly shrewd. "Your goal will be Fairwood Priory, I have no doubt?"

Gervase had been leaning over the back of the chair where the spaniel lay, idly tickling the dog's silky ears, but at that he came quickly erect again, a frown between his brows.

"Why Fairwood, sir?" he asked abruptly, and his host's eyebrows lifted.

"Because in extremity such as yours it is natural for a man to seek the sanctuary of his own home," he explained mildly. "You are Gervase Ashbourne, are you not?"

For an instant Gervase neither moved nor spoke. Then, with a gesture of defeat, he said quietly: "I am, sir, though I do not know how you discovered it. We are not, I think, acquainted?"

The other smiled. "I was a guest at your wedding, Mr. Ashbourne, though among so many it is not likely that you remarked me. There have been reports that you were with Monmouth. Also you wear a ring bearing the Ashbourne crest."

Gervase lifted his hand and looked ruefully at the gold signet. "I had forgotten that," he remarked. "My grandfather gave it to me when I first went to Court, and I have worn it ever since." He shrugged, and glanced again at his companion. "You have discovered my name, sir, and my destination, but that alters nothing. I must still leave your house as soon as I can do so without being observed. Every minute I spend here places your household in deeper danger."

"Fairwood lies some miles from here," the other man said reflectively, "and the country is thick with troops engaged in tracking down fugitives such as yourself. You must, of course, do as you think best, but I have a plan to lay before you which I hope you will consider carefully before making any decision."

"I should be an ingrate, sir, to do aught else," Gervase replied. "If it lessens the danger of your kindness to me being discovered, I shall be happy to adopt it."

His host made no comment upon this, but leaned back in his chair and, removing his spectacles, polished them thoughtfully on the skirt of his coat. He appeared to be choosing his next words with care.

"My niece," he said at length, "whom you encountered last night in the garden, has been spending a visit with me. She returns home tomorrow, and her road lies by way of your grandfather's estate. I suggest that you ride with her, disguised as a servant. Thus you will attract less attention than if you attempt to make the journey alone and in your present attire."

Gervase had listened with astonishment and growing dismay to this ingenious plan, and as soon as the speaker paused, said emphatically: "It is out of the question! My dear sir, do you not realize what your niece would be risking? If such an imposture were discovered she would be flung into prison, perhaps even charged with treason. I would ask no one, least of all a woman, to risk so much on my account, and, with respect, you have no right to ask it of her either."

"I ask nothing of her," his host replied calmly. "The plan is hers, not mine."

"Then, sir, as her uncle, you must forbid it! Why should she place herself in such peril for a stranger?" He paused, regarding the other's placid face with deep perturbation, and after a moment went on, less vehemently but quite as earnestly: "Do not think me ungrateful. I am more honoured than I can say that she should wish to help me, but she must be made to see that what she suggests is impossible. An impulse of pity for a hunted man must not be allowed to place her in such danger."

For a moment or two the other man studied him without speaking. Then, as though coming to a decision, he replaced his spectacles and rose to his feet.

"Believe me, Mr. Ashbourne, I have pointed out to her all the perils of the course she suggests, but my niece is a very resolute young woman. She will pay no heed to my warnings. Perhaps you can succeed where I have failed."

So saying, and without waiting for a reply, he hurried out of the room. Gervase remained where he was, tapping his fingers on the back of the chair and frowning with mingled exasperation and concern, until after a few minutes the sound of someone entering made him turn.

She had closed the door and was coming slowly towards him across the book-filled room, a graceful girl in a riding-dress of apricot-coloured velvet, its richness contrasting sharply with her shabby surroundings. Her head was bare, and the thick waves and curls of her dark hair showed glints of reddish-bronze where the light touched them; her eyes were of a clear amber-gold, fringed with long lashes and set beneath straight, dark brows. An unusual face, not beautiful by ordinary standards, but striking in its contrast between broad, serene forehead and the warm vitality of eyes and lips.

That was his first thought, and then his attention was caught by a brooch fastened in the creamy lace beneath her chin and a sharp sense of shock drove everything else from his mind. That intricate design of rubies and pearls was familiar to him; he had seen it time and again in the portrait of his grandmother which hung in Sir William's bedchamber at Fairwood.

"Who are you?" he demanded, and his voice was husky and unsteady. "In God's name, tell me who you are!"

She halted before him, and the amber-coloured eyes lifted to meet his in a look which was at once pleading and uncertain. She was breathing quickly, and the hand she lifted to touch the brooch trembled a little. "You have already begun to guess, I think," she said in a whisper. "I am Elinor—your wife!"

2

Challenge from a Lady

GERVASE stood motionless, staring at her, hardly able to believe that he had heard aright. Could this indeed be the insignificant child whom he had led to the altar five years before? Could so short a time have transformed that timid little girl into a serene and self-possessed young woman who could calmly propose to lead a rebel officer in disguise through a countryside thick with Royal troops?

"I do not understand," he said slowly at last. "How come you here? What house is this?"

The spaniel, which had roused at the sound of her voice, was now standing on its hind legs on the chair, its forepaws scrabbling at her dress to demand attention. She picked it up, holding it tightly as though seeking reassurance from its eager welcome, and Gervase realized that she was far less composed than had appeared at first glance.

"It is Mead House, my mother's old home," she replied breathlessly. "It belongs now to her brother,

Robert Seddon, whom you have seen. As to the 'why' of my presence here, I came in search of you."

"In search of me?" he repeated incredulously. "But you could not have known—"

"That I would find you here?" she broke in hurriedly. "No, of course not, but during these past weeks many rumours have reached us, that you were with Monmouth. We tried by every means in our power, your brother and I, to discover if it were true, and to make contact with you if it were so, but all to no avail. At length it was decided between us that I should set out in search of you."

Gervase frowned. "It would have been more fitting, surely, for Hubert to have made the search, if search were needful."

She shook her head.

"These are dangerous times for a man to be absent from home," she replied gravely, "but no one could suspect me of joining Monmouth. Besides, Sir William would never have permitted Hubert to leave Fairwood at present without some reasonable excuse, and he had none, whereas I had only to pretend that my uncle was ill and in need of me. It has happened before."

"So my grandfather remains in ignorance of your purpose," Gervase remarked grimly. "I thought it unlikely that he would countenance so foolhardy a scheme."

"No, he does not know." Elinor turned away and sat down in the chair, taking the puppy on her lap. Gervase could no longer see her face. "I came here first to seek my uncle's advice, and to find out whether anything concerning you was to be learned in Bridgewater or Taunton. It was on Sunday evening that I arrived here. Yesterday forenoon word reached us that the rebel army had been destroyed in a night battle at Westonzoyland. We sent a servant to discover if the rumour were true, and he brought back news that it was indeed so. Hundreds had been killed, and hundreds more made prisoner. It seemed then that I had come too late."

She paused, but Gervase made no reply. Her words had conjured up again the memory of that scene of destruction and defeat, so that his earlier optimism was engulfed once more in a rising tide of despondency.

After a few moments Elinor went on: "When Duchess discovered you last night in the garden, and you admitted that you were a rebel officer, my first thought was that you might be able to give me the news I sought—for I did not recognize you then. It was not until after my uncle brought you into the house that he realized who you were, but you were so weary that he thought it best to let all explanations wait until you had recovered from your ordeal."

Silence fell again upon the room. Elinor was still looking down at the little dog in her lap, and Gervase moved slowly to seat himself in the other chair, his eyes searching her half-averted face. There was an uneasiness growing in his mind, born more of all that she had left unsaid than of any words she had uttered, but for the moment he could not bring himself to voice it. Instead he said abruptly: "You have changed, Elinor!"

She looked up at that, a clear, direct glance from those amber-coloured eyes, and a slight smile which held just the faintest tinge of bitterness touched her lips for an instant. "I have grown up," she replied quietly, and bent again over her pet, leaving the words to hang like an accusation or a challenge between them.

Gervase bit his lip, and a faint flush darkened his cheeks. As a rule he was not easily put out of countenance, especially by young women, but for one tiny fraction of time he had seen his grandfather look at him out of a girl's fresh young face. That cool, level glance, the dry inflection of the voice, had been Sir William's very own.

The fear within him had grown until it could no longer be concealed. Reluctantly, because of the answer he might be given, he asked: "How fares it at home? Is my grandfather well?"

"No, he is not!" Her voice was low and fierce, and her eyes, lifted again to meet his, blazed with an intensity of feeling that startled him. Clearly his question had released some pent-up flood of emotion, and she was no longer calm and self-controlled. "Gracious God! do you need to ask? Sir William is eighty years old, and his every hope for the future was bound up in you. For you he schemed and planned, fought to restore Fairwood to its former glory, denied himself so that every opportunity might be placed in your way, and how have you rewarded him? By ignoring his advice, denying his wishes, and binding yourself irrevocably to a cause which he has always despised! Worst of all, by years of deliberate, heartless neglect! Yet now you dare to ask me if he is well, as though you had parted from him but a sennight since."

"Madam, you forget yourself!" Gervase came swiftly to his feet, white with an anger the more fierce because he knew that her accusations were justified. "Whatever differences may lie between my grandfather and myself concern us alone, and will be settled between us."

"You alone!" she repeated with biting scorn. "What of those who have been close to him these past few years, and have seen him worn down by anxiety on your behalf, watched him eating his heart out for some word from you, some sign that the faith he had in you was not wholly unjustified? Oh, he has said nothing! He is too proud and stern to disclose what is in his heart, but we guessed it, we who love him, and it has near broken our own hearts that we were powerless to bring him comfort."

There were tears shining in her eyes now, and some of Gervase's anger was overwhelmed by surprise. He said curiously: "I did not know that my grandfather was so dear to you."

"How could you know?" she retorted bitterly. "Five years ago I near died of fright if he so much as spoke to me. I thought I should never learn to be at ease in his presence. Then after you returned to London he made me come often to the Priory, and I grew to know him, and so to love him. When my father died, no one could have been more patient, more gentle!" She paused to brush the tears impatiently from her eyes. "I owe so much to Sir William, and I would do anything in the world for him. It was for his sake that I set out in search of you, and your brother permitted me to do so. Your grandfather is dying, Gervase, and the only thing that can bring him peace in his latter days is reconciliation with you."

He stared at her, his anger forgotten, and the fear which had been briefly lost in anger crystallized into brutal certainty. Yet it was a certainty which at first his mind could not completely accept. Sir William had always been there in the background of his existence, apparently invulnerable to time and misfortune alike, and it seemed unbelievable that the indomitable spirit was failing at last.

"But has nothing been done?" he asked incredulously. "No physician consulted?"

Elinor made a gesture of impatience. "There is no physic, sir, for your grandfather's malady," she said scornfully. "He is not ailing in the sense that you mean, but he is old and tired and very lonely. Can you not comprehend how bitter a thing it is for a man of his years to see his dearest hopes so wantonly laid waste?" She broke off, studying his stricken face, and when she spoke again her voice had softened. "I believe that you do love him, in spite of all, so can you not understand how it has grieved me to see him growing feebler every day, and to know that nothing I could do would lighten his burden? Only you can do that."

"I?" Gervase said bitterly. "What comfort can it bring him to know that his grandson is a hunted fugitive, and ripe for the gallows if King James's men discover him? Better to let him believe that I perished on Weston Moor. That were at least a soldier's death."

Her eyes challenged him. "Have you no wish to see Sir William again?"

"My wishes do not matter. Do you not realize that as one of Monmouth's officers my life is forfeit, and that any who aid me or give me shelter do so at their peril? By my mere presence in this house I place both you and your uncle in danger."

She shrugged. "That risk we accepted when we took

you in, and Sir William would accept it as readily for a sight of you. Politics are not important now. It is the bond of love and kinship between you which should be remembered."

"Politics would be important enough to destroy us all if I were found at Fairwood," he replied grimly. "There will be no mercy shown to any who had a hand in the rebellion."

"If we are cautious, you need not be found there. You can ride with me as my servant, and then lie hidden somewhere until it is safe for you to visit Sir William. No one need know of your presence at Fairwood save we three, and your brother."

He shook his head. "The danger is too great. What if I were recognized during our journey? No, I will not permit you to take so grave a risk."

Elinor lifted Duchess to the ground and rose to her feet. Scorn was smouldering afresh in her changeful eyes, and once again that almost indefinable bitterness had etched itself about her lips.

"Such concern for me is gratifying, sir, but unconvincing. Let us have honesty in its place. You seek an excuse to avoid seeing your grandfather, and since I do not believe it is fear for yourself that prompts you, it must be pride. Pride, and reluctance to admit that through all these years his judgment has been sound, and yours at fault." She laughed with bitter mockery. "Gracious God, how monstrous is your vanity! Even with the shadow of the gallows upon you, you will not own that you were wrong, but would rather let a good old man die in loneliness and sorrow."

"By God, madam, you go too far!" Gervase exclaimed furiously, stung to fresh anger by the contemptuous challenge in her voice and eyes. "Sir William must be failing indeed to tolerate such impudence as yours. It is a weakness I do not share."

"Am I then to cry pardon for it?" she flashed. "A wife should strive to please her husband, I know, but I have had scant opportunity these five years past to learn what does or does not please mine!"

They stood staring at each other, he tight-lipped and white of face, she with flushed cheeks and blazing eyes, but before either could speak again the door was flung open. Robert Seddon hurried into the room, the old serving-man at his heels.

"Children, children!" Mr. Seddon's voice was sharp with urgency. "This is no time for trifling quarrels. King James's men are at the gate!"

Elinor uttered a little, choking cry and Gervase swung round, his hand flashing to his sword-hilt in a gesture as instinctive as it was futile. Mr. Seddon shook his head.

"No, that will not serve," he said impatiently. "Concealment is the only answer now. Elinor, the priest-hole, quickly! You know the trick of it."

She nodded without speaking, and, catching Gervase by the hand, pulled him towards the door. He followed her without protest, only saying urgently over his shoulder: "What of the room where I slept?"

"All set to rights, sir, as soon as you left it," the servant replied. He seemed undisturbed by the imminence of danger, and his phlegmatic calm was reassuring. "There's naught to show it's been used these six months."

Elinor dragged Gervase across the stone-flagged hall to the dining-parlour on its farther side, and pushed aside a big carved chair which stood against the wall. Some hidden mechanism yielded to her trembling fingers and a narrow section of the panelling slid aside, disclosing a dark aperture.

"No stranger has ever discovered this secret yet," she said hurriedly. "Bide still and quiet, and you will be safe enough." She caught him by the sleeve as he was about to step into the hiding-place, and saw with surprise that there were tears in her eyes again. "Gervase, forgive me! I should not have spoken as I did just now."

An imperative knocking sounded upon the front door, and in the study the dog began to bark shrilly. He laid his hand over hers for an instant, and felt the slender fingers cold and trembling beneath his own. Then he stepped into the priest-hole and the panel slid shut again, leaving him in darkness.

Elinor thrust the chair into its place and ran out of the room as the servant made his leisurely way across the hall towards the door, which was shaking now beneath a fusillade of blows. He observed her white face and trembling lips, and patted her arm reassuringly.

"Rest easy now, Miss Nell," he whispered. "These be no local troops, and they'll know naught of any priest-hole. The young master'll not be taken this day."

She flashed him a tremulous, grateful smile and darted on into the room where her uncle still waited. As she closed the door the thunderous knocking ceased abruptly, and a moment later a man's voice spoke in loud, hectoring tones.

"Bestir yourself, you doddering greybeard, or your

master will find his door beaten down. What house is this? How many rebels do you shelter here?"

The servant's reply was lost in a fresh outburst from Duchess. Elinor picked her up and looked anxiously at her uncle, who had seated himself in one of the elbow-chairs with a large book open on his knees. He motioned to her to stand beside him, and thus they were found by the scarlet-coated officer who a minute or two later came swaggering into the room.

He was a young man, probably no older than Gervase himself, with a large-featured, somewhat fleshy face which was good-looking in a florid, sensual way. He strode in without ceremony, spurs jingling and his sword arrogantly upthrust behind him by the weight of his hand on its hilt, for the Royal troops were masters of Somerset that day, and even a junior officer held the power of life and death. No General entering a captured city ever swaggered it more boldly that the Captain of the Tangier Regiment who now came clattering and jingling into that quiet, book-lined room.

He halted just within the door, his menacing glance passing from the old gentleman in the chair to the white-faced girl with the struggling dog in her arms, but he made no attempt to acknowledge her presence. To Seddon he said brusquely: "There are still too many damned rebels skulking in these parts, and if you harbour any here I charge you to disclose them. I am Captain Blake of Colonel Kirke's dragoons."

Mr. Seddon peered at him over the top of his spectacles, the embodiment of vague, mild innocence.

"I take no part in politics, young man, nor do I harbour rebels in my house. However, you have my permission to search it if you please."

An unpleasant sneer twisted the soldier's full lips.

"We'll search, my friend, with your permission or without it. The King's business waits upon no man's pleasure, and there are grave penalties for aiding these Monmouth dogs. You, I take it, are Robert Seddon?"

Mr. Seddon admitted it placidly, and Captain Blake's dark eyes turned again to Elinor.

"This is your daughter?"

"No, sir, my niece. Mrs. Elinor Ashbourne."

"Ashbourne, eh?" The Captain's eyes narrowed. "I have heard that name before."

"No doubt you have," Mr. Seddon agreed amiably. "My niece is grand-daughter by marriage to Sir William Ashbourne of Fairwood Priory." He paused, and then added with no change of tone: "A gentleman noted for his Royalist sympathies."

"So I have heard!" Blake strode forward and flung himself down in the other chair, disregarding the fact that Elinor was still standing. "What does she here?"

"I visit my uncle," Elinor said coldly before Seddon could reply. The intruder's rudeness was making her angry, and helping her to overcome her dread of what his presence might lead to. "Are such domestic matters also of interest to His Majesty?"

"To His Majesty's loyal servants, perhaps, if they lead to the capture of even one of these accursed rebels," he informed her ominously. "Where is your husband, ma'am?"

She forced herself not to flinch at the question, to continue to meet the hostile eyes with no change of expression in her own, although her heart was thumping with a violence which seemed to shake her whole body.

"I do not know," she said steadily. "We were married five years ago, when I was but a child, and afterwards he went back to the Court. I have not seen him since."

"So?" The soldier's heavy brows lifted, and his gaze travelled over her in a slow, appraising way which brought the hot colour to her cheeks. "The more fool he, to be so neglectful!" He paused, enjoying the confusion he had provoked in her, and then his voice sharpened again. "What of your brothers, the other menfolk of your family?"

"I have neither brother nor sister, and my parents are dead. As for my husband's family, you will find his younger brother at Fairwood, with Sir William. There is no one else."

He made no reply, but continued to study her with impudent familiarity, his lips curving to a smile which she found vaguely disquieting. Feigning an indifference she did not feel, she moved away to sit on the deep window-seat, half turning her back upon him yet still uncomfortably conscious of his regard.

Elsewhere in the house the soldiers could be heard making their search, jack-boots clattering on the old oaken floors, doors slamming, and the occasional crash of glass or sound of splintering wood to serve as brutal reminders that to the Royal army the West Country was a conquered enemy territory, to be subjected to the most violent penalties of defeat and occupation. Elinor sat as still as death, forcing herself to outward calm though fear lay like a cold weight on her heart. The priest-hole was cunningly hidden; it had defied detection for more than a century, even though its existence was common knowledge in the locality, yet discovery was an ever-present possibility. Of the consequences of discovery she did not dare to think. As early as yesterday the hangman's rope had begun to take its ghastly toll.

At last, when she was beginning to feel that she could endure no more, heavy footsteps approached the room and a sergeant made his appearance.

The Captain spoke from the chair where he still lounged. "What have you found?"

"Nothing, sir," the sergeant replied with a trace of regret in his voice. "We've been through the house from cellar to attic, and the garden and outbuildings, too. There's no rebels hidden here."

Blake heaved himself to his feet and looked down sardonically at Mr. Seddon, who had remained apparently immersed in his book while the dragoons ransacked his house. The old gentleman returned the glance blandly.

"As I informed you at the outset, Captain, I take no part in politics," he remarked mildly. "I fear you have had a wasted hour."

For a moment or two the soldier made no reply. From Seddon his glance shifted to Elinor, and then he looked away through the doors which his men had left standing wide to the dining-parlour on the far side of the hall. The cloth had already been spread on the table when the dragoons arrived, and now the serving-man was moving stolidly about the room as he resumed the interrupted preparations for the evening meal.

Blake laughed softly on a sneering note. "We'll bide for supper," he said abruptly. "As a loyal subject of King James, Mr. Seddon will not grudge His Majesty's servants a meal."

Elinor shot a glance of swift dismay at her uncle, but he was not looking at her. He was smiling amiably up at the big young man in the scarlet coat who towered so threateningly over him.

"I shall be honoured, sir," he said placidly. "Elinor, my dear, be good enough to tell Hezekiah to set a place for the Captain, and bid them in the kitchen see to the comfort of his men."

Elinor stared at him, feeling herself incapable of movement yet knowing that her uncle had made the only possible reply. Blake had turned, and was watching her with mocking eyes, and, feeling that this was part of some macabre nightmare, she got up and crossed the hall to the parlour.

A nightmare the evening remained thereafter, both at the time and in the memory of it which was to linger in her mind for years to come. The panelled dining-parlour, familiar to her since her childhood; the table with its white napery, and pewter gleaming dully in the candle-light; Hezekiah moving quietly to attend to their needs, and her uncle discoursing with learned courtesy to an unwelcome guest whose indifference could not have been more clearly shown. The guest himself, bold-eyed and forceful, growing less and less restrained as the wine sank lower, drawing his chair closer to hers, lowering his voice to a note of hateful intimacy as he paid her compliments remarkable more for fulsomeness than for propriety. She sat like a statue, knowing that her uncle and the servant were as powerless to help her as she was to help herself; that they were all three bound hand and foot by their shared knowledge of the priest-hole and the perilous secret it held.

From where she sat the panel was clearly visible, and it exerted a dreadful fascination upon her. She found her eyes returning to it again and again, no matter how often or how resolutely she turned them elsewhere. Her thoughts returned as constantly to Gervase in his cramped prison, and beyond the picture of him her imagination conjured up she seemed to see the gaunt and weary face of the old man who lay dying at Fairwood, lonely and defeated in his unspoken sorrow. For their sake she forced herself to live through the ordeal without shrinking, turning a deaf ear to murmured improprieties, remaining impassive even when Blake took her hand in his to kiss and fondle it, leaning so close to her that she felt his wine-laden breath on her cheek.

Would he never leave? The candles were burning down, and beyond the windows twilight had given place to the luminous darkness of the summer night, but Captain Blake showed no disposition to resume the duties which he had earlier been so prompt to assert. In spite of what he had said then, it seemed that the King's business could very well wait upon the Captain's pleasure.

An alarm which could not be denied was growing within her, for in the present turbulent state of the country even the innocent dare not provoke the Royal soldiers too far, and her uncle's few servants would be helpless in the presence of the military. Mr. Seddon sat silent now at the head of the table, his lips tightly compressed as he watched Blake's increasingly impudent advances, while from his place at the other end of the room, Hezekiah glared impotently in the same direction. Elinor's gaze turned again towards the secret panel, and she prayed silently and desperately for deliverance.

It came at last from an unexpected quarter. An urgent knocking on the front door startled them all out of their preoccupation, and after a small commotion in the hall, and the sound of voices engaged in indistinguishable argument, the sergeant presented himself at the parlour door with the village constable trailing eagerly at his heels. Both appeared to be labouring under some excitement.

"Word's just come, sir, of a pair o' rebels skulking in a cottage a couple o' miles from here," the sergeant reported eagerly. " 'Tis thought that one of 'em may be Monmouth himself."

Blake slewed himself round in his chair to glare at the speaker. It was plain that the interruption was unwelcome.

"Impossible!" he said scornfully. "Monmouth would not be fool enough to tarry in these parts. You are so eager to capture him that you see him in every damned plough-boy who marched with his army."

"Your pardon, Captain!" The constable pushed past the sergeant into the room. "The man who brought the news be trusty enough, and he's seen Monmouth more nor once these past days. I've been seeking aid this hour past."

Blake continued to glare at him. The news could not have come at a more inopportune moment, but he was soldier enough to know that he dare not ignore the summons. Though he had little faith in the fugitive's supposed identity, every possibility must be investigated as long as the rebel Duke remained at large. He swore comprehensively and got to his feet.

"Get the men to horse," he commanded, "and mount this fellow behind one of them if he came on foot. We'll take a look at these two bashful gentlemen."

Sergeant and constable withdrew, and the Captain remained for a few moments apparently lost in thought, staring before him with lower lip out-thrust. At length he picked up his glass again and tossed off what remained of the wine.

"Devil take Monmouth and all rebel dogs!" he said thickly, and turned again to Elinor, setting a hand on the back of her chair and leaning down towards her. "May our next meeting be soon, sweetheart, and less rudely ended. Plague on't if I ever answered a call to duty with such reluctance!"

He bent lower and kissed her lingeringly upon the lips, and then without another glance at her uncle swaggered from the room. In response to a sign from Mr. Seddon, Hezekiah followed him, but uncle and niece sat in tense silence throughout all the disturbance of the soldiers' departure.

At last, when all was quiet again and Hezekiah came back into the room, his master asked quietly: "Have they gone?"

"Aye, sir, thanks be to God, and the gates locked behind 'em," the servant replied grimly. "We'll have warning enough if they come again."

"I trust they will not return," Mr. Seddon retorted. He got up, and stood watching the other man, who without waiting for instruction had gone straight to close and curtain the windows. "They have searched the house and found nothing, and that should be sufficient."

The windows were securely shrouded now. He went across to the secret panel, and Elinor's gaze followed him wearily as he released the hidden catch and the section of wall slid aside.

"Come, Mr. Ashbourne," he said quietly. "Your imprisonment has lasted longer than we thought, but better a few hours' discomfort than discovery and arrest."

Gervase emerged from the priest-hole with a word of thanks, but it was towards Elinor that he looked first. There were spy-holes in the panel, skillfully concealed in the rich carving, and though the view they afforded of the parlour was necessarily limited, he had seen and heard enough of what went on in the room to know that it was upon her that the heaviest burden of the evening had fallen. He went round the table to stand beside her, as Captain Blake had stood so short a while before.

"What can I say?" he asked in a low voice. "I am in need of your forgiveness for many things, Elinor, and not least of all for the insults you have endured this night. Had I not known that my presence here would expose you to even worse danger, I would have disclosed it long since."

She lifted her head to look up at him. Her face was white and exhausted and there were dark shadows beneath her eyes, for the strain of the evening had taken heavy toll of her endurance.

"Captain Blake's conduct demeaned him more than it humiliated me," she said quietly, "and it was a small price to pay for your safety, though I will own that I have never wished so earnestly to be rid of anyone's company. I fear, though, that our deliverance means some other poor soul's misfortune. Do you think the man they seek may really be the Duke?"

Gervase shook his head. "If I thought it possible I should not be lingering here. Depend upon it, His Grace is many miles away by now, and the men Blake seeks merely some poor fugitives who, like myself, escaped the slaughter on Weston Moor. God grant them another escape tonight!"

"Amen to that!" She got up slowly, pushing her hair back from her forehead with a weary gesture. "Ah, how tired I am!"

"Go to your bed, my child," Mr. Seddon said gently. "I think we have no more to fear tonight."

"You have no more to fear from my presence, sir, at any time," Gervase corrected him firmly. "You all stand in too much danger while I am in this house. I will find me some other hiding-place, which, if it is discovered, will involve no one else in my ill-fortune."

"No!" Elinor spoke sharply, but there was a sob in her voice. "My uncle is right! They will not come here again, but elsewhere you could be betrayed by any chance passer-by." She laid an urgent, compelling hand on his arm. "Gervase, I beg of you! Promise me that you will stay here—for Sir William's sake, if you will not for your own."

"He will stay, Elinor," Mr. Seddon assured her tranquilly, "and tomorrow you shall both set out for Fairwood in the manner you devised. Now, a truce to this foolishness, and get you to bed. You will have need of all your wits if you are to bring your husband safely to his grandfather's house."

Still she hesitated, looking anxiously at Gervase. He cast a dubious glance at Mr. Seddon, who met the troubled gaze with one of compelling calm. Gervase made a little gesture of defeat.

"I will stay," he agreed resignedly. "You have my word upon that. For the rest, we will talk of it again tomorrow." He lifted her hand from his arm and put it to his lips. "Perhaps then we may agree more easily than we did today."

She smiled faintly, but made no reply, and, bidding them both goodnight, went slowly towards the door which Hezekiah had opened for her. The spaniel pup scrambled up from the mat where it had been lying and pattered after her, its paws slipping and scrabbling on the oaken floor.

3

Enterprise Perilous

So Gervase passed a second night beneath the roof of Mead House, a night undisturbed by any further alarms. He and Robert Seddon sat talking for a long time after Elinor had retired, and before they parted Gervase had agreed, albeit reluctantly and with deep misgiving, to adopt the plan devised for his escape.

"Though I cannot like it, sir," he said emphatically. "The danger to Elinor is too great. Better by far for her to return alone to Fairwood, and I make my way there as best I may."

"I do not agree," Mr. Seddon replied calmly. "There is danger, I grant you, but if you play your part adequately no one should suspect you. The distance is not great. You will be at Fairwood before nightfall."

"Yes, and what then?" Gervase got up and began to move restlessly about the room; there was bitterness in his voice. "There, more than anywhere, I shall stand in danger of recognition, and if that happens I drag my whole family to destruction. Already, you tell me, they are hanging the rank and file of our army. How much less hope of mercy have we who helped to plan the rebellion, and who came with the Duke from Holland! The law holds that he who knowingly aids a traitor is himself guilty of treason, and that law will be enforced to the last letter, make no doubt of that. It would have been enforced here tonight had they discovered my presence. For what other reason do you suppose I remained quietly in hiding while that drunken oaf forced his damned attentions upon my wife?"

Mr. Seddon took off his spectacles and polished them. It appeared to be his habit whenever he was thoughtful or perturbed.

"I am deeply attached to Elinor, Mr. Ashbourne," he said mildly, "and I trust that you will not take it amiss when I say that, while your present concern for her welfare does you credit, it is regrettable that it has been so long delayed."

Gervase halted and turned to face him, a dark flush rising in his cheeks. "I am aware of it, Mr. Seddon," he replied in a low voice, "but since we are dealing in frankness I will say also that the marriage was none of my seeking, and my wishes consulted not at all. I offer that as explanation, not excuse. I have failed most miserably in my duty towards her, not least in the trouble I have brought upon her now. That is why I say it will be better if I go at once, and take my chance alone. That way I involve nobody in my peril, and if I am taken, then at least Elinor will be free of the bonds imposed upon her by expediency and ambition."

"You gave her your word that you would stay," the other reminded him quietly.

"Aye, so I did! Devil take it, was there ever such a coil?" He looked up ruefully, meeting the elder man's eyes. "Advise me, sir, I beg of you! In which course lies the greater villainy?"

For a moment or two Robert Seddon continued to regard him, and his shrewd yet faded eyes were not altogether unkindly.

"I have harboured some harsh thoughts of you, young man, during the past five years," he said at length, "but perhaps they were not entirely justified. You spoke just now of your duty to Elinor. As I see it, that duty at present lies in giving her the protection of which I fear she may shortly stand in need."

"With all my heart, sir," Gervase responded readily, "but what protection can a fugitive rebel give, and against whom? What danger threatens her?"

Mr. Seddon frowned, and polished the ill-used spectacles more vigorously that before.

"Captain Blake, and others of his kind," he said bluntly. "The Royal army rules Somerset today, and you have seen how inadequate is the protection that I can offer her. Once she reaches Fairwood she will be safe, but I cannot permit her to make the journey with no other escort than Hezekiah. He would lay down his life for Nell, for he has been in our service since before her mother was born, but he is too old to bear the responsibility alone."

Gervase looked blank.

"What of the servants she brought with her from Fairwood?"

"She brought none save Hezekiah," Mr. Seddon explained patiently. "He is not my man now, but hers. He entered Thomas Dane's service at the time of my sister's marriage, and when Thomas died, Sir William found a place at Fairwood for Hezekiah and his wife. Elinor chose him to accompany her because he is the servant she trusts above all others, but in the present state of the country, trustworthiness alone is not enough. She may have need of a strong arm also before her journey is over."

Gervase made a gesture of defeat. "You leave me no choice, sir. I will go with her, of course, and I pray God that my presence brings no harm to her."

In accordance with this plan, Hezekiah roused him early on the following day, and showed him the garments which were to provide his disguise. These were of the humblest country fashion, rough homespun designed more for service than for show, with a leathern jacket, and a shapeless hat which had seen better days. When he had put them on, Gervase, regarding himself with rueful humour, reflected that he was unlikely to be identified as an Ashbourne of Fairwood and a captain in Monmouth's army; whether he would escape all suspicion of having been concerned in the rebellion was another matter.

He followed the servant down to the study and found Elinor there with her uncle. She appeared to have recovered from her unpleasant experiences of the previous day and greeted him composedly, looking him over in a critical fashion. Mr. Seddon, too, studied him closely, and after a moment or two remarked with satisfaction:

"That is very well, I think. An excellent disguise!"

"The dress is excellent," Elinor agreed slowly, "but there is more to a disguise than donning homespun and laying aside a sword." She went across to him and stood looking up into his face. "I could wish you less like your grandfather, Gervase! Any who know him will recognize you for an Ashbourne even if they have never seen you before."

She reached up and pulled off the battered hat. He had discarded his periwig with the rest of his soldier's garb and his own short dark hair was revealed, curling crisply about his ears. Elinor rearranged it with deft fingers, drawing it forward across his forehead, and then replaced the hat in such a way that it cast a shadow across his features.

"There, that is better! If you will remember to hang your head when we encounter anyone it may pass muster. And try to hold yourself less soldierly, or we shall be betrayed at the outset."

He looked down at her with a trace of amusement, discovering again in voice and manner that elusive likeness to Sir William. It was strange, he reflected, that one personality could so leave its stamp upon another.

"Tell me something of the part I am to play," he suggested, "for you have, I feel sure, provided me with a name and a character."

"Of course," she agreed calmly. "You are Jacob Hunt, son of Samuel Hunt who is my uncle's gardener, and you have been sent back to Fairwood with me because in the present troubled times my uncle fears for my safety unless I have some stronger escort than Hezekiah. You will spend the night at Hezekiah's cottage and tomorrow return home alone."

Gervase nodded. "I understand. Tell me, does such a person as Jacob Hunt exist, or is he merely a figment of your imagination?"

"Certainly he exists. Those are his clothes you are wearing now, for in size and colouring you are not unlike him, and 'twas that which first suggested this plan to my mind. Jacob, like his father, is in my uncle's service."

"Then he was seen yesterday by the soldiers who searched the house?"

Mr. Seddon broke his prolonged silence. "For a few moments only, and they are not likely to have paid much heed to him. He was out in the cow-byre tending a sick beast all the while they were here, so they had small chance to observe his looks."

"His father will keep Jacob out of sight until tomorrow evening," Elinor put in, "and impress upon him where he is supposed to have been meanwhile. If 'tis told to him often enough he will not forget." Her tone was dry, and Gervase detected a gleam of mockery in her eyes as she added deliberately: "Jacob is loyalty itself, but somewhat wanting in wit."

"My thanks to you, madam!" He bowed, matching mockery with mockery. "A weak head but a strong arm—such a part should not be beyond my power to play convincingly."

She chuckled, her eyes approving him, yet, jest though they might, both knew that they would be tak-

ing their lives in their hands once the shelter of
Mead House was left behind them. That knowledge lay
heavily on all their minds as they ate a hurried meal,
and then went out to where Samuel Hunt, forsaking
the post of gardener for that of groom, was waiting
with the horses. Elinor and Hezekiah had their own
mounts, and Mr. Seddon had provided for Gervase the
stout old grey which he himself used on his rare jaunts
abroad. Gervase eyed it rather ruefully, reflecting that
if his imposture were discovered and he found it necessary to make a dash for liberty, he would have small
chance of escape on so staid and elderly a beast.

He lifted Elinor on to the back of her dainty bay
mare, and watched her uncle hand up to her the wrig-
gling spaniel. As she settled the little dog comfortably
in her lap, he asked curiously: "What in the name of
Heaven possessed you to bring a dog on such an er-
rand as you had in mind?"

"I had no choice," she replied frankly. "Duchess is
with me so constantly that it would have aroused suspicion at the Priory had I left her behind, and that I
could not risk. It was my intention to leave her in my
uncle's care while I went in search of you."

He nodded, and turned to mount his own horse, for
they had taken leave of Mr. Seddon within the house
and there was little more to say. Hezekiah, it seemed,
had been thinking along similar lines to Gervase, for he
laid hold of the grey's bridle and said in a low voice:
"Take my horse, sir! Pray 'God there'll be no need for
it, but if the need does arise 'twill serve you better than
this old fellow."

Mr. Seddon nodded his approval, and with a word
of thanks Gervase swung up into the saddle. The Ash-

bourne stables were justly famous, and both Elinor's
mount and her servant's had obviously been chosen for
the journey with an eye to speed and endurance alike.
With such a horse beneath him, Gervase felt that his
chances of escape were considerably improved.

Mr. Seddon bade them God-speed, and stood at the
door to watch them out of sight, while Samuel hurried
ahead to open the gates. He secured them again as
soon as the riders had passed through, and the grating
of the rusty lock brought home to Elinor, as nothing
else had yet done, the danger of the enterprise on
which she had embarked. For a moment her heart mis-
gave her and she felt an overpowering desire to turn
back, but she conquered it resolutely, reminding herself
that the seeming safety of her uncle's house was a mere
illusion, as Captain Blake's intrusion the previous day
had proved. Sir William Ashbourne's name should protect her and her companions if they were challenged,
and no one in Somerset had seen Gervase since his
brief stay there five years ago. Even her uncle had not
recognized him at first—Elinor uttered a sudden exclamation of dismay and drew rein.

Her companions did likewise; Gervase said sharply:
"What is it?"

"Your ring!" Her voice was shaken. "Oh, how could
we have forgotten? You are still wearing it!"

He rapped out an oath and at once began to tug at
the gold signet, which at first resisted all his efforts to
remove it. After a struggle he succeeded in pulling it
off, and held it out to Elinor. "You had best keep it for
me," he said quietly. "Thank God you remembered it!
It could have betrayed us all."

She took the ring and bestowed it in an inner

pocket, and the journey was resumed, but though no further mention was made of it, the incident had disturbed them all. So small a thing, so easily overlooked, and yet the Ashbourne crest on the finger of a supposed serving-man would have brought complete disaster had it been observed by hostile eyes. Was there anything else, each one of them was thinking, which had been forgotten and yet which could bring discovery?

The first part of their journey was accomplished with only one other disquieting incident, for Hezekiah knew every inch of the country, and led them for the most part by unfrequented ways. Once, however, when for a short distance they were obliged to follow the high-road, they rounded a bend to come face to face with a disturbing and melancholy sight.

A file of prisoners, pinioned two and two, some of them wounded and all sunk in a dull apathy of despair, trudging along under the guard of red-coated militia. Behind them came the most tragic sight of all, two farm-carts drawn by plodding horses, into which had been cast all those whose injuries prevented them from going on foot. Although two days had passed since the battle, they lay with reeking wounds untended under the summer sun, so crowded together that they could not even brush away the flies which hovered in tormenting clouds about them, while their cries and groans fell unheeded upon the ears of their captors.

The officer in charge of the party rode up to Elinor and saluted her. He was very young, hardly more than a boy, and he looked with undisguised admiration at this richly-dressed young lady.

"Your pardon, madam," he said apologetically,

"May I be permitted to know your name, and whither you are bound?"

She had been watching with fascinated horror the approach of those two dreadful carts, but at his words she dragged her gaze away from them towards her questioner. She was very pale, but that was easily accounted for by the sight before her.

"I am Elinor Ashbourne," she replied tonelessly, "and I am on my way home to my grandfather's house. He is Sir William Ashbourne of Fairwood Priory."

The young officer looked relieved.

"Sir William's loyalty is known to all," he remarked. "You may ride on, madam, and my apologies for hindering you." He glanced without curiosity at her companions. "Have a care for your lady, fellows! There are still some accursed rebels at large."

He reined his horse back to let them pass and they rode on, too disturbed by what they had just seen to appreciate the irony of that well-meant advice. After a little, Hezekiah turned aside once more from the highroad and led the way along a narrow, tree-shaded track which wound its way up a steep hillside. Gervase brought his horse alongside Elinor's, and saw that tears were glistening on her white cheeks while her lips moved soundlessly as though in prayer. After a few moments, becoming aware of his regard, she turned to look at him.

"Those poor, misguided creatures!" she said in a low voice, "Ah, Gervase, what an infinity of suffering this rebellion has let loose upon the West!"

He could not deny it. Hitherto he had thought of the campaign merely in terms of success or failure, of triumph or defeat for the Protestant cause, and the men who composed the rebel army had been to him but the means to an end. Now, through Elinor's words and her compassionate tears, he saw them for the first time as individuals, as human beings who believed and suffered, who loved and were beloved by the families and friends from whom they had been so rudely sundered. It was, he thought, as though a stone had been hurled violently into a placid pool, spreading ripples of disaster which reached ever outward to engulf people who had never even seen the Duke of Monmouth and who cared little who sat upon the throne of England as long as they were permitted to live out their lives in peace and quietude. In that moment the whole tragedy and futility of the rebellion bore down upon him, as he realized the terrible responsibility which must for ever rest upon that small group of zealous or ambitious men who, like himself, had helped to plan and finance the expedition.

"There was one I knew in that unhappy throng," Elinor continued after a pause. "His father worked for mine, and I knew him when we were children in Taunton. He was the merriest lad I have ever known— laughter was never far from his heart or from his lips. Yet now he trudges there in bonds, and his face is the face of an old man. Why, Gervase? Why did he leave his home and family to follow Monmouth? Why did you?"

He tried to answer her and could not. "For England," he should have said, "because we will not tolerate a Popish tyranny, and because we believed that Monmouth was the man to deliver us from it." The words would have sounded with a fine flourish, and two days ago he would have uttered them with wholehearted conviction. Yet now, with this new, uncomfortable perception which had been granted him, he realized that they were only a part, and the lesser part at that, of the whole truth. He had flung himself into politics as an escape from personal unhappiness, and turned to the Duke's party because he liked Monmouth as a man and admired him as a soldier. He admitted this to himself now for the first time, but he could not yet admit it to Elinor.

"Does the reason matter now?" he said at last. "We failed, and your old play-fellow is a prisoner, and I may be in like case before the day is out, and it will concern our captors not at all why we acted as we did. A rebel is a rebel, whether his motive for being so is noble or base."

She sighed, but said no more, and for another mile or so they rode in silence. The track brought them up over the crest of a low ridge of hills, and in its descent of the farther side presently joined a broader road. They had ridden along this for perhaps half-a-mile when they saw another party of militia ahead of them. These were grouped about the gate of a small farm which they had apparently been engaged in searching, and though most of them were foot-soldiers, the figure of a mounted officer loomed conspicuously among them.

"They have seen us," Gervase said quietly as Elinor drew rein. "Ride on, my dear! There is nothing else to be done."

She obeyed without question, and the officer detached himself from his men and moved forward a little to meet them. As they drew near enough to distinguish his features, Elinor uttered a swiftly-stifled gasp of dismay. Gervase guessed that the man must be known to her, and cursed silently at the ill-fortune which had cast this additional danger in their way.

4

The Colonel of Militia

OBVIOUSLY recognition had been mutual, for as they came up to him the officer bowed with slightly exaggerated courtesy, and addressed Elinor by name.

"Give you good-day, Mrs. Ashbourne. You are strangely far from Fairwood, are you not?"

"None so great a distance, surely, Colonel Venner," Elinor replied rather coldly. "I am on my way home from a visit to my uncle, Mr. Seddon, at Mead House."

"You choose unseasonable times to go a-visiting, madam. When rebellion is abroad 'tis wiser for honest folk to bide at home."

"My uncle's housekeeper, sir, sent me word that he was ailing. I am his only kin, and it was my duty to go to him. Happily, his indisposition proved less serious than I feared, and so I am free to return to Fairwood, where my presence is more urgently required."

"To nurse its dying master, I suppose," Venner said brutally. "You divide your time, it seems, between two old and ailing gentlemen, and that is a poor life for a young woman. You have my sympathy, Mrs. Ashbourne!"

"I have not sought it, sir," she retorted, "any more than I sought this conversation. Will you have the goodness to let me pass?"

He ignored the request and continued to regard her with faintly malevolent mockery, while Gervase, slouching awkwardly in the saddle and doing his best to look like a slow-witted yokel, covertly studied him in his turn. He saw a tall man a year or two on the young side of forty, with a pale, austerely-featured face between the curls of a flaxen periwig. Thin, high-bridged nose, high cheek-bones and thin yet well-shaped lips formed a countenance undeniably handsome, yet repellent in its total lack of emotion or humanity. Such a man could no doubt be a dangerous enemy and it was clear that no love was lost between him and Elinor. Their antagonism was as strong as it was unmistakable.

"Bear with me a few minutes longer, Mrs. Ashbourne," Venner said smoothly. "I would like to know more of this visit to your uncle. Mead House is not far from Bridgewater, where the rebel army was encamped."

Gervase stole ā glance at his wife. Her face, shadowed by the broad, plumed hat, was pale but composed, the brows lifted a fraction in disdainful inquiry.

"What of it, sir? Neither my uncle nor I have ever supported the pretensions of the Duke of Monmouth."

"Yet it is common knowledge that your husband was close in his counsels," Venner replied with a sneer. "Or do you ask me to believe that you were unaware of it?"

"We have heard rumours to that effect, but no certain news," Elinor said levelly. "As you are no doubt aware, my husband has not visited Fairwood for close upon five years, so if you have any sure tidings of him, Colonel Venner, I shall be grateful if you will inform me of them."

The sneer deepened about the Colonel's thin lips.

"I'll warrant you will," he said unpleasantly. "It must be irksome to be neither maid nor wife. I am sure that Mr. Hubert, too, is eager to know whether or not he may step—lawfully—into his brother's place."

The bay mare snorted and backed as Elinor's hand tightened angrily on the rein, and Duchess gave a protesting yelp. Venner leaned forward and gripped the mare's bridle above the bit, forcing her to be still, while his cold, blue-grey eyes looked mockingly into Elinor's face, as flushed now as it had been pale before. She was not, however, at a loss for a retort.

"Be good enough, if you please, to confine your attention to my husband's politics," she said fiercely, "and leave family matters to those whose concern they are. Now let me pass! It is intolerable that I should be insulted in this fashion."

"You should have remained at your uncle's house, madam, until the countryside became less turbulent." His voice sharpened with sudden suspicion. "Why did you not? These are times when no gentlewoman would ride abroad from choice."

This was the moment of danger. Gervase glanced surreptitiously at the cluster of militia-men, and wondered what chance two unarmed men and a woman would have of breaking through the group and making their escape. Very little, he thought grimly, with Venner's horse blocking the road and Venner's hand still firmly gripping the bridle of Elinor's mount.

"I did not stay at Mead House, sir, because even there I was not safe from unmannerly importunities," Elinor replied sharply. "His Majesty's officers, it seems, do not deal in courtesy, and it is clear that only at Fairwood can I hope to be safe from further indignities."

"To be sure!" Venner was sneering again. "It would be a bold man who, even upon the King's business, dared to violate the sacred precincts of Fairwood Priory."

"The King's business, sir, has not, nor ever will, meet with any hindrance at Fairwood," Elinor retorted promptly, "but boldness and impudence alone will never open the doors of Sir William's house. You, I believe, have already found that out!"

To Gervase the words were cryptic, but it was obvious that their import was very clear to the Colonel— and to at least one other person within earshot, for a snigger, hastily stifled, came from the group about the farmhouse gate. Venner released the mare's bridle as though it had suddenly become red-hot, and jerked upright, his face distorted by an anger so swift and murderous that it was almost shocking by contrast with his former impassivity. For a moment he seemed incapable of speech, and then he said in a voice thick with fury:

"If I do come to Fairwood again, madam, it will be upon the King's business, and Heaven help you all if I find your rebel husband skulking there!" He reined back his horse and flung out a pointing hand. "Your road is open! May it lead to a humbling of the damned Ashbourne pride!"

Elinor ignored both the words and the threat implicit in them, and sent the bay mare bounding forward at a reckless pace along the uneven road, with Gervase and Hezekiah thundering after her. Not until the farmhouse had been left well behind them did she slacken speed, and when at length she halted in the shade of a clump of trees, Gervase, who had followed close behind her all the while, saw that anger still lingered in her flushed cheeks and stormy eyes. It was an anger which had served them well, but before he could utter either praise or inquiry, she said sharply: "Where is Hezekiah?"

He realized then that the two of them were alone, and that along the way they had come there was neither sight nor sound of the servant. He was conscious of a stab of misgiving, but said easily: "That horse of his would be hard put to it to keep pace with these. I will ride back to meet him."

"We will both go," she replied briefly, and turning the mare about, trotted back along the winding road. Within a minute or two they came in sight of Hezekiah, approaching them on foot and leading Mr. Seddon's horse by the bridle.

"Oh, what now?" Elinor exclaimed, and beneath the exasperation in the low-voiced question Gervase caught for the first time a hint of fraying nerves. It touched him strangely, reminding him of the frightened child of five years ago rather than the self-possessed young woman whose level gaze and direct, challenging remarks had aroused such doubts and self-questioning in his own mind.

"At least his delay was not occasioned by the military," he said reassuringly. "Some mishap has befallen his horse."

When they came up to the serving-man, they found

that the grey had cast a shoe and would have to be re-shod before it could complete the journey. Fortunately there was a village close at hand, but since it had been Hezekiah's intention to make a detour to avoid it, he suggested that Elinor and Gervase should ride on by that route while he took the grey to the smith, and that he should follow them as soon as might be.

"I do not know," Elinor said doubtfully. "I am not as familiar with the country as you are, Hezekiah, and we might miss the path." She turned to Gervase. "What are we to do?"

He considered the question for a moment or two before replying. "What would you do in these circumstances if I were indeed Jacob Hunt?" he asked at length.

She shrugged. "I should go into the village with Hezekiah, and wait at the inn while the grey was shod."

"Then that is what you will do," Gervase said decisively. "We have come this far in safety because we have behaved in a natural manner, and it will be best if we continue to do so."

She agreed somewhat dubiously, and they resumed their journey at walking pace. Another half-mile brought them to the village, where, leaving Hezekiah with the grey horse at the smithy, Elinor and Gervase rode on to the inn. They were now less than five miles from Fairwood, and the inn-keeper who came bustling out to greet them recognized Elinor at once. With an air of impatience which was only partly assumed she explained the cause of the delay, and allowed herself to be conducted to the neat little-used parlour.

"I will take a glass of wine while I am waiting," she

informed the landlord. "You may give it to Jacob to bring to me."

The inn-keeper looked curiously at the tall, roughly-dressed young man who had followed them into the parlour, but if he thought it strange that Mrs. Ashbourne should have so uncouth an attendant he made no comment, merely signing to Gervase to go with him. Left alone, Elinor endured some five minutes of agonized suspense until the door opened again and her husband came back into the room with a flask of wine and a glass on a tray.

"Is all well?" she asked as soon as the door was closed, and he nodded.

"I believe so. He seems to accept me for what I profess to be." He set the tray down, filled the glass and carried it across to her. "At all events, he asked no questions."

She had sunk down into a chair and covered her eyes with her hand, and replied without looking up. "I do not want the wine. It was the only excuse I could think of to bring you back here."

Gervase took her other hand and curved the fingers firmly about the glass. "Drink it," he said quietly. "I think you need it." He watched until she had taken a few reluctant sips, and then turned aside to lean against the edge of the table. Still watching her, he asked the question which had been foremost in his mind for some while. "Who is this Colonel Venner who speaks you so unmannerly?"

There was a palpable pause before Elinor replied. At last, looking down at the glass in her hand, she said in a low voice: "He is cousin to Geoffrey Marsham. He was at one time an officer in the regular army; now, as you saw, he holds a commission in the Wiltshire Militia. His home is in that county, but—" she hesitated, as though choosing her next words with care "—he has been a good deal in Somerset of late."

"Marsham?" Gervase repeated. "You mean Priscilla's husband?"

Another pause, then: "Her late husband," Elinor said very quietly. "She was widowed six months ago."

This time the pause became a silence which seemed to last for ever. Elinor endured it for as long as she could, but at length something stronger than her will compelled her to look up at Gervase. He had not moved, and though his face was pale, its expression told her nothing, but she saw that his hands were gripped hard on the edge of the table on either side of him.

As their eyes met at last, he said hoarsely: "How did it happen?"

"It was an accident," she replied reluctantly. "He came home late one snowy night, when the rest of the household had retired, and his foot must have slipped as he mounted the stairs. They found him next morning, lying dead in the hall below." She paused, nervously moistening her lips. "He . . . he was an excessively heavy drinker, I believe."

"Oh, my God!" Gervase was scarcely aware that he had spoken the words aloud. He moved across to the window and stood staring blindly out, while his imagination conjured up a thousand things which Elinor had left unsaid.

At last, after another long and painful silence, her voice came to him again, low and diffident. "Do not stand there, Gervase, I beg of you! You may be seen and recognized."

He came back to the table, impelled more by the need to question her than by concern for his own safety. The picture he had built up of Priscilla as a contented housewife had been rudely shattered, and he could not bring himself to contemplate that suggested in its place.

"I do not understand," he said desperately. "How could my grandfather let her be married to such a man? Or did he not care as long as she was wed?"

Elinor did not reply at once. She was not looking at him, but down at the empty glass which she was twisting between her hands.

"You know as well as I do," she said quietly at length, "that that is unjust. Mr. Marsham was well-born and possessed a comfortable fortune, and was, so I have heard, Priscilla's most persistent suitor. It was only recently, certainly not more than a year before his death, that he began to drink to excess, and that Sir William could not possibly have foreseen."

He made no reply, but he knew that what she said was true. For a minute or two he brooded over the intolerable thought of Priscilla married to an inveterate drunkard, and then the original subject of the conversation recurred to his mind.

"And Venner?" he asked abruptly. "What part does he play in all this?"

Again there was that curious hesitation before she replied.

"He was a frequent visitor to his cousin's house," she said slowly, "and after Mr. Marsham's death his visits became more rather than less frequent. Sir

William believes that he cherishes a hope of marrying Priscilla himself, for his own fortune is small and there are no children to inherit the Marsham estate."

Gervase stared. "But you said that Marsham is only six months dead."

"That is not likely to weigh with Colonel Venner," Elinor said dryly, "but when Sir William heard how often he was visiting Priscilla he thought it best that she should come back to the Priory to live, and leave her own house in the care of her sister-in-law, Miss Thomasine. Since then the Colonel has not seen her. He came to Fairwood once, but Sir William gave orders that he was not to be admitted."

"So that was the meaning of the taunt you flung at him," Gervase remarked thoughtfully. "Small wonder it provoked him to such fury against us all. Unless I am mistaken, he will make good that threat if it lies within his power."

"I should have tried to curb my temper," Elinor said remorsefully, "but I do dislike him so very much. He came to Fairwood once with Priscilla and Mr. Marsham, and once I met him at their house, and he always seems to be sneering at me behind that cold mask of a face."

"You had ample provocation for your anger today," Gervase replied absently, "and it served us well in that Venner was so enraged that he let us pass without questioning me. I doubt whether I could have maintained the deception if he had."

He moved restlessly away from the table again, not towards the window this time, but to the fireplace, where he stood resting his hands against the great beam above it and staring down at the empty hearth.

Silence settled again upon the room, broken only by the eager snuffling and scratching of Duchess, who had found a mousehole in the wainscot and was doing her best to extricate its occupant.

Gervase's thoughts and emotions were in wild confusion, provoked by the news he had just heard. So Priscilla was at Fairwood! He would see her again, which until this moment had seemed a dream impossible of fulfilment, for from the Priory he must make his way at once towards the coast in an endeavour to slip undetected out of England. He would see her, and she was no longer a wife but a widow, free at last of a husband for whom she could surely have felt no affection and little respect.

He checked himself sharply, realizing with a faint sense of shock the line his thoughts were taking and the futility of them. Priscilla might be free, but he was not, nor was his wife any longer a shadowy, childish figure he scarcely remembered. She was the woman who had sheltered him and saved his life, and who was now risking her own to lead him to safety. He turned his head to look at her, and saw that she had taken off her broad-brimmed hat and was sitting with closed eyes, her head turned slightly away from him as it rested against the back of her chair. Seen thus unawares, she seemed touchingly defenceless, and he realized with a stab of remorse how young she was. Not yet eighteen, if his memory served him aright, though the self-possession she had learned at Fairwood made her seem older at times; too young by far to bear the burdens which had been thrust upon her.

They were both roused at last by the clatter of hoofs and jingle of accoutrements in the village street, and a flash of red coats went past the window. Gervase swung round, and Elinor started up out of her chair to stare at him with wide, apprehensive eyes.

"Venner?" she questioned breathlessly, but he shook his head.

"No, not this time. Those are dragoons, not militia."

The soldiers had halted at the inn. An angle of the building hid them from the couple in the parlour, but the sound of their arrival was unmistakable. Elinor caught Gervase by the arm.

"Go and saddle the horses, and wait in the stable until they have gone, for it will not do for them to find you here with me. If danger threatens you, try to make your escape. I shall be safe enough with Hezekiah."

He looked at her strangely. "You think I would leave you?"

"What good could you do by staying? I am close enough now to Fairwood to invoke Sir William's authority if they challenge me. Go, for the love of God! You must not be found here!"

He saw the wisdom of her words and obeyed them, although with the utmost unwillingness. When he had gone, Elinor sat down again and tried to assume the outward aspect of composure, in spite of the frightened thumping of her heart. She called Duchess to her and lifted the little dog on to her lap, trying to draw some comfort from the contact.

The minutes dragged by, but at last spurred feet sounded in the passage outside and the door was thrust unceremoniously open. Elinor looked round, assuming the air of affronted dignity proper to the occasion, but then the colour drained from her face and a feeling of sick dismay laid hold upon her. Confronting her on the threshold was the large, scarlet-coated figure and bold, florid face of Captain Blake of the Tangier Regiment.

5

The Servants of the King

He kicked the door shut behind him and sauntered across the room, his dark eyes mocking her dismay. Elinor resisted an impulse to shrink from him, and looked at him with an assurance she did not feel.

"It seems, sir, that you have little use for courtesy," she greeted him coldly. "This is the second time that you have thrust yourself unasked into my presence."

He laughed, in no way discomposed by the criticism.

"Nor is it likely to be the last, my dear, unless you come to look upon me with more kindness. If I waited to be invited into your presence I fancy I might wait till doomsday."

Elinor's lips tightened. As at their previous encounter, his discourtesy was rousing her to an anger that cast out fear.

"A gentleman, Captain Blake, would spare me the necessity of pointing that out to him."

"And a gentlewoman, Mrs. Ashbourne, should be more cautious than to risk imprisonment by hindering the King's servants in their lawful duty. You deceived me finely yesterday, did you not?"

A cold hand seemed to close sharply on her heart. Was this then a deliberate pursuit, with sure knowledge of the quarry he hunted?

"I do not understand," she said faintly, and scarcely recognized the voice that spoke as her own. "How did I deceive you?"

He did not reply at once, but paused to set one foot on the chair beside him and lean his elbow on his bent knee. For the space of a few seconds he studied her in silence, and then he said softly:

"By pretending to know nothing of your husband's present whereabouts, or the manner in which he has occupied himself during the past few weeks." He leaned forward, his voice becoming harsher and more menacing. "Gervase Ashbourne, madam, came with Monmouth from Holland, and was still with him when he marched out of Bridgewater to attack us three nights ago. That much I have learned from rebels already taken prisoner. If he survived the battle I believe that he will try to return to his home."

Elinor sat very still, her hands resting on the spaniel's silky fur, while she considered what answer to make to this. The situation was not, perhaps, as desperate as she had feared, for unless Captain Blake was playing cat-and-mouse with her, he had as yet no more than suspicion to go upon.

She said, in as level a tone as she could command: "That is not likely. Sir William Ashbourne is strong against Monmouth and would aid none of his followers, not even his own grandson. In fact, my husband quarrelled with him on that very subject some time ago and has been estranged from him ever since."

Blake grinned unpleasantly. "Yet there might be others willing to help him. Yourself, for example, or your uncle, Mr. Seddon. Oh, I know we have searched Mead House and found nothing, but I have learned since of a priest-hole hidden somewhere within its walls. The constable told me of it last night."

Elinor achieved a sigh and an affectation of weary boredom. "Does that legend still persist? These old tales die hard in country places, and I have no doubt that the constable spoke in good faith, but if you indeed believed him, sir, why did you not return?"

"I might have done, madam, had those two other rebels not led me so merry a dance before I ran them to earth. As it was, I could not have reached Mead House again before morning and by then, as well I knew, it would be too late. If the priest-hole does exist, your uncle would guess that I should hear of it, and would know that it would not serve a second time. Had I discovered it yesterday it might have been a very different matter."

"Since my husband is unacquainted either with my uncle or with the reputed resources of Mead House, it is unlikely that he would seek refuge there even if it were within his power to do so," Elinor retorted promptly. "You pursue shadows, Captain Blake, as I fancy you did last night when you sought Monmouth himself."

The soldier's face darkened with anger. "Shadows may yet lead to the substance, madam! I did make a second visit to your uncle's house, only to find that you had fled. Why did you leave in such haste?"

Elinor got up, letting Duchess jump to the floor. There was contempt in her eyes and voice. "Look for the answer to that question in your own conduct, sir! Unless your memory is too clouded by wine, you may recall that last night you used me with intolerable familiarity. I sought to avoid a repetition of so disagreeable an experience."

"So?" Blake took his foot from the chair and stood upright. "You fled from me, did you? Are you sure that the purpose of your journey is not rather to bear news of your husband to Sir William Ashbourne?" He moved towards her as he spoke, and his hands came down on her shoulders, frustrating her attempt to retreat. "There are harsh penalties, my dear, for aiding these rebel rogues, and neither rank nor youth nor beauty will save you from them." She tried to break free, but he only laughed and pulled her into his arms. "Yet it is possible that even a rebel officer might elude pursuit, if his wife exerted herself to distract the attention of his pursuer."

Elinor struggled, but she was trapped by the heavy table behind her, and further hampered by Duchess, who was yelping and leaping in a frenzy of excitement against her skirts. The noise the dog was making drowned any sound of approaching footsteps, and when the door was flung open, crashing back on its hinges, it took Captain Blake so completely by surprise that he let Elinor go and swung round in a fury to learn the cause of the interruption. Discovering the intruder to be a tall young fellow in rough country garb, his face congested with rage.

"Get out, you blundering oaf!" he roared. "Get out, damn you!"

The words were scarcely uttered before the new-comer launched himself across the room at the Captain and seized him by the throat. For a moment they struggled together, and then Blake went over backwards into the hearth with an appalling clatter of fire-irons; his head struck the side of the fireplace with a sickening crack and he lay still.

Elinor uttered a faint cry, and Gervase turned quickly to her. She was so pale that he feared she was about to collapse and caught her by the arms to steady her, speaking her name in an urgent undertone while she clutched at the front of his jacket and fought desperately for self-control.

The landlord of the inn must have been close at Gervase's heels, for the clatter of Blake's fall had scarcely died away before he was in the room. He shut the door and went quickly to kneel by the prostrate figure, thrusting a hand inside the scarlet coat. For a moment he remained thus, and then he looked up at the white-faced girl and the roughly-clad young man supporting her. Gervase's hat had been knocked off in the brief struggle, and his features were now clearly revealed.

"He's suffered no worse than a broken head," the inn-keeper said in a low, hurried voice, "but there'll be the devil to pay when he comes to himself. For the love of God, sir, get yourself and your lady away from here while you may!"

"You know me?" Gervase queried sharply, and the other man smiled grimly as he got to his feet.

"I've lived in these parts long enough, sir, to know an Ashbourne when I see him," he said, "but you've no call to fear betrayal from me. Reckon I owe more loyalty to Sir William's family than I do to these catch-poll red-coats."

"It will not be forgotten, I promise you," Gervase assured him gratefully, "but for the present know me only as Jacob Hunt, servant to Mrs. Ashbourne. Where are the soldiers now?"

"Swilling ale in the tap-room, and small hope I have of seeing payment for it," the landlord said bitterly. It was plain in which direction his political sympathies lay. "Like master, like man, I reckon! None of 'em care aught for duty if there's pleasure to be had."

"As well for us that it is so," Gervase retorted dryly. He picked up his hat, pulled it on again, and turned to Elinor. "Are you recovered, my dear? Our good friend here is right when he says that it is perilous to linger."

She nodded wordlessly, picking up her own hat with trembling hands and placing it on her head. Gervase scooped Duchess up under his arm, and with the inn-keeper to guide them they went quietly out of the parlour and through the domestic quarters to the stable-yard. Their horses, which Gervase had already saddled, were waiting in their stalls, but as he led them out, Elinor said suddenly: "Hezekiah is still at the forge!"

"Rest easy, mistress!" the inn-keeper assured her. "I'll send word to him to follow you."

She looked gratefully at him. "Then will you tell him to meet us at his own cottage? We will wait for him there."

Gervase lifted her into the saddle, handed her the little dog, and turned to the inn-keeper. "No words of mine can express our gratitude for your aid," he said.

"You risk much to help us. God grant you do not suffer for it!"

The other man grinned. "Leave that to me, sir! When all's done they'll not believe I knew aught o' what happened, and 'twill give me rare pleasure to cozen 'em. Aye, that it will!"

With that assurance they had to be content, and, mindful as they were that every moment's delay increased the danger of discovery, they lost no time in setting out on the last stage of their journey. The innkeeper pointed out to them a road which would lead them clear of the village, and stood at his gate to watch them out of sight. Then he turned and went back into the house.

Captain Blake, making a slow and painful return to consciousness, became aware first of the throbbing torment of his head, and secondly of a commotion which seemed to be going on all around him to aggravate it. He opened his eyes, and after a momentary difficulty in focussing them, discovered the chief authors of the disturbance to be his sergeant and the inn-keeper, each of whom was occupied in loudly denouncing the other for the misfortune which had befallen the Captain.

"And I say that if a man keeps an inn, 'tis for him to see what manner o' people come into it," the sergeant announced belligerently. "A fine state of affairs it is when a gentleman can be knocked over the head in the parlour and no one the wiser!"

"No one the wiser?" the landlord retorted indignantly. "Didn't I give the alarm the minute I found him lying here? As for the rest, half a score o' soldiers in the tap-room should be enough to keep order in any house. If they was doing their duty, that is!"

"Peace, the pair of you, in God's name!" Captain Blake besought them feebly. "What of the woman, and the man who struck me down?"

"Gone, sir, thanks to this blundering numbskull here," the sergeant admitted reluctantly. "He let 'em walk out through the back door wi' no questions asked."

"How was I know what had happened?" the inn-keeper demanded bitterly. " 'Twas the lady as gave the orders, and 'twas not for me to gainsay her, and her close kin to Sir William himself."

The sergeant made an attempt at sarcasm. "A lady o' quality in these parts always goes by way o' the kitchen and stable-yard, I suppose?"

"She said she didn't want to pass the tap-room. Seems she'd already suffered some rough treatment from you red-coats, and had no wish for a second encounter. Who's to blame her for that?"

Captain Blake dragged himself into a sitting position on the settle to which they had carried him, and took his throbbing head between his hands, endeavouring to recall the scene which had immediately preceded his discomfiture. Slowly, in disjointed fragments, memory returned to him. He had accused the alluring Mrs. Ashbourne of knowing more than she pretended of the present whereabouts of her rebel husband, and had been about to press the advantage thus gained when that hulking oaf of a servant came blundering into the room to ruin all. Now the lady had fled, and her attendant with her. He could, of course, follow her to her home, but it was gradually being borne in upon him, chiefly by the words and attitude of the inn-keeper, that he would need to tread warily. He was in a district

where great influence was wielded by the Ashbourne
family, and it would not do to provoke them too bla-
tantly, particularly since, with the exception of the
renegade Gervase, their loyalty to the Crown was un-
questioned.

It was plain that for the moment his hands were
tied, and if there was a way out of the impasse he was
at present in no fit state to perceive it. Irritably he dismissed the inn-keeper, commanded the sergeant to
search the whole village lest any fugitives had contrived
to get so far from the scene of the rebel defeat, and sub-
mitted impatiently to the ministrations of the landlord's
wife when she came to dress his injury.

This was less severe than it might have been, since
the thick curls of his periwig had afforded him a certain amount of protection, but it was sufficient to leave
him with a pounding headache and a disinclination to
pursue the quest for stray rebels any farther that day.
Since the people of the inn had allowed this outrage to
be committed in their house, they should pay for it by
giving hospitality for the night to himself and his men.

During the early part of the evening, when Captain
Blake, having dined with less than his usual appetite,
was sitting alone in the parlour and trying to alleviate
his discomfort with brandy, there was a sudden clatter
of hoofs and tramp of marching feet in the village
street. These sounds ceased outside the inn, orders
which the Captain could not distinguish were given,
and a few minutes later footsteps approached the parlour and the landlord ushered a newcomer into the
room.

Captain Blake, looking up in some annoyance, found
himself confronting a tall, coldly-handsome man in the

uniform of a Colonel of Militia, and came hurriedly to his feet. The Colonel dismissed the inn-keeper with a disdainful gesture and advanced into the room

"Do not disturb yourself, Captain Blake," he said pleasantly, "for I understand that you have recently sustained an injury. That is so, is it not?"

Blake's fingers strayed involuntarily to the bandage which was just visible beneath his periwig, and he admitted, somewhat uneasily, that it was. The Colonel nodded sympathetically.

"You received that hurt at the hands of a serving-man, so the landlord tells me," he continued, halting by the table to pull off his gloves. "The servant, it seems, of a certain Mrs. Elinor Ashbourne." The gloves were dropped on to the table, the Colonel's hat followed them, and a pair of singularly hard blue-grey eyes fixed their gaze upon the Captain's face. "I am Venner of the Wiltshire Militia, Captain Blake, and I have some acquaintance with the lady in question. I should like to know more of the affair, if you please."

Captain Blake's heart sank. The foreboding that trouble might arise from his pursuit of Elinor Ashbourne was apparently justified, but not even at his most pessimistic had he visualized a situation such as this. Any protests, he fancied, would come from the Ashbournes themselves; he had certainly not expected to be called upon to explain his conduct to an officer of rank superior to his own.

Somewhat haltingly, unnerved by the penetrating gaze of those cold eyes, he described his fruitless search of Mead House the previous day, his later chance discovery that a priest-hole was said to be concealed within its walls, and his conviction that a second search would now be as barren as the first. He spoke of the suspicions aroused in him by Mrs. Ashbourne's precipitate departure from her uncle's house, and the pursuit which had been the result of those suspicions. He had been questioning her, he explained, concerning the whereabouts of the rebel, Gervase Ashbourne, when her servant burst into the room and attacked him.

"Such violence on his part might almost suggest that your pursuit was of the wife rather than of the husband," the Colonel commented acidly, but to Blake's relief he did not pursue that train of thought. "So you suspected her of carrying a message from Gervase Ashbourne to his grandfather. Why?"

The Captain shrugged. "As I have told you, sir, so sudden a departure savoured of flight, or of some compelling reason for her journey. Mead House is close enough to Weston Moor to provide shelter for a fugitive from the battle, but from what I have heard, Fairwood Priory is more likely to provide the means for complete escape."

"Sound enough reasoning, I admit. Some compelling reason, you say!" For a space Venner was silent, drumming his fingers on the table while Blake waited respectfully and reflected that so far he had come off better than he had expected. At length the Colonel said thoughtfully, "Describe to me the servant who attacked you."

This was more difficult, for Captain Blake had had only the most hazy impression of his assailant as the fellow flung himself upon him. However, he did his best.

"Young, I believe, and tall and strongly-made. A rough-looking oaf to be in attendance upon a lady."

Colonel Venner nodded. "I encountered Mrs. Ashbourne myself earlier today, but I paid little heed to her servants. Perhaps the inn-keeper can tell us more about him."

The inn-keeper, summoned to their presence, was voluble on the subject of Mrs. Ashbourne's attendant. Certainly he had seen and spoken with him. He was Jacob Hunt, servant to Mr. Seddon of Mead House, who was uncle to Mrs. Ashbourne. Mr. Seddon had sent Jacob to protect the young lady during her journey, so the elder servant had told him, and if he had exceeded his duty in attacking the Captain it was only out of devotion to the family he served.

Colonel Venner cut short this loquaciousness and dismissed the man. When they were once more alone, he looked ironically across the room at Captain Blake.

"I grow increasingly certain, Captain, that both you and I have today been guilty of gross carelessness. That we have permitted a notable rebel to slip through our fingers."

"A notable rebel?" Blake repeated blankly. "You mean . . ."

"I mean Gervase Ashbourne, Captain Blake. It is my belief that his wife was not the bearer of a message from him, but an escort and a disguise for the man himself. Ashbourne has not lived in these parts since he was a boy, and his last visit was close upon five years ago. The risk of recognition would not be so very great."

Blake regarded him doubtfully. "But to ride with

him through our patrols! Would any woman venture that?"

"Elinor Ashbourne would," Venner replied briefly. "I dislike the lady intensely, but that does not blind me to her mettle." He rose from his chair and began to pace to and fro across the room. "This is no more than a suspicion, a premonition, if you will, and yet I would stake all I possess upon its being so! All that remains is to verify it."

"I could follow them to Fairwood Priory, sir," Blake suggested eagerly. "After what happened here, it is the natural thing for me to do."

Venner shook his head. "You would gain nothing by that, I am certain. Even if the house itself contains no secret hiding-place—and we cannot be sure that it does not—there are the Priory ruins and the crypt beneath them, to say nothing of the various outbuildings. The place is like a village in miniature, and would offer a dozen places where a man might hide. No, we must find some other means of discovering the truth."

Blake lapsed into crestfallen silence, and the Colonel resumed his measured pacing. Perhaps ten minutes were passed thus, and then with an air of decision Venner returned to the table and drew up a chair, signing to his subordinate to do the same.

"Look you, Captain Blake," he said briskly when they were seated, "I do not know whether your pursuit of Elinor Ashbourne was prompted by duty or your own desires, though the violence you suffered at her husband's hands might lead me to hazard a guess. However, obey me implicitly and we will say no more of that. We are both, I hope, loyal servants of the

King, and our most pressing duty is to make prisoner this confounded rebel. You understand me, I hope?"

The Captain assured him that he did, and was happy to place himself and his men under the Colonel's orders. These orders Venner then proceeded to give.

"Tomorrow morning you will go, with your men, to Fairwood, and demand Jacob Hunt. They will have some story ready, no doubt, that he has returned to his home, or some such thing, and so you will order a search to be made, both for Hunt and for Gervase Ashbourne. Finding nothing, you will depart, though not without making such threats as seem suitable to the occasion. The empty threats, Captain Blake, of a baffled and angry man."

He paused there, and the Captain nodded his understanding.

"I'll play my part well, sir, never fear! What next?"

Colonel Venner shook his head. "As far as you are concerned, nothing! I desire only to lull them into a sense of false security, and that will be the end of your part in the affair—save that you will reveal to no one what has been said in this room tonight. This is no ordinary situation, Captain, and direct and ordinary methods will not prevail." He paused, staring at the candle-flames, a faint, sneering smile playing about his lips although his eyes remained as bleak as ice. "I have a very particular reason for wishing to bring this matter to a satisfactory conclusion, and I think—yes, I think I possess also the means to accomplish it."

6

Return to Fairwood

THE afternoon sunshine was warm on the mellow bricks of Fairwood Priory when Elinor at last drew rein before its door, and beyond the gardens the chapel with its surrounding fragments of ruined monastic buildings could be glimpsed between the trees. Clearly her approach had been observed, for she had scarcely dismounted when swift footsteps sounded within the house, and from the great double doors, set wide to the summer day, Hubert emerged eagerly to greet her.

They met at the foot of the steps, and he kissed her hand and then her cheek, uttering conventional words of welcome and of surprise at her early return, but she could see a veiled anxiety in his eyes. In his elder brother's absence, Hubert's responsibilities had increased as his grandfather's health declined, and his own ill-health had laid an additional burden upon him, so that he looked a good deal older than his four-and-twenty years. Elinor regarded him with affectionate concern as they went into the house.

"You look so tired, Hubert," she said gently. "Have things gone badly here during these past few days?"

He glanced at her with a swift, warm smile which for a moment restored the lost boyishness to his face.

"We have missed you, Nell," he said simply. "My grandfather most of all. Fairwood is quick to feel the absence of its mistress."

"How is it with Sir William?"

Hubert hesitated for a moment. "Less well, I fear," he said gravely at length. "As I say, he has missed you sadly, though the news of your return seems to have restored him a little. I was with him when they brought me word of your approach."

"I will go to him at once!" Elinor ⬛⬛⬛⬛ her pace as she turned towards the stairs, but on the lowest step she paused again, her hand on the carved newel-post, to look with sudden misgiving at her companion.

"Hubert, you do not think that he . . ." she left the question unfinished, but he had no doubt of her meaning.

"I don't know, Nell," he said quietly. "I pray that it is not so, and yet," he paused to glance swiftly about them, and then added in a lower voice, "last night he spoke to me of my brother."

"Of Gervase?" Elinor was startled, for this was the first time in two years that any mention of his elder grandson had passed Sir William's lips. "What said he?"

"He asked for news of him." Hubert took her arm and drew her with him up the stairs; his voice was muted so that it was barely audible. "When I replied that nothing certain was known of his present whereabouts, he said that inquiries must be made, that we must discover what has become of him. I think it was the news of the rebel defeat which prompted him to speak at last."

"Hubert!" Elinor's voice was reproachful. "You did not tell him of that?"

"Priscilla let it fall by chance while she was sitting with him." An impatient exclamation from Elinor interrupted him, and he added as though in excuse, "I should have foreseen the possibility, I suppose. She has never learned to guard her tongue, and word of the battle had just reached us, so that it was foremost in all our minds."

"Perhaps it has happened for the best," Elinor said thoughtfully. "You did not tell him, did you, that I had already set out to look for Gervase?"

Hubert shook his head. "No, though I did say that being at Mead House and so in the neighborhood of the battlefield, you would doubtless cause inquiries to be made. That seemed to ease his mind a little."

"Hubert, what are his feelings towards Gervase? Has he forgiven him, do you think?"

He moved his hands in a helpless gesture.

"Who save my grandfather himself can tell you that? He spoke only of the necessity of discovering what has become of him, for the sake of Fairwood and of our family. If any accident has befallen Gervase, then the future of both become my responsibility, and God knows how little I am fitted to bear it!" He halted, turning to her with a sort of desperation, "Nell, tell me, in pity's name! Have you brought news of my brother?"

"Yes," she whispered. "Yes, Hubert, I have, and it is good news, my dear, so do not look so careworn. He is alive and well and, for the present, safe. I will tell you more when we come to Sir William and there is no risk that we may be overheard."

With this he had to be content until they came to Sir William's bedchamber. They were met at the door by Mercer, his personal servant, and with a word of greeting to him Elinor went quickly and quietly across the room to the great bed where the old man lay.

Three years had seen a vast change in Sir William Ashbourne. His face now was sunken, so that skin the colour of parchment was stretched tightly across prominent bones, lending to the aquiline countenance the aspect of an aged bird of prey. He lay very still, his sparse white hair covered by a linen cap, yellowed, claw-like hands inert upon the rich coverlet, and yet the dim reflection of earlier fires gleamed still in the faded blue of his single eye. He smiled faintly as Elinor bent over him.

"You are soon returned, my child," the weak old voice greeted her. "How fares your good uncle?"

"Well enough, sir," she replied. "His servants grow over careful and summoned me without real cause."

"I am glad to hear it. You spend too much time already by the sick-bed of an old man."

"You know that I begrudge no moment of it, Sir William," she chided him gently. "It is a duty which is also a happiness to me."

"Sir!" Hubert had come to stand beside her, and now spoke in soft, urgent tones. "Elinor brings the news you desired to have. News of Gervase."

Sir William's glance, which had turned towards the speaker, came back to Elinor's face. There was eagerness in its expression, and anxiety also, and she spoke quickly to reassure him. Save for the servant, there was no one to overhear, and Mercer could be trusted implicitly.

"Better than mere news, Sir William," she said softly. "I bring Gervase himself."

She heard Hubert gasp, but did not turn to look at him. The carven lines of Sir William's face betrayed no trace of emotion, but his hands had closed, as though involuntarily, into quivering fists. After a long moment of silence he said haltingly: "Was he . . . with Monmouth?"

Elinor hesitated. It had been impossible to keep all news of the rebellion from the old man, and though they had spoken of it only when he questioned them, and then had told him as little as they dared, she knew that he had been able to form at least a general idea of the progress of the insurrection. Priscilla had let fall the news of the Royal victory on Sedgemoor. It would be worse than useless to attempt to deceive him now.

"He came with the Duke from Holland," she replied gently, "and served as one of his officers throughout the campaign. After the rebel defeat he became a fugitive, and it is thus that he comes to you now."

"But, Nell, where is he?" Hubert broke in urgently. "How did you find him?"

Sir William was waiting with a faint frown for her reply; the servant had drawn near and was listening as expectantly as his master. Briefly, and passing lightly over the moments of peril, Elinor described her meeting with Gervase and all that had followed it.

"After we left the inn," she concluded, "we made all speed to Hezekiah's cottage, and reached it with no further misadventures. When he joined us there, it was agreed that he and Martha should hide Gervase for the present. It would have been too dangerous for him to come to the Priory by daylight, nor will he do so at all until he receives permission from you, Sir William."

"So in his extremity he remembers the duty he owes me!" The old man's voice was bitter. "His recollection of it comes somewhat late!"

Elinor's heart sank at the tone, and for the first time a qualm of doubt assailed her. Had she done right to bring Gervase to Fairwood, to urge him so emphatically to seek a reconciliation with his grandfather? She had felt convinced that both desired it, however much they might pretend otherwise, but she might have been mistaken, deceived by her own ardent desire to see peace made between them. She dropped to her knees beside the bed, taking one of Sir William's withered hands in both her own.

"But not too late, sir?" she pleaded. "You will see him, will you not? Please, I beg of you!"

His expression softened, and he turned his head on the pillow to look at her. "If you are his advocate, child, I cannot refuse. For your sake, I will see him—though, mark you, I promise nothing."

"That you receive him is all I ask," she replied unsteadily, getting to her feet. "Now you must rest. Hubert and I will arrange everything, will we not, Hubert?"

"With all my heart," he responded promptly. "This is better news than ever I dared to hope for!"

So it was that late that same night, when most of the household was asleep, Hubert Ashbourne waited anxiously at a side door of the Priory. Every possible precaution had been taken to keep secret Gervase's presence on the estate and his intended visit to the house itself, for no one was in any doubt of the dread consequences of discovery. Relief at the fugitive's present safety, and gladness at his return, must inevitably be tempered with misgiving.

A furtive figure came silently through the garden towards the door, and a moment later the brothers' hands had met in a firm clasp by which each tried to convey the meaning of the words which for caution's sake they dare not utter. Then Hubert drew Gervase into the house, barred the door, and took up the candle which, with its flame carefully shrouded, had been kept in readiness.

The light revealed them to each other at last, and Hubert felt a faint sense of shock at sight of the rough clothes and cropped hair of the man before him, so different from the courtly figure he remembered, and which made his own laced coat and flowing curls seem suddenly incongruous. Gervase, for his part, was shocked by his brother's altered looks, and felt a sharp stab of remorse that the younger man had been left to shoulder burdens which should by right have been his own responsibility. None of this, however, was it possible to say; Hubert gestured to him to be silent, and led the way through the familiar rooms and corridors to the door of Sir William's bedchamber. There he paused for a moment and turned to his brother.

"You must prepare yourself for a shock, Gervase," he warned him softly. "You will find him greatly changed."

He opened the door and they went quietly into the big room. Candles were burning on either side of the bed, and as they entered, Elinor rose from a chair there and came forward to meet them. She had changed her riding-dress for a gown of amber satin

which echoed the colour of her eyes, flattering the
creamy-gold of her skin and the rich darkness of her
hair, and there were pearls about her throat and in her
ears. Her smooth shoulders were bare above the filmy
lace edging the low-cut bodice, and her skirt was slit in
front and caught back to reveal an embroidered petti-
coat shimmering with gold thread. Hubert thought he
had never seen her look so beautiful, and, divining the
reason for it, glanced curiously at his brother.

His expression revealed nothing. Gervase took his
wife's hand and bore it to his lips with a courtliness
which immediately gave the lie to his humble attire,
but neither spoke as she led him towards the massive
four-poster in the middle of the room. Bending over its
occupant, she said softly: "Gervase is here, Sir
William."

The old man's head turned slowly towards them,
and as she moved back Elinor knew by Gervase's sudden shocked stillness that not even the warning which
she had urged Hubert to give him had wholly prepared
him for the change he now beheld in his grandfather.
For a long moment the two men regarded each other,
and then the younger dropped to one knee beside the
bed, his dark head bent in a sudden, impulsive surrender of pride and self-will. Sir William's gnarled hand
moved to touch and grip the bowed shoulder, and thus,
with no word spoken, peace was made between them.
After a little, Sir William looked again at Elinor.

"I thank you, my child," he said quietly. "Now go
with Hubert into the next room. I would like to be
alone for a while with Gervase."

She nodded silently, too deeply moved to speak, and
with Hubert beside her went softly from the room.

As the door closed behind them Gervase lifted his head. "Grandfather" he said haltingly, "what can I say—" but Sir William's hand was raised to interrupt him.

"Of the past, Gervase, nothing! All that lies behind us, and it is of the future that we must speak, for this is likely to be our last meeting in this world." Gervase made a gesture of protest and denial, and the old man smiled faintly. "No need for pretence between us, boy! I shall not rise from this bed again, and you must not tarry here longer than is necessary to make provision for your escape. Until you are out of England, you go in mortal peril."

Gervase rose to his feet. "I leave Fairwood again tonight, sir," he replied firmly. "What becomes of me is not important—I have never deluded myself regarding the price of failure—but my presence here imperils you all. I do not know how much Elinor has told you—"

"Enough to convince me that you are safest here until some plan has been made for your escape," Sir William broke in. "Unless, of course, you have already made some such plan."

Gervase shrugged. "I must try to reach the coast, sir, that much is certain. If Hubert can furnish me with a mount and a fresh disguise, I can be away from here before daybreak."

"To ride straight into the arms of your enemies," Sir William added dryly. "That will not serve."

"That I should not be captured here, sir, is what matters most. To shelter a traitor is to share his guilt in the eyes of the law, and already I have involved too many people in my danger. Henceforth I must take my chance alone."

There was a pause, and then Sir William said quietly, "Draw up yon chair, Gervase, and listen to what I have to say." He waited until this command had been obeyed, and then continued: "Now heed me carefully. You say that your personal safety is unimportant, but you are wrong. Your life does not belong to you alone. When I am gone, it will be for you to take up the responsibilities which I have laid aside."

"Sir, even if I escape I shall be forced to live in exile. So many know me for a rebel that nothing else will be possible."

"Even rebels have been pardoned ere now, Gervase, and it may be that I still have some small measure of influence. Yet even if a pardon is not forthcoming I do not think your exile will last for ever. Monmouth had no shadow of right to the throne and I would never support his pretensions, but that does not mean that I am content with our present ruler; and there are hundreds—nay, thousands—like me throughout the kingdom. The time will come when you may return in peace to Fairwood."

"God grant it may be so," Gervase responded soberly. "I have been neglectful of my duty in the past, I know."

"Perhaps I am in part to blame for that," Sir William said with a sigh. "It may be that I should have acted differently five years ago."

Gervase, who had been staring down at his clasped hands, looked up sharply. "It was necessary, sir, that I should marry Elinor."

"It was," his grandfather agreed, "but it was a thousand pities that your duty could not match your inclination." He smiled faintly at Gervase's look of blank astonishment. "Oh, I know 'twas your cousin you hankered after then, and if nothing more than a fair face and an empty head had been needful in your bride I might perhaps have let you have your way. I wonder, though, how much of your desire for her sprang from resentment of the match I had made for you."

He paused, but Gervase made no reply. Surprise and dismay that an attachment which he had supposed a secret should have been so readily detected was tinged now with a faint, uneasy suspicion that what his grandfather said was true. He had resented the demands made upon him, and the necessity which bound him to a rich child-bride; had then his feelings for Priscilla, which he had accounted the one true love of his life, been no more than a defiance flung in the face of authority? The thought was a humiliating one, yet strangely enough, it lacked any real hurtfulness.

"I realize now that I was too high-handed in my dealings with you," Sir William resumed after a moment. "You had been so long away that I had forgotten you were no longer the boy I took to London, but a man with the right to be consulted upon a matter which touched you so closely. I would have brooked no refusal—my need of Thomas Dane's fortune was too pressing for that—but I might have been content with a formal betrothal, and to delay the marriage-ceremony until Elinor was older. For mark this, Gervase! I am certain that were you now free to choose between her and Priscilla, there is no doubt upon whom your choice would fall. Elinor is all, and more, than I hoped she would be, and has brought to Fairwood far more than her father's gold. I never thought to find a woman to match my own Elizabeth, but by Heaven! in your wife I see her live again."

His glance had gone to a portrait which hung nearby, and Gervase looked in the same direction. The light was too dim to reveal more than its shadowy outline, but memory served him where his eyes could not, and he realized with an odd sense of discovery that Sir William spoke the truth. There was no physical likeness, for the portrait showed his grandmother as plump and fair, but in her face, as in Elinor's, there was that strange blend of vitality and serenity, and an unfaltering courage which would face hardship and danger without complaint.

"She has brought me greater comfort than I can ever tell!" Sir William's tone was musing. "Hers is a rare spirit, Gervase, as you will learn in days to come. As, perhaps, you have already begun to learn. I served both myself and you better than I knew when I chose your bride."

There was another, longer pause. Gervase's thoughts were upon the days just past, and the part which Elinor had played in them. He saw her again in the shadowy garden of Mead House, compassionately aiding an exhausted fugitive; in her uncle's study, challenging him with flashing eyes and fearless words to see his grandfather again; on the road to Fairwood, boldly facing the menace of Colonel Venner and his attendant soldiers when discovery would have meant imprisonment. Yes, he had indeed begun to learn.

"I had hoped to hold a son of yours in my arms before I died!" Sir William's voice broke in upon his thoughts. "Ah well, a man of my years has learned to relinquish his dreams without bitterness, but remember,

Gervase, you owe a duty to the name you bear. There has been an Ashbourne at Fairwood since our ancestor received the estate at King Henry's hands, and it would be a grievous thing if strangers came to take possession here."

"I am not the last of our name, sir," Gervase reminded him gently, "My brother—"

"Hubert will never marry," Sir William stated, and there was an odd note of finality in his voice. "He is as obdurate in that as he is dutiful in all other things. Unlike you, Gervase, who have been dutiful in nothing else."

Gervase bit his lip. "No reproach which you could utter, sir, can exceed those I heap upon myself," he said in a low voice, "but if it pleases God to bring me safely through my present danger I shall endeavour to mend matters in the future. That I swear to you."

"It is enough!" Sir William's voice was weaker now, but filled with contentment. "I have been grievously troubled since you went abroad, but tonight the shadow is lifted from my heart. You will come safely through this peril, of that I am convinced. Stay with Hezekiah for the present. The soldiers are less likely to seek you there, and if they do, you have the open country at the door. We will find some means of getting you out of England. There are smuggling vessels which ply along our southern coasts and whose masters will take any risk if the price is right." His voice trailed into silence, and he smiled wearily at his grandson. "We must bid each other farewell now, Gervase. I grow very tired, and it is best that you do not linger here too long." He put out one frail hand, and Gervase took it between his own. "God bless you, dear lad, and bring you safely home!"

"I have been blessed already, sir, more richly than I deserve." Gervase replied unsteadily. "I will strive to be more worthy in the future."

Sir William did not reply. He had fallen into one of the sudden dozes of extreme age, and after a moment or two Gervase lifted the withered hand to his lips and then laid it gently down upon the coverlet. Moving very quietly in order not to disturb his grandfather, he went out of the room and into another close by, guided by the glimmer of light beneath its door.

Elinor and Hubert were sitting at a small table where a single branch of candles made a pool of radiance in the shadows. They were talking in low tones, but they broke off as he entered and turned their faces towards him. Seeing them thus together, sensing the bond of affection and comradeship between them, he was conscious of a swift, inexplicable feeling of desolation, as though he were a stranger intruding upon a close-knit family circle where he had no right to be. He went forward to stand by Elinor's chair, resting one hand on its back.

"My grandfather is asleep," he said awkwardly. "You are right, Hubert, he is greatly changed."

"But all is well between you, is it not?" Elinor asked anxiously. "Your differences are at an end?"

"Yes, all is well," he replied, "and I know, I think, whom I have to thank for it. You were right, Elinor, in every word you said to me. I deserve all your reproaches, and more."

She coloured slightly. "If I spoke harshly, it was only because I so ardently desired to see peace made between you," she said in a low voice. "For your sake as well as Sir William's."

"What now, Gervase?" Hubert spoke abruptly, not looking at them. "Do you return to the cottage?"

"For the present!" Gervase glanced curiously at his brother, surprised by the change in his manner. "If I can lie hidden for a while there is a chance that I may reach the coast undetected. My grandfather suggests that I may find a smuggling craft willing to give me a passage to France."

"Of course!" Elinor exclaimed eagerly. "The ports will be watched, but they cannot keep guard along the whole coast. If we could find a way—"

"Perhaps we will, but not tonight," Gervase broke in quietly. "It is late, and this day's adventures have already made heavy demands upon you. You must be very weary." He took her hands and drew her to her feet, and held her so, looking down at her. "Though, by my faith, you show no sign of it! I vow that Captain Blake's ardour is understandable, however deplorable his manner of expressing it."

Colour rushed into her face, and the gold-brown eyes faltered away from his. Withdrawing her hands, she murmured a breathless good night and turned quickly towards the door. Hubert moved silently to open it for her, and, pausing only to exchange a word with him, she went softly out of the room, leaving the two men alone.

When Hubert turned towards him again, Gervase was still standing by the table, staring down at the candle-flames. His face revealed nothing, but he was considering, with surprise and some dismay, the explanation which had been vouchsafed him of the sudden constraint in his brother's manner and of Sir William's firm conviction that Hubert would not marry. It had been clearly revealed to him in one unguarded moment as the younger man watched Elinor go past him out of the room.

The memory of that look stayed with him as, with few words spoken on either side, they retraced their steps to the door by which Gervase had entered the house, and he was still pondering on all that it implied as he made his way cautiously across garden and parkland to Hezekiah's cottage at the edge of the wood. Not until he was secure once more in his improvised hiding-place did the realization dawn upon him that his visit to the Priory had come and gone, and he had seen nothing of Priscilla.

7

The Brothers

SIR WILLIAM was very tired next day, but those closest to him, Elinor and Hubert and the servant, Mercer, could see that he was easier in his mind. He slept a good deal, but in his wakeful moments seemed eager to talk of Gervase, as though now that his years of silence had been broken he wished to make amends for them.

During the forenoon Elinor was sitting beside his bed. She had been reading to him from the book which still lay open in her lap, but seeing that the old man had fallen asleep she had paused, and sat now with her gaze resting on the trees and sky visible beyond the window, and her thoughts dwelling, as they had dwelt almost constantly during the past few days, on the man who now lay hidden in the little cottage beyond the park. The first part of her self-imposed task had been accomplished, but until she knew that Gervase was safely beyond the sea there could be no peace or reassurance in her mind.

And in her heart? She smiled a little at the thought, with wistfulness and resignation, for peace had been a stranger there for many a day. It had fled from her on her wedding-day, when she discovered that the marriage which had seemed to her like a fairy-tale was no more than a heartless bargain, a trading of the proud Ashbourne name for her father's gold. She had put childhood from her in the same moment, and taken a resolve that Priscilla's cruel gibes should not for long be justified. Merchant's daughter though she was, she would learn to be worthy of the name she now bore, and one day the husband who now cared nothing for her would look at her with love and pride.

To that end she had striven ever since, sparing no effort to become everything that the mistress of Fairwood Priory should be. The determination and diligence which had raised Thomas Dane from obscurity to a position of wealth and influence were not lacking in his only child, and with Sir William's help, and Hubert's, she had overcome the difficulties which at times had seemed insurmountable, until now the reins of the great house rested firmly in her hands, and it was to her that all problems were brought, all decisions referred.

She had waited, patiently at first and then with deepening misgivings, for Gervase to come home, and as time passed a bitterness she could not conquer took possession of her. It was for Sir William's sake alone that she had set out to search for her husband in the rebel ranks, believing that his neglect of her had brought about an answering indifference in her own heart. The two days just past had taught her how mistaken she was, and now a tentative glimmer of hope awakened as she remembered the fury of his attack on Captain Blake, and how last night he had looked at her with more than kindness in his eyes. Some day, surely, that hope must be fulfilled.

The sound of the door being softly opened disturbed her thoughts, and she looked round as Mercer came into the room. Seeing that his master was asleep, he put a finger to his lips to enjoin silence and beckoned urgently to her. In swift concern she laid aside the book and followed him soundlessly into the corridor.

"Soldiers, madam," he replied in answer to her anxious, low-voiced question. "A score or more dragoons under an officer who demands to search the house."

Elinor's lips tightened. "My old acquaintance, Captain Blake, no doubt," she remarked. "Well, he will find nothing, search he never so closely. Does Mr. Hubert know that he is here?"

"He was on his way to meet the soldiers, madam, when he sent me to warn you of their presence."

She nodded. "I will go down. Stay with Sir William, Mercer, and you had best wake him and tell him that the dragoons are here. It is not likely that we can persuade them to abandon their search."

Mercer bowed and withdrew into the bedchamber, while Elinor went quickly towards the hall. At the head of the stairs she encountered Priscilla, in a state of mingled excitement and agitation.

"Elinor, is it true?" she exclaimed. "My woman tells me that the house is to be searched."

"True enough, unless Hubert can fob them off," Elinor replied briefly. "You had better come with me. Some of these dragoons are not over-nice in their manners."

"But why should they search this house?" Priscilla demanded as she followed the other girl down the stairs. "What can they hope to find here?"

Elinor shrugged with assumed indifference. "Who can tell? Everyone in Somerset is suspect today, and they may have heard the rumours of Gervase being with Monmouth. It would be enough."

They came into the hall by way of a door below the minstrels' gallery, and halted there unobserved to study the scene before them. In the middle of the great room Hubert was confronting Captain Blake, his slight figure seemingly overpowered by the soldier's scarlet-coated bulk, while behind the Captain his men awaited the order to commence their search.

"It is intolerable!" Hubert was saying angrily as the girls entered the room. "Not once since this house was built has the loyalty of its occupants been questioned! My grandfather is very old, and lies sick in his bed. Is this his reward for a lifetime of devotion to the Crown? By God, sir, your accusations are more than discourteous! They are indecent!"

Elinor spoke quietly from her place by the door, in a voice icy with scorn. "You waste your breath, Hubert, when you appeal to Captain Blake on the grounds of courtesy or decency. He admits the demands of neither."

Blake swung round towards her, an angry flush darkening his face, but paused a moment before delivering any reply to that uncompromising speech. The two girls made an admirable picture there between the carved pillars of the gallery; Elinor slim and straight in her saffron-coloured gown, Priscilla's golden, more voluptuous prettiness enhanced by her widow's weeds and veil, and the Captain was not the man to let it go unappreciated. After a moment or two, however, he recalled his attention to the business in hand, and said ominously:

"Bold words, madam, but I warned you yesterday of the perils threatening those who hinder the King's servants in their duty. You may account yourself safe here, but I would remind you that Fairwood Priory is no more sacred than any other house that aids rebellion or harbours traitors."

"Fairwood has done neither," Hubert broke in heatedly. "Not a single sword, not a penny piece did Monmouth have of us, nor did one man of ours march with his army."

"No?" Blake's voice was filled with heavy scorn. "You lie, Mr. Ashbourne! What of your brother, who not only marched with Monmouth, but held a commission in his army?"

"My brother, sir, is a renegade and a traitor," Hubert replied steadily, "and if he was indeed out with Monmouth he had no aid from us, nor ever will."

"That we shall see!" Blake said with a sneer. "If you are indeed innocent of succouring this rebel you have nothing to fear from a search of your house and buildings." He turned his head to toss an order to his men. "Be about it with no more delay, and see to it that the search is thorough."

Hubert opened his mouth to protest again, but Elinor, who had moved forward to his side, laid a hand on his arm.

"Parley with him no more, Hubert," she said contemptuously. "It is to no avail, and the sooner the search is begun the sooner it will be ended." She looked past the Captain to the dragoons, already dispersing under the sergeant's orders, and raised her voice a little so that all might hear her next words. "All I ask is that his men remember that Sir William Ashbourne is an old man, and ill, and to treat him with the respect which his years command."

They gave no sign that they had heard her, but went clattering off in different directions. Elinor's lips tightened, and a troubled frown creased her brow. For a moment she hesitated, then, saying quietly to Hubert, "I will go back to Sir William," she turned again to the door by which she had entered.

"One moment, Mrs. Ashbourne!" Blake's hectoring tones halted her after only a few paces. "There is another matter to be settled between us before you go. The matter of a certain loutish servant of yours named, so I am told, Jacob Hunt."

Elinor had paused at his first words, and faced him with a look of disdainful inquiry. Now she shook her head.

"He is not here, Captain Blake," she said scornfully.

"Did you suppose I would let him linger within reach of your vindictiveness, when he acted as he did merely in my defence? I am not so lacking in gratitude."

"Nor in audacity, madam, it seems, since you so wantonly impede the course of justice."

"From justice, sir, Jacob has nothing to fear, and I would not have troubled to remove him from its reach," Elinor retorted coldly, "but malice allied with power, however transient that power may be, is a different and far more deadly thing. You shamed yourself yesterday by the conduct which provoked Jacob's attack upon you. You shame yourself today by seeking vengeance for your discomfiture. Now I am going to Sir William who may have need of me. Come, Priscilla!"

She turned her back upon the furious and chastened soldier and swept from the hall, and Mrs. Marsham, after a moment's hesitation, followed her in silence. Captain Blake, very red in the face, stood glaring after them until the door closed behind them, and then transferred his enraged glance to Hubert. Mr. Ashbourne returned the look blandly, and the Captain, finding no outlet there for the fury which was consuming him, spun round on his heel and began to pace up and down the hall in a manner which was a sufficient indication of his feelings.

The search, which was intensive and prolonged, naturally yielded nothing to the exasperated dragoons. Sir William bore with commendable fortitude their invasion of his bedchamber, and lay propped against his pillows, watching their earnest endeavours with his one faded but sardonic eye. The soldiers had entered boldly enough, with as much clatter and swagger as their Captain commonly displayed, but something in the quietness of that impressive room, the compelling personality of the gaunt old man in the great bed, and the disdainful indifference of the slim, dark girl at his side, subdued them immediately. They made their search hurriedly, almost apologetically, and withdrew with obvious relief as soon as it was done.

Captain Blake, receiving repeated reports of failure in the great hall, had no need to feign the anger required of him by Colonel Venner's plan. His rage was overmastering, the more so because he could find no excuse to vent it, and the threats which he poured out against Fairwood and all its occupants, the elusive Gervase Ashbourne, and especially the supposed Jacob Hunt, were spoken with a passionate sincerity which came from the bottom of his heart. Only the certainty, born of Colonel Venner's confidence, that before long they would all suffer the fate which he was now cheated of meting out to them, enabled him to retain the least semblance of self-control.

When at last he and his men had taken their sullen departure, Elinor came to join Hubert at the door whence he had watched them ride away. They looked at each other, and without a word slowly descended the steps and paced across the wide sweep of gravel before the house, where no one could approach them unobserved and they could talk without danger of being overheard.

"They were satisfied, were they not?" Elinor asked anxiously. "We need not fear that they will come again?"

Hubert shook his head. "I do not think it likely, though they may keep watch on the approaches to the house in the hope that Gervase will try to come to us. I will confess, though, that my heart was in my mouth when you baited Blake as you did. I feared that you might provoke him too far."

She flashed him a smile which was at once rueful and mischievous. "My temper betrayed me, as it so often does, and yet there was method in it also. Surely only the consciousness of innocence could prompt a woman to speak so at such a time? Besides, your own manner was not precisely conciliatory."

"The charge is just," he agreed, smiling, "and one thing at least seems certain. That accursed red-coat has no suspicion of the true identity of Jacob Hunt."

"Heaven be praised for it!" Elinor replied earnestly. "Hubert, do you think all is well with Gervase? They will not have searched the cottages?"

"I think not, but I will ride over directly, so that your mind may be set at ease. It is better that I should go. For you to do so might arouse suspicion."

She agreed, and thanked him so warmly that he was filled with secret shame, for he knew that the impulse which had prompted him to make the suggestion was as unworthy as it was futile. He did not want her to go seeking Gervase. The memory of the perils which she had already dared for his sake, and the radiance which, subdued by anxiety though it was, had clung about her ever since her return to the Priory, provoked in him a jealousy which filled him with dismay.

His love for her was no sudden thing; it had grown slowly, almost imperceptibly, through the years, so that by the time he was fully aware of it his heart was lost beyond recall and all he could do was to try to keep the fact a secret. His was a love which hoped for nothing, demanded nothing. Even now, when the smallest indiscretion, or one incautious word, might betray Gervase and set Elinor free, he had used his utmost endeavours to protect him, and would continue to do so as long as it lay within his power. To do anything else had not even occurred to him.

Yet at the same time the thought of them together was more than he could bear, and though he realized the futility of his actions it seemed inevitable that he should do all he could to keep Elinor and Gervase apart. So he ordered a horse to be saddled, and rode off in the same direction as that taken by the dragoons, whom he followed as far as the village. To his relief they passed through it without a halt, and a few questions here and there assured him that only the Priory itself had been searched. He expressed his satisfaction that no harm had been done, urged the villagers to send word to him at once if those or any other soldiers molested them, and rode back, casually enough, by way of Hezekiah's cottage.

The old man must have been keeping watch, for as Hubert approached he emerged from the house and came forward to take his horse.

Hubert, dismounting, asked quietly: "Have the soldiers been here?"

Hezekiah shook his head. "Not within a quarter of a mile, sir. I caught a glimpse of them as they crossed the park, and the young master slipped out into the wood lest they come this way. He has but just returned.

Hubert thanked him and went on into the cottage, where Hezekiah's stout, grey-haired wife bobbed him a curtsy before hurrying out to join her husband.

Gervase was standing in the middle of the dark, low-ceilinged kitchen, and almost before his brother was into the room he asked sharply, "What happened at the Priory?"

Hubert told him as briefly as he could, for he could imagine what torments a man must endure when he was obliged to lie in hiding, not knowing what violence his family might be suffering for his sake, powerless to aid them because his mere presence would be enough to condemn them utterly. To accept, willy-nilly, the aid and protection of those dearest to him, knowing that if their efforts failed they, as well as he, must bear the punishment.

"I followed them to the village, and when I was certain that they had gone, I came here," he concluded, and added, on an impulse of self-torture which he could not resist, "Elinor is anxious for your safety."

His brother's back was towards the light, and Hubert could not see what effect, if any, the words had upon him.

Gervase said quietly, "As it happened, anxiety was needless. When Hezekiah warned me of Blake's presence I went out to the wood, for I have no wish to incriminate these good people by being found in their house. That, too, as it proved, was needless."

Hubert nodded. "Only the Priory itself was searched. They did not even draw rein in the village."

"I would feel happier if they had," Gervase said slowly. "Does it not seem strange to you that when a house-to-house search is the order of the day, our people alone should be spared?"

Hubert did not reply at once, for until that moment such a thought had not occurred to him, but now he was aware of a pang of uneasiness. After a little he said uncertainly, "Perhaps Blake was concerned only with settling his private grudge against Jacob Hunt. He may have had no real suspicion that you were at Fairwood."

"You think he used my part in the rebellion merely as an excuse to continue his pursuit of Elinor? That having been baulked of success in that, and also in his desire for revenge upon her supposed servant, he had no thought to spare for his duty?"

"It is possible."

"But is it? Could any professional soldier be so neglectful? He was ruthless enough in his quest elsewhere."

"Then he must have learned what is, after all, common knowledge—that Monmouth had no support from Fairwood. Why then should he look for fugitives here?"

"Perhaps you are right!" Gervase turned away and threw himself down on the settle beside the hearth. "Blake, after all, is nothing but a swaggering bully and unlikely to have any deep and sinister motive behind his actions. If it were the other officer we encountered yesterday there might be real need for uneasiness. He, I fancy, could be dangerous."

Hubert gave him an odd look. "Do you mean Lionel Venner?"

Gervase nodded. "Yes, the Colonel of Militia who is kin to the Marsham family. How well do you know him?"

"Well enough to dislike him," Hubert said curtly, "and to know that the dislike is mutual. It was I who had the pleasure of informing him that my grandfather would not permit him to set foot inside the house. I have never seen a man so murderously angry. There's a wicked temper beneath that cold exterior."

"That I can believe," Gervase agreed, remembering the fury in Venner's face the previous day, "but what sort of reception did he expect, in God's name? If a man forces unwanted attentions upon a woman newly widowed, is her family to make him welcome?"

"Unwanted attentions!" Hubert stared, and then added abruptly, "Is that what Elinor told you?"

"Why, yes!" Gervase broke off, a sudden doubt assailing him. Was that what Elinor had said? "That is, she told me that my grandfather suspected Venner of coveting the Marsham fortune, and I assumed that Priscilla was brought to Fairwood to shield her from the fellow's importunities."

"She was brought to Fairwood because she was scandalising the whole neighbourhood with her conduct," Hubert said bluntly. "Gossip was linking her name with Venner's even before her husband died, and Marsham was scarce cold in his grave before his cousin was ruffling it in his house as though he were already master there." He paused, looking quickly at his brother's face and then away again. "I am sorry, Gervase! I believe you had some fondness for Priscilla at one time, but it is right that you should know the truth, and neither Elinor nor my grandfather is likely to tell you."

Gervase sat staring at his brother while yet another picture of Priscilla lost shape and disappeared. From imagining her as contented, if not happy, in her marriage he had passed to envisaging her as the loyal, long-suffering wife of a drunkard, but now it seemed that that, too, was no more than an illusion. What, then, was the truth?

He said with an effort: "Elinor told me that Marsham drank to excess. If Priscilla found life with him so unbearable that she sought consolation elsewhere, whose is the greater blame, hers, or theirs who bound her to him in the first place?"

" 'Sdeath, Gervase! are you still so besotted that you must be seeking excuses for her even now?" There was bitterness as well as exasperation in Hubert's voice. "It was not Marsham's drunkenness that thrust Priscilla into Venner's arms, but her light conduct which drove him to the bottle. As God is my witness, that is the truth! I watched it happen."

He came slowly across the room until he stood facing Gervase in the light of the fire which crackled and glowed beneath the big iron pot suspended above it. He was pale, his lips tightly compressed, his hands clenched hard on his riding-whip as he fought to subdue the storm of resentment which had suddenly taken possession of him. It was an unspoken, unacknowledged resentment which had been growing throughout all the years when, fettered by his own physical weaknesses and his grandfather's increasing need of him, he had stayed quietly at home while his elder brother dwelt in the great world, experiencing the intrigues of Court life and the excitement and danger of war. That was a life which Hubert had longed to share, for he had full measure of the bold, adventurous Ashbourne spirit even though he lacked the bodily strength to indulge it. He knew that he might have found peace and happiness in marriage, but the only woman he had ever loved was his brother's wife. Gervase had been granted that gift along with all the rest, and prized it, it seemed, no more than he prized the others.

"What do you know of Priscilla, or for that matter of any of us?" Hubert asked now, his voice low and fierce. "A few short weeks five years ago, when you were angry and resentful at the match made for you, and she flattered because you admired her! Secret meetings and stolen kisses—did they show her to you as she really is? Do you know that within a month of your departure she was dallying with another man, or that our grandfather had to hurry her into marriage with Marsham because her waywardness was ruining every chance she had of finding a husband? I doubt whether she has thought of you once in a twelvemonth, yet you must still moon over her like a lovesick schoolboy, and picture her as the innocent victim of a drunken husband and a heartless family."

He paused, breathing quickly, his hands still twisting and wrenching at the whip as though it were some living, hated thing. Gervase made no reply. He was no longer looking at his brother, but with set lips and frowning brow was staring into the fire as though what he saw there was distasteful to him.

"Geoffrey Marsham was a coward," Hubert went on more calmly, "and though we may despise him for it, what right have we to judge him? He was mortally afraid of Venner, of his tongue, his temper and his sword. Venner knew it, and missed no opportunity of baiting him. When rumours first started of an intrigue between Venner and Priscilla, Marsham did not dare to call his kinsman to account, but he was at least man enough to realize how craven his conduct was. He began to drink excessively, but whether in search of forgetfulness or the courage he lacked, no one will ever know. All that the poor fool found was death."

Again he paused, and still Gervase did not speak. Hubert sighed and, letting fall the whip, dropped down on the settle beside him.

"I have no grudge against Priscilla," he said wearily. "I have lived beside her all her life, and know that she is not to blame because she is as she is, and I believe, God help her, that she truly cares for Venner. For Marsham she felt only contempt, and their marriage was doomed to failure from the very first. Miss Thomasine made sure of that."

"Thomasine?" Gervase roused himself with an effort and turned towards his brother. "Thomasine Marsham?"

Hubert nodded. "Aye, Geoffrey's sister, a sour-faced stick of a woman. She must be past forty now, for there was fifteen years between them. She was the eldest, he the youngest of the family, and their mother died when he was born. Miss Thomasine never married, but remained to keep house for her father and see to the education of the younger children, but Geoffrey was her favourite, and a cosseted, pampered weakling she made of him. She hated Priscilla even before they met, for she had been mistress of that house for more than twenty years and now a girl of sixteen was coming to take her place. That in itself was bad enough, but Priscilla was pretty and gay and Marsham doted on her then. She and Miss Thomasine quarrelled incessantly, and he, poor devil, was caught between the two. I don't doubt he was regretting his marriage even before Venner came on the scene."

Gervase was frowning. "What did Miss Marsham hope to gain? Priscilla was his wife, and nothing could alter that."

"I doubt whether she had any thought of gain. It was all malice, I believe, and a desire to make mischief. I have often wondered whether it was she who first spread the stories about Priscilla and Venner, for she was very prompt to inform my grandfather of Venner's visits to Priscilla after Marsham's death. She is a strange woman, bigoted as a Puritan yet violent in her moods, and some say she is half-crazed. Even her brother was afraid of her, in spite of her fondness for him."

"A happy household that must have been," Gervase said bitterly, "and worse, no doubt, after Marsham died. Surely Priscilla is more to be pitied than blamed, and I cannot see the need to keep her here as though she were a prisoner."

"I did not say that she is to blame," Hubert replied with a sigh. "Her life since her marriage has not been happy, and if only she and Venner had behaved with decorum, I dare say they might have married after a year or so and nothing would have been said."

"Except by Miss Marsham," Gervase added sardonically. "She would scarcely welcome any man who stepped into her brother's shoes."

Hubert got up and began to move restlessly about the room, while Gervase sat staring morosely before him, his hands clasped between his knees. There was a lengthy silence, but at last the younger brother ceased his uneasy prowling and swung round to face the elder, gripping the edge of the rough wooden table with both hands and leaning forward across it.

"Gervase," he said in a low, strained voice, "there is something else, something which I have not yet disclosed to my grandfather or to the girls, though it cannot be kept from them much longer. The gossip about Priscilla and Venner was bad enough, but now something even uglier is afoot, and I fear it may stem from the same source." He paused, and then added reluctantly, as though the words were forced out of him against his will: "It is being whispered that Geoffrey Marsham's death was not the accident that it was made to appear."

8

"Unborn Tomorrow and Dead Yesterday"

On the day following Captain Blake's descent upon Fairwood Priory and Hubert's visit to his brother's hiding-place, Gervase sat alone in the cottage kitchen and tried to decide upon some plan which would offer him a reasonable chance of escape. His grandfather's suggestion of a smugglers' craft was still in his mind, but to act upon it he would first have to reach the coast. For that a guide would be necessary, since he would be obliged to travel by night across unfamiliar country, and where could a guide be found whose loyalty was unquestionable?

The most prudent course would undoubtedly be to remain in his present hiding-place until the search for rebels became less intense, but apart from the danger his presence meant to everyone at Fairwood, the enforced inactivity was already beginning to tell upon him. The past two days had seemed interminable. He longed for some action, however perilous, however futile, to break the monotony of his voluntary imprisonment and afford him some refuge from his thoughts.

He sighed, and resting his elbows on the table, leaned his head on his hands, running his fingers deep into his hair. A profound melancholy swept over him, and he wondered with bitter irony why he was striving so earnestly to preserve a life which had become empty and meaningless, its political ambitions lost in the welter of ruin in which the rebellion had ended, its romantic dreams brought to a like desolation.

Remembering how on the night after Sedgemoor he had thought of Priscilla and of Fairwood as the only reality left to him, he laughed softly in mirthless mockery of that delusion. At Fairwood he was a stranger, an intruder in his own home, and Priscilla had forgotten him long ago. What, then, remained? Life without warmth, without purpose; a thousand tomorrows as empty as today.

He was still sitting there, head bowed upon his hands, when the door opened softly to admit Elinor, a basket on her arm and her little dog frisking at her heels. As Gervase looked up with a start, she said gravely: "You should keep better watch than this. What if I had been one of the King's men?"

"You would be less light of foot, and so I should have had warning of your approach," he replied with an attempt at lightness, and got up to take her burden from her. "How fares my grandfather today?"

"The same," she replied with a sigh. "Very weary, but more contented, I think, since his talk with you." She glanced round the room and then back to him again. "Are you alone?"

He nodded. "Hezekiah, as you may know, is at the Priory. His wife has gone to stay at Long Willow Farm. It seems that the goodwife there was brought to bed last night, and two of the elder children are sick." He broke off, his eyes searching her face, reading the trouble there. "What is it, Elinor?"

Duchess was frisking and fawning at his feet, clamouring for attention, and Elinor spoke sharply to her before answering the question. Then, lifting her eyes again to his face, she said in a low voice: "I am the bearer of ill news, Gervase. The Duke of Monmouth is made prisoner."

He stood staring at her, not speaking, the colour draining from his face. So fate, it seemed, could deal yet another blow, even when one supposed that the burden was already too great to bear. Like so many of the rebels, both captive and fugitive, he had drawn a measure of comfort from the thought that the leader himself had escaped.

"Are you certain?" he asked unsteadily at last. Elinor nodded, watching him with compassionate eyes.

"The news came to us from a sure source. He was taken in Dorset early on Wednesday morning, by men of the Sussex militia under Lord Lumley and Sir

William Portman. He was disguised as a countryman and trying to reach the south coast."

She paused, but he had the impression that this was not the whole story, and said abruptly: "Go on! Tell me all you know."

"He and a companion were seen the previous evening by a cottage woman, who informed the militia," Elinor continued reluctantly. "They kept watch all night, and in the morning the other man was taken. He admitted that he had not long parted from the Duke, and the search was resumed." She hesitated, and then added in a voice little louder than a whisper: "They found him hiding in a ditch, under an ash tree."

"Oh, my God!" Gervase turned abruptly away from her and dropped down again on the bench by the table, burying his face in his hands. So that was how it had ended, the bold attempt to set a Protestant king on England's throne! With a weary, ill-clad fugitive dragged ignominiously from a ditch to imprisonment and death. Now there could be no second chance, and hundreds of honest, deluded fools had died and would yet die in vain. In a voice he hardly recognized as his own, he said hoarsely: "What followed?"

"They took him before a magistrate, and then he was sent under escort to London."

"To be sure!" Gervase's voice was harsh with bitterness and grief. "King James will wish to savour his triumph to the full. He has always hated and feared the Duke."

Elinor had moved forward until she stood close beside him. He was aware of her presence even though he did not look at her.

"Is there no hope?" she asked hesitantly.

"None at all! There need not even be a trial, for a Bill of Attainder was passed by Parliament immediately they heard of his landing in England. Lumley and Portman would have been within their rights had they executed him on the spot." His voice broke, and he added wretchedly, " 'Twould have been more merciful, perhaps, if they had."

Filled with pity for his grief, her heart wrung by the helpless anguish in his voice, Elinor laid a timid hand on his arm. For an instant he seemed to withdraw resentfully from the touch, but then, in a blind need for comfort, he turned towards her, burying his head against her shoulder.

Elinor stood very still, her arms about him, her whole being filled with a curious mingling of joy and sorrow. Joy that it was to her he turned in search of solace, sorrow for the tragic circumstances which had brought him to it. Disjointed pictures rose in her memory. Monmouth as she had seen him five years ago, in the heyday of his popularity and success; a lad who had been her merry playmate stumbling along a dusty road with dazed eyes and fetters on his wrists; Gervase, her husband, an exhausted fugitive with soldiers at his heels. Tears filled her eyes for the pity of it all, for everything which these past few weeks had seen destroyed.

Nor was it over even yet. Involuntarily her arms tightened about him, for danger still lurked everywhere, as much—she knew it instinctively—in his restless, impatient spirit as in the curious eyes and unguarded tongues of others. How long would he be willing to remain in hiding while others fought his battles for him and faced the perils which were rightly his?

"What is there left," he said at length in a muffled voice, not lifting his head. "A traitor's death here, or exile in a foreign land, exile with no work to do, no prospect of return! We came to set England free, and we have accomplished nothing, nothing but ruin and defeat for those who trusted us! King James will wreak a terrible vengeance upon the West Country for this summer's work. It is only just beginning."

Elinor had learned enough of politics from Sir William to realize the truth of what he said, and though her heart ached for him she could find no words of comfort. She stood silent, stroking his dark, dishevelled hair, while the tears ran unheeded down her cheeks, and Duchess, sensing her distress, rose on hind legs and pawed anxiously at her skirts.

Gervase moved at last, and lifted his head to look at her with haggard eyes. "I have made you weep," he said remorsefully, "and 'tis not for the first time, I know. It was a bad bargain they made for you, Elinor, when they planned our marriage."

She shook her head and tried to smile. "I would not have had it otherwise," she replied gently. "This is a black and bitter time, my dear, but it is not the end of all things. One day you will come back to Fairwood. Sir William is certain of it, and he is very wise, Gervase, wiser than you or I. Trust him and obey him, as I have learned to do, and trust, too, in the infinite mercy of God. You have been saved thus far, in the face of many dangers. Is not that a sign?"

He sighed, and drew her down on to the bench beside him.

"Would that I had your faith," he said slowly. "All I can think of is the danger my presence here means to all who know of it, and the ease with which it could be discovered. It is not right that you should take such risks on my behalf."

"We are trying to find someone who can be trusted to guide you to the coast," she assured him, hiding her dismay at this hint that her fears were justified, "but you must be patient. It is not easy, and meanwhile you are safer here than you would be anywhere else. The soldiers have searched and found nothing, so what more have we to fear?"

Gervase agreed, saying nothing of his own lingering suspicion that the authorities were not so easily satisfied, for Elinor had enough to bear without being burdened with his uneasy thoughts. For a few minutes longer they discussed the all-important topic of his escape, and then she rose reluctantly to her feet.

"I must go now," she said regretfully. "It is just possible that I was seen coming here, and if I tarry too long it will arouse suspicion, especially if Martha is away."

She lifted the cloth from her basket and began to unpack the provisions it contained, setting them neatly on the table. Last of all she produced two books which she laid before Gervase.

"I brought them for you," she said with a hint of shyness. " 'Tis little enough, but may help to beguile the tedium of being hidden here."

He was touched by this evidence of thoughtfulness and thanked her gratefully, but for the present did no more than glance at the books. Instead he came round the table and stood beside her, finding himself oddly unwilling to let her go.

"You will come again?" he questioned, and she nodded.

"Tomorrow, if I can, but we must go warily." She looked up at him, anxiety in her eyes. "Promise me that you will be patient, Gervase, and stay in hiding until we can make some plan which holds at least the hope of success."

"I have given my word to my grandfather, and now I give it to you." Gervase took both of her hands in his and stood looking down into her eyes. "Can you not trust me to keep it?"

A faint smile flickered across her face.

"I trust your intention to do so," she told him candidly, "but my fear is that you will do something reckless out of sheer boredom. Idleness makes the time drag heavily."

"You know me better than I supposed," he said ruefully, "but put your trust in this. I might stake my own life on a slender chance, but I will never gamble with yours, or my grandfather's, or Hubert's." He paused, still grasping her hands but looking now above her head, a faint frown on his brow. "These past few days have taught me many things, but above all they have shown me the extent of my selfishness. For years I have allowed my own feelings and beliefs to rule my life, without pausing to consider whether they were either worthy or right. I shall not do so again."

The smile quivered once more at the corners of her mouth, but Gervase did not observe it, or the loving perception of the glance she turned upon him. She might have said again that she trusted the intention

more than the performance, but she was wise enough
to hold her peace. It would not be easy for so imperious
and headstrong a nature to abide by such a decision,
and it would not help him if she showed the doubt she
felt.

So she bade him farewell and departed, the spaniel
bounding joyously before her, while Gervase, prevented
by the dictates of caution from watching her go, returned to his seat by the table.

He fingered the books which she had brought him,
but did not open them, for his mind was busy with
other things. In spite of the grave news she had
brought, her visit had done much to relieve the black
depression of his spirits. Perhaps, after all, there was
some hope for the future. One day Fairwood would be
his, and if his grandfather was right in the conviction
that a second exile would not be of long duration, he
would devote the rest of his life to caring for the estate
with each generation of Ashbournes was taught to regard as a sacred trust. He had forgotten that lesson for
a while, but he would not do so again.

There was comfort in the thought, and more than
comfort in the knowledge that Elinor would be beside
him in that future life. The "rare spirit," Sir William
had called her, and Gervase knew that the old man had
spoken truly. He was ashamed now of the despair he
had felt a short while since, and from the bottom of his
heart gave thanks that the folly of five years ago had
not gone to such lengths as to raise an insuperable bar-
rier between himself and his wife. It had not been easy
then to resist temptation, but at least Elinor need never
know how close he had come to yielding to it; need

never, in fact, know that the temptation had ever existed.

A faint sound roused him from his thoughts and made him instantly alert. The windows of the cottage were small, and set so high in the thick walls that it was impossible to see into the house at a casual glance, but the sound which had disturbed him was such as a curious person might have made had he tried to raise himself against the wall to look within. Gervase did not move, or give any indication that he had heard it, but strained his ears to detect any repetition of the noise.

At length, when none came, he rose soundlessly to his feet and moved softly to the door, intending to shoot the bolt into place against any surprise attack. His hand was actually upon it when the sound of a stealthy footfall reached his ears.

He left the bolt drawn and stepped back a pace, standing with his back against the wall so that he would be hidden by the opening door if the unknown ventured into the cottage. He was unarmed, but given the advantage of surprise was confident of his ability to overcome a single adversary, and the sounds he had heard did not suggest that there was more than one person outside the house. There was a brief, nerve-racking pause, and then very slowly the latch lifted and the door began to swing inwards.

A footstep on the threshold and a shadow darkening the entrance. Gervase braced himself, waited a moment longer and then sprang, slamming the door shut and seizing the intruder from behind. There was a scream; he realized with a shock that his arms were encircling a supple feminine form, and glimpsed golden hair beneath a black veil. Abruptly he released her and she stumbled away from him, turning towards him the white, terrified face and wide blue eyes of Priscilla.

For a few seconds they stared at each other in silence, but it was the silence of astonishment and dismay rather than of rapturous recognition. Gervase, waiting for a surge of emotion, for some echo of the fierce desire which had possessed him five years before, found that he waited in vain. He saw only a pretty, rather plump young woman in widow's weeds, upon whom he could look with complete indifference, while the thought foremost in his mind was an uneasy query as to the purpose of her presence there.

He saw that she was trembling and close to tears, and realised belatedly how severe a shock it must have been to her to find herself so roughly handled. He took her arm and led her across to the settle and made her sit down there.

"I am sorry, Priscilla," he said quietly. "I did not mean to frighten you, but what the devil made you come creeping in here so furtively?"

It was some moments before she was sufficiently in command of herself to answer. Coming from bright sunlight into this small, dim room, sustaining the shock of being brutally seized by an unknown assailant, had so scattered her wits that at first she had not realized who he was, and only when he spoke did the worst of her alarm subside. Now she sat staring at him with a sort of incredulous dismay. This surely could not be Gervase, this stranger with cropped hair, and the rough, greasy clothes of a cowherd or a shepherd. This was not as she remembered him, and the shock of seeing him thus changed was as great in its way as that which she had already undergone.

Gervase repeated his question, a hint of impatience in his voice, and this time she made shift to answer him. Pressing one hand against her side, for her heart was still beating uncomfortably fast, she said breathlessly: "I followed Elinor. It seemed strange to me that she returned so soon from her uncle's house, and when those soldiers came to the Priory yesterday I began to suspect the reason. I wanted to be sure."

"And now that you are sure," Gervase said bluntly, "what do you mean to do? Betray me to the authorities?"

Priscilla looked frightened. "No, no! Why should I? I wish you no harm, Gervase. You know that."

"Do I?" His tone was uncompromising. "Why, then, were you so eager to be certain that I was here?"

"I was curious, that is all," she replied tearfully. "The days are so long! You do not know what it is like to be mewed up there, with naught to do but read or sew or wait upon Sir William. Sometimes I think I shall go mad with boredom."

"Elinor seems to support such a life without complaint."

"Oh, Elinor is a paragon of virtue, I know!" Priscilla's voice was waspish now. "That is impressed upon me from morn till night by Hubert and his grandfather, but I scarcely thought to hear it from you. Besides, she is mistress of the house and has much to occupy her. I am but a guest, and an unwelcome one at that!"

Understandably so, Gervase thought grimly, if this was how she behaved. Aloud he said: "You still have not told me what use you mean to make of your discovery."

"Why should I wish to make any use of it at all? If I

had to come creeping upon you like a thief it was Elinor's fault, and Hubert's. They should have told me that you were here. I am a member of the family, am I not?"

"God's light, Priscilla! this is not a game we are playing." Gervase was growing angry now. "Or if it is, the stakes are life and death! Do you not realize what would follow if my presence here became known, and the fact that I have been given aid and shelter? We should all be hauled off to prison—you and Elinor and my grandfather as well as Hubert and myself. Would you be so eager to claim kinship with us then?"

"There is no need to try to frighten me," Priscilla said indignantly. "I do not want to see you captured, and you have no right to suppose that I would betray you. Why, it would be like betraying my own brother!"

"Your brother!" he repeated and laughed. There was no amusement in his mirth, but a mockery directed both at himself and at her. "It was not as a brother you looked upon me five years ago."

A little colour came back to her face, but she met his eyes squarely.

"That was a folly which would never have endured," she said. "I do not mourn its passing, Gervase. Do you?"

"No," he replied, and was astounded to discover that he spoke the simple truth. Their love had been a fragile and fleeting thing, doomed from the moment of its birth, and now at last he could admit that, to himself as well as to her. "No, I do not mourn it, nor did I seriously believe that you would deliberately betray me. Yet so much depends upon keeping this secret, and one indiscreet word could bring disaster. Try to forget that you ever came here today. Will you do that, Priscilla?"

She nodded, looking curiously at him. "I suppose it was you who attacked that officer the other day? You were Elinor's supposed servant?"

"Yes, I was Jacob Hunt," he said shortly, "but that, too, you would do well to forget. Knowledge of such things can be dangerous in times like these."

"Yet Elinor is permitted to share it, is she not?"

"Were it not for Elinor, I should be dead or captive by now," Gervase said soberly, "but do not suppose that the risks she is taking on my behalf lie easily on my mind or conscience. I would have kept her from them if I could, but since that was not possible I trust to her resourcefulness and discretion. She lacks neither."

"And I lack both! Is that what you would say?"

"I am told that your conduct has not been remarkable for the latter."

Priscilla tossed her head. "By Elinor, I suppose! Oh, you are all the same! Why can I not be left in peace to manage my own affairs in my own way?"

"Because, it seems, you cannot do so in a manner becoming to an Ashbourne of Fairwood." Gervase retorted angrily. "There are some decencies, Priscilla, which must be observed."

"Decencies!" she repeated in a voice shrill with scorn. "Say rather 'hypocrisy.' Why should I pretend a sorrow I do not feel, and swathe myself in black for a man I always despised? I endured four years of marriage with him, and now that I am free of him I am still imprisoned in a cage of meaningless conventions. Oh, it is not for my sake Sir William brought me here and forbade me to see Lionel! It is for the sake of his own selfish pride, lest any breath of scandal touch the precious, the sacred names of Ashbourne or of Fairwood." She beat her hands together and rocked to and fro, her voice rising hysterically. "Sometimes I think this place has bewitched you all. I hate it! I would be glad to see it destroyed!"

One swift stride took Gervase to the settle. He grasped Priscilla by the wrists and jerked her to her feet with a violence that smote her into silence.

"And I think that you are out of your mind!" he said sternly. "Do you dare to say that to me, when I know you to possess the means for its destruction? By Heaven, Priscilla! you will swear to me now that you will say nothing of what you have learned today, or I will keep you here until Hezekiah returns, and then send word to my grandfather of what you intend. He will know how to deal with you, I have no doubt!"

As he had expected, that threat had the desired effect. Priscilla burst into tears and tried vainly to free herself from his grasp.

"I did not mean it!" she sobbed. "Let me go, Gervase, you are hurting me! I did not mean it!"

"Swear it!" he said relentlessly. "Swear before God that you will reveal this secret to no one." She made no reply, and he tightened his hold on her wrists, giving them a little shake. "Swear it, if you want to leave this house alone."

With the utmost reluctance, her voice choked with sobs, she did as he commanded. When the solemn words had been spoken he let her go and stepped back.

"Remember it," he said grimly, "and remember this also! Your husband did not die in his bed, and though

I have no doubt that his death was the accident it seemed, there may be others less ready to believe it. So do not make a boast of your scorn for him, or it may recoil on your own head. Already, so I have heard, there are ugly rumours abroad, so set a guard on your words and on your deeds—for your own sake, if not for the sake of the home and family you so despise."

For a long moment Priscilla stood staring at him, the back of one hand pressed against her mouth, her eyes wide and dark with horror in a face the colour of ashes. Then with an inarticulate cry she stumbled across the room, flung open the door and fled through the cottage garden, her black veil floating behind her.

Gervase closed and bolted the door and stood resting his forehead against the rough wood. He felt suddenly very tired, and sick at heart because of the danger threatening those he loved, danger which he had brought upon them and was now powerless to avert.

9

Devil's Counsel

ELINOR returned to the Priory in a very thoughtful mood, and confided to Hubert her fears of what Gervase might do if his present imprisonment were too prolonged. She hoped for reassurance, for a dismissal of those fears by one who was more closely acquainted with him than she could yet claim to be, but to her dismay she found Hubert disposed to agree with her. Moreover, it seemed that Sir William himself was not blind to the danger.

"He spoke to me of this less than a hour ago," Hubert said with a troubled frown, "when I told him that you had gone to break the news of Monmouth's capture to Gervase." He looked anxiously at her. "How did he receive it?"

"With grief and dismay, as we expected." Elinor replied briefly. Those moments at the cottage, when Gervase had turned so naturally to her for comfort, were too precious to discuss even with Hubert. "At present, concern for our safety holds him in check, but this inactivity is driving him to distraction; and it will be worse now, for he is certain to brood over the Duke's fate."

Hubert nodded. "God send we find a guide for him ere long," he said gravely. "My grandfather advises me to seek aid in that from Master Ember, for if any man can furnish what we need, it is he. 'Tis too late to visit him today, but I will set out first thing tomorrow morning."

Elias Ember lived in the nearest market-town. He was a merchant now, and a prosperous one at that, but in his time he had been many things, most of them disreputable. With advancing age, however, it seemed that he had repented of his sins and turned to the ways of honesty. He was not many years younger than Sir William, and they had been well known to each other for more than fifty years, so it was to be supposed that the latter knew whether or not Master Ember was to be trusted.

Even so, Elinor was not entirely happy at the proposal to consult him, and said doubtfully, "Is it wise, do you think, to admit him to the secret?"

"Sir William thinks so," Hubert replied reassuringly, "and 'tis unlikely that Master Ember will be reluctant to defy the law. It would not be for the first time, I'll be bound! In fact, it would not surprise me to learn that he could put Gervase in the way of finding a smugglers' craft to ship him across the Channel, for I'll warrant that not all the goods Master Ember buys and sells come into this country by way of the ports."

"Oh, if only he could!" Elinor exclaimed fervently. "But will he, Hubert? Gervase has not simply broken the law. He is guilty of treason and armed rebellion."

Hubert sighed, rubbing his hand across his forehead as he always did if he were tired or harassed.

"That we shall not know until tomorrow, Nell! Ember has always held aloof from politics, and there is no way of knowing where his sympathies lie, though I've a suspicion they will always be with the fugitive rather than the pursuer, no matter what the reason for the chase. We can only trust to that, and to my grandfather's judgment of the man. He is not often mistaken."

With that she had to be content, but it was with mingled feelings that she watched Hubert ride away from the house next day. Though she hoped devoutly that his mission would succeed, success would mean the departure of Gervase, and the thought of letting him go from her into untold danger seemed to tear savagely at her heart. Even if he won through to safety, how long would it be before she saw him again?

Hubert, too, was in the grip of conflicting emotions as he covered the eight miles between Fairwood and the town, but none of it was visible in his face when he dismounted before the handsome timbered front of Master Ember's house. He was no stranger to the place, for the Ashbournes had frequent business dealings with the merchant, and out of consideration for Ember's advancing years Hubert often visited him rather than give him the trouble of traveling to Fairwood. It would therefore occasion no remark that he called at Ember's house.

A deferential serving-man admitted him, and conducted him to a room where the old merchant heaved himself out of his chair to greet him. He was a big man, inclining sadly to corpulence, with shrewd grey eyes in a wrinkled, weatherbeaten face which was just now wreathed in a beaming smile of welcome.

"Mr. Ashbourne, sir, 'tis a pleasure to see you!" he announced heartily. "Sit you down and take a glass of wine or a mug of ale to wash the dust from your throat. How is it, sir, with your honoured grandfather?"

Hubert accepted the chair thrust forward for him, expressed a preference for ale, and after an exchange of courtesies broached the trifling matter of business he had invented as an excuse for his visit. This was soon disposed of, and after a few moments of silence, during which his host studied him with shrewd, twinkling eyes, Elias said bluntly: "You did not ride eight miles on a hot summer's day, Mr. Ashbourne, for the sake of a trifle o' business you might well have dealt with in a letter. Be there some other way I can serve you?"

"Perhaps!" Hubert's eyes were intent on the inch or

so of ale remaining in the pewter tankard he held. "Your interests, so it is said, are wide and far-reaching."

"That's so," Elias agreed, and Hubert's gaze lifted suddenly to meet his.

"As far as the coast, Master Ember?" he asked softly.

There was a little silence. A fly buzzed angrily against the window-pane and a child's laughter came faintly to them from the street.

Elias stroked his grizzled beard and regarded Hubert consideringly. "What part o' the coast, sir?" he asked at length.

"That is immaterial. The nearer and the less populous the better."

Elias noddcd. "You'rc wishful, maybe, to send summat out o' the country?" Hubert nodded, and the old man went on; "Might it be, in a manner of speaking, livestock?"

"In a manner of speaking," Hubert agreed levelly, "it is!"

"Aye!" The gnarled fingers were still moving rhythmically over the beard. "There be many in the West today, sir, as'd like to ship a cargo o' that sort across the Channel and precious few as will be able to do it. Precious few!"

"That I know, Master Ember," Hubert set down the tankard and leaned forward in his chair, speaking in a low, earnest voice. "But this—cargo—is very precious to us all at Fairwood, and my grandfather bade me ask your help if you can give it, as a favour to him and for the sake of the long acquaintance between you."

"To be sure, I've had more than one favour from Sir

William in the past," Elias remarked reflectively, "and I'd be glad of a chance to repay 'em. What had ye in mind, sir?"

"A night journey to the coast, and a ship where gold is the answer to all questions and a trifle of danger not greatly considered," Hubert replied briefly. "The cost is unimportant. We will pay whatever you ask."

"My own part I'll do for naught, out o' respect for Sir William and all his family," Elias replied with dignity, "but there'll be others, o' course, as will expect payment for the risks they take. But I'll not let you be cheated, Mr. Ashbourne. A fair price 'twill be, a fair price!"

"That, too, I know," Hubert replied with a smile. "We have always had fair dealing from you, Master Ember. And thank you, my friend! You put us deeply in your debt."

"Thank me when the deed be done, sir," Elias retorted brusquely. "Now let's see! 'Twill mean the Devon coast, or even Cornwall, for there's ships patrolling the Bristol Channel, and the risk'd be too great even though the journey by land would be shorter."

Hubert looked at him with astonishment. "How do you know of the ships?"

Elias chuckled wickedly. "I have my own ways o' finding out, sir. My interest be far-reaching, as you said yourself. Leave all to me, Mr. Ashbourne, and I'll send you word as soon as it be rightly settled."

"Thank you, Master Ember," Hubert got up and held out his hand. "You will make all possible speed, will you not?"

"Impatient to be gone, is he?" Elias remarked understandingly, gripping the proffered hand. "Well, 'tis natural enough, and I'll not delay longer than is needful. Look to hear from me in a day or two."

Hubert thanked him again and took his leave, feeling easier in his mind than he had done for several days. There was something about Elias Ember that inspired confidence.

This sanguine mood lasted until six miles of the homeward journey lay behind him, and he was once more approaching the boundaries of Sir William's land. Then, as he drew near to a small hedge-tavern which stood by itself at a fork in the road, the sight of scarlet coats about its door struck a shrewd blow at his new-found confidence.

Instinctively he drew rein, then, reminding himself that he had nothing to fear from these militia-men, as he now perceived them to be, rode forward again. The sound of his approach had already attracted their attention, and as he drew close to the tavern two of them stepped into the road to bar his way. For the second time he brought his horse to a halt.

"Well, what is it?" he said impatiently. "What do you want?"

One of the men laid hold of the bridle; the other said stolidly; "Colonel's orders, sir. We'm to let no one pass without questioning 'em."

"Confound it, you fool, I am Hubert Ashbourne of Fairwood Priory! Can a man not go about his lawful business now without being hampered at every turn by any impertinent jackanapes who chances to wear a red coat?"

"We, too, have our work to do, Mr. Ashbourne!" The cold, ironical voice came from the tavern, and Hubert swung round in the saddle to see Lionel Venner standing at the open window. "Bear with us, I beg of you, while we endeavour to do it."

A caution born of his brother's conviction, and his own instinctive certainty, that this man was dangerous, cooled Hubert's anger a little but could not disguise his dislike. He said shortly: "Since you are aware of my identity, sir, you will realize the absurdity of detaining me. Pray order your men to let me pass."

"Come, Mr. Ashbourne, such heat in the heat of the day is imprudent," Venner retorted mockingly. "Dismount and take a glass of wine with me. Corporal, have one of the men stable Mr. Ashbourne's horse."

Hubert started to protest, recognized the threat behind the mock cordiality of the invitation, and dismounted, seething with silent fury. Venner had the means to enforce obedience, and to follow his natural inclination for defiance would result only in his own discomfiture and increased danger for his family.

He entered the tavern, and Venner moved away from the window to open the door of the room and beckon him within. Then, filling two glasses from the bottle which stood, half empty, on the table, he handed one to Hubert and raised the other in salutation. "To the damnation of all rebels," he said deliberately. "May they rot in Hell!"

Acutely conscious of the watchfulness behind the mockery in the blue-grey eyes, Hubert honoured the brutal toast, recklessly draining his glass to the dregs.

Venner laughed softly. "You evidently find that sentiment to your liking, Mr. Ashbourne," he said lightly. "I wonder whether your enthusiasm springs from loyalty or from self-interest." Hubert began an angry question, but the Colonel went on without giving him a chance to finish it. "You have heard, perhaps, of the capture of the so-called Protestant champion?"

"We have heard that the Duke of Monmouth was taken on Wednesday morning," Hubert replied carefully. It had dawned on him suddenly that Venner was furiously angry. For once held rigidly under control, masked by the urbane mockery of voice and manner, the man's evil temper was seething just below the surface like a savage hound held precariously in leash. It would be fatally easy to snap that insecure restraint, and then, Heaven help them all! "In Dorset, I believe?"

"Yes, scuttling for safety, and leaving the fools who followed him to bear the consequences of armed insurrection," Venner said with a sneer. "A noble leader, i' faith! They are all the same, these ambitious adventurers, gambling for high stakes and then trying to evade payment of their debts when the game goes against them."

Hubert returned a non-committal reply, wondering what had happened to put Venner in so ugly a mood and what purpose could lie behind his own detention. On that latter point, however, he was not to wonder for long.

"But let us turn to more personal matters," Venner resumed after a moment, filling the glasses again. "How is it with my cousin, Mrs. Marsham?"

"She is well, I believe," Hubert replied shortly.

"And Mrs. Ashbourne and Sir William? The lady was blooming when I had the good fortune to encounter her a few days ago."

"My sister-in-law is in excellent health!" This time the words were spoken even more curtly than before.

"As for Sir William, he is as well as a man of his years can hope to be."

"A remarkable old gentlemen, to be sure!" The Colonel lifted his glass to his lips, watching Hubert closely above it. "And what of your brother, Mr. Ashbourne? How fares he?"

"My brother?" Hubert started, and in spite of his determination to remain calm, the words came out just a little more loudly and sharply than he intended. "How can I tell you that? He has not been at home these five years."

Venner set down his glass and rested both hands on the table, leaning forward across it. His thin, handsome face remained impassive, but there was a baleful glitter in his eyes.

"I am not a fool, Mr. Ashbourne," he said in a cold, clipped voice. "Gervase Ashbourne was with Monmouth, and since he has not yet been captured, and it is unlikely that he has been able to leave the country, he must be in hiding somewhere. And where more likely than Fairwood Priory?"

Hubert shrugged, trying to dissemble his dismay. "There was a captain of dragoons who entertained a similar suspicion. His men searched the house two days ago and found nothing."

"Captain Blake is a blundering young fool," Venner retorted contemptuously. "Able enough, no doubt, on the battlefield, but too easily swayed by his own passions, and prone to use the bludgeon of bullying rather than the rapier of reason."

Hubert picked up his glass and sipped reflectively at its contents, seeking a moment's respite in which to marshal his thoughts. So Venner knew of Blake's visit to Fairwood, and was even acquainted with the man himself, as that shrewd summing-up of his character revealed. Remembering his brother's migivings because the dragoons had restricted their search to the Priory itself, and his relief that it was Blake rather than Venner who commanded them, Hubert began to feel extremely uneasy.

"In this instance, Colonel Venner," he said at last, "the rapier achieves no more than the bludgeon. My brother is not at Fairwood."

"Think again, Mr. Ashbourne!" Venner's voice was soft now, and gently persuasive. "Your brother Gervase is a known rebel who has borne arms against his King and incited others to do likewise. His life is forfeit. He has no more hope of escape than Monmouth himself. Why should you involve yourself in his crimes? You have nothing to gain by protecting him, and everything to lose."

Hubert stood rigid, staring at him, repelled by the loathsome suggestion in the words, and repelled even more by the thought which had flashed unbidden and unwanted into his mind. The thought that what Lionel Venner said was true.

"What claim, after all, has he upon you?" Venner continued quietly. "He is almost a stranger to you. For years he has left you to bear responsibilites which are rightly his, and to husband an estate and a fortune which he will claim when Sir William dies. Is Fairwood not more truly yours than his? You have been kept prisoner here by your grandfather's need of you, when you might have been carving a career for yourself at Court or in politics, for is it not usually the younger son who goes forth to make his fortune, while the elder bides at home and cares for his inheritance? Yet your youth is being wasted here, and what can you hope for in the future save to be your brother's pensioner?"

Hubert set down his glass so suddenly and violently that the stem snapped, spilling the wine in a dark pool across the table. He paid no heed, but turned abruptly away and stood with bent head, overwhelmed by a horror greater than he had ever known, not because Venner was suggesting that he should betray his brother, but because he had been assailed by a hideous temptation to agree.

"That he is not hidden in the Priory itself I know," the hateful voice continued, and now it seemed to Hubert that it was no longer the voice of Venner but of his own worse self, and the words not spoken by another but forming themselves in his own mind. "You need not fear, then, that any there would suffer for giving him shelter. That I promise you, and if you need assurance of my good faith, you have it in the fact that Priscilla dwells beneath your roof. I would not let any harm come to her. All I need to know is where your brother is skulking. My men are here! He could be captive within the hour, and none to know who spoke the word that led me to him. One word, Ashbourne, but it could mean so much to you!"

He paused, and in the heavy silence the steady drip of the wine from table to floor sounded like the measured ticking of a clock, or the beat of a troubled, tempted heart. Hubert's hand was clenched hard on the hilt of his sword, his face white to the lips and beaded with sweat as he fought against the monstrous force of temptation arrayed against him.

"So much for both of us," Venner went on after a

moment, "For me, Priscilla and her fortune—for it is not likely that a man as old and infirm as Sir William could survive the shock of his grandson's arrest. For you, Ashbourne, your brother's inheritance, his title and"—the smooth voice sank even lower, became the voice of temptation itself—"his wife!"

"Elinor!" Hubert spoke the name under his breath, in a tone that made of it a supplication, a desperate appeal for help in his silent battle, nor did he utter it in vain. He closed his eyes, and the image of her rose in his mind as clearly as though she stood beside him. Elinor, who had risked her life to bring Gervase to Fairwood, and who would risk it again and again, without hesitation as long as any danger threatened him. He could never face her again, much less take her in marriage, if he did the monstrous thing that the soft, insidious voice was suggesting.

He opened his eyes again, rubbing his hand across his brow, and looking dazedly about him as though awakening from a nightmare. Barely a minute had passed; Venner still leaned upon the table, watching him with coldly glittering eyes; the wine still dripped with a faint sound on to the floor, yet Hubert felt that he had lived through an eternity of temptation. Now the brief madness had passed and he was himself again.

"My brother is not at Fairwood," he said distinctly, "but if he were, Venner, I would see you in Hell before I told you where to find him."

A spasm of fury twisted the elder man's face, and for an instant it seemed that the leashed demon of his temper would break its slender bonds. He said in a voice shaking with passion: "You are likely to rot in

Hell before me, my young friend, along with your rebel brother and that impudent jade, his wife! Do you know the punishment prescribed by law for a woman convicted of treason, Ashbourne? It is burning alive."

Hubert did know it, and had endeavoured to put the knowledge from his mind, but Venner's brutal words conjured up a picture so vivid and so horrible that it provoked in him an actual feeling of nausea. He gripped the back of a nearby chair for support and said, more faintly but no less defiantly: "His Majesty's officers excel in uttering bombastic threats. Captain Blake's annoyance at the failure of his search found similar expression to your own."

"You will find that what we threaten we can perform," Venner retorted ominously. "You are a fool, Ashbourne, an improvident, quixotic fool! Your brother will be captured in the end, and three lives—nay, four, if we take Sir William into account—be sacrificed where one would have sufficed."

"Five!" Hubert said laconically. "You forget Priscilla. Since you are so determined to incriminate all at Fairwood in my brother's crimes, even though he is not there, you cannot pick and choose between members of the family. You must destroy us all."

He thought then that Venner would strike him, and even braced himself for the blow, but it did not come. With a tremendous effort the Colonel maintained his self-control, and merely said thickly: "It is not likely that you would admit Priscilla to your family secrets. Whatever else my cousin Marsham may have been, he was at least loyal to his King, and she will have learned nothing of treason in his house. No, Ashbourne, you cannot scare me off in that matter. I will take Gervase

Ashbourne, and I will take him at Fairwood, along with those who have given him aid and shelter."

Somehow Hubert contrived to laugh. He let go the chair and moved to seat himself in it, looking up scornfully at Venner. "My dear Colonel," he said, "if you had any knowledge of my brother's whereabouts you would be on your way to arrest him, and not wasting your time here by trying to trick me with your devil's counsel into admitting something which I do not know. Fairwood is a loyal house. No rebels are harboured there."

Before Venner had time to reply the door opened to admit the corporal. He saluted, and held out a folded paper which Venner accepted with an eagerness apparent even to Hubert. He glanced rapidly through the message it contained and then thrust it into his pocket.

"Have my horse saddled, and order the men to make ready to march," he commanded. "This is the information for which I have been waiting."

The man saluted again and withdrew. Venner looked across at Hubert. "Duty compels me to leave you now, Mr. Ashbourne." All the mocking urbanity was back in his manner, and his ill-temper had disappeared, charmed away, it seemed, by whatever message the paper contained. "Do not suppose, however, that I have threatened idly today, and when you feel the rope tightening about your neck, remember that you could have avoided it, and at considerable profit to yourself!"

He went out, leaving Hubert a prey to greater uneasiness than before, for the Colonel's sudden change of mood, far from reassuring him, seemed like an omen of disaster. He remained where he was until he heard the little troop march away from the tavern, and then, hurrying to the window, he saw that they had taken the road which led to Fairwood.

Spurred by that discovery to frantic action, he raced to the stables thrust out of his way a startled lad who was working there, and saddled his horse with trembling hands. A few minutes later, thanking God for his life-long familiarity with every path and hedgerow, he was galloping across country towards the little cottage at the edge of the wood.

10

A Secret Discovered

ELINOR, meanwhile, had occupied the early part of the day with some of the innumerable duties which were the lot of the mistress of a great country house. After she had taken leave of Hubert she paid her usual morning visit to Sir William and sat with him for half-an-hour, though by tacit consent neither spoke of the subject nearest to their hearts. On leaving the old gentleman, she summoned the housekeeper and was occupied with her for another hour or so in a discussion of various domestic matters, so that the morning was well advanced before she realized that she had seen nothing of Priscilla.

Inquiries brought the information that Mrs. Marsham was lying late a-bed, and as this was sufficiently unusual to be disquieting, Elinor hastened to her room. She recalled that the previous evening Priscilla had looked pale and distraught and had retired early, and this fact, together with her unaccustomed tardiness in rising, suggested that she might be unwell. On reaching the bedchamber, however, she found it occupied only by Mrs. Marsham's woman, who volunteered the information that after rising late, her mistress had gone out for a walk.

Elinor shrugged, and betook herself again to her household tasks, for if Priscilla felt well enough to go out there was obviously no need for concern. The elder girl reappeared in time for dinner, but she still looked pale and troubled, though Elinor was too preoccupied with her own problems to pay much heed to Priscilla's. They made a silent meal of it, and parted again immediately it was done.

Half-an-hour later Elinor was busy in the still-room when the door was flung violently open and Priscilla appeared on the threshold, white-faced and agitated. "Elinor," she exclaimed, "what shall I do? Thomasine Marsham has just driven up to the door."

"Miss Marsham?" Elinor repeated in astonishment. "What in the world brings her here?"

"I cannot tell, but 'tis certain to cause trouble, whatever the reason! I will not see her!"

"Nonsense! Of course you must see her!" Elinor said briskly, putting aside the list of medicines with which she had been occupied. "Something may have happened at your home which requires your attention. Come, we will go together!"

"I am afraid of her," Priscilla said miserably as they made their way along the corridor. "You do not know her, Elinor! I am sure they are right who say she is half-crazed."

"Well, there is no need to be afraid of her now," Elinor pointed out. "She can scarcely browbeat you in this house, whatever she might try to do in your own."

A few minutes later, however, greeting her guest in the West Parlour, Elinor began to wonder if she had spoken too soon. Miss Marsham was a thin, angular woman, her pale, rather bony face framed by iron-grey hair beneath a linen cap, her forbidding aspect increased by the deep mourning in which she was clad from head to foot. She replied civilly enough to the words of welcome, but her eyes, cold and hard as pebbles in her pallid face, looked balefully past Elinor to Priscilla, who hovered nervously near the door as though contemplating flight.

Her alarm was not altogether surprising, Elinor reflected, watching the apprehensive way in which she greeted her sister-in-law. Thomasine Marsham must always have been plain, even as a girl, and now, with her prominent features, cold, pale eyes and compressed, down-curving lips, her countenance was of a grimness which might have quailed a bolder spirit than Priscilla's. As though to indicate her disapproval of the frivolities of the world, Thomasine affected a style of dress reminiscent of the most extreme Puritans, and a gleam of their fanaticism seemed to burn in her eyes, though whether this indicated religious fervour or a more worldly emotion was difficult to tell. There seemed to be in her nature a tinge of the ruthlessness which characterised her kinsman, Lionel Venner, and Elinor liked the one as little as the other.

The fact remained, however, that the woman was at

present a guest at Fairwood, and must be treated with the hospitality for which the Priory was noted. Miss Marsham, for her part, seemed equally mindful of the demands of etiquette, and inquired meticulously after the health of Sir William and of Hubert, and had a word to say on the subject of the rebellion and the present violent doings throughout the county.

Then, with the air of one who had fulfilled her social obligations to the letter, she said with a subtle change of tone: "It is time that I came to the business which brought me here, for no doubt, Mrs. Ashbourne, you are wondering why I should come a-visiting in these troublous times." She looked at Priscilla and added grimly: "Hannah Pennan is dead."

"Oh!" Priscilla said vaguely; then, apparently feeling that some further comment was called for, she added: "When did she die?"

"We buried her yesterday. I should explain, Mrs. Ashbourne," she went on, turning to Elinor, "that Hannah Pennan was an old and valued servant of my family. She was my brother's nurse, and remained devoted to him throughout his life."

"You have my sympathy, Miss Marsham," Elinor said cautiously, for she felt that this news in itself was not the real reason for Thomasine's visit. "It is almost as distressing to lose a faithful servant as to lose one's own kin."

"Hannah had exceeded her allotted span," Miss Marsham said harshly. She was looking at Priscilla again, and the gleam in her eyes was more pronounced than ever. "She lived a long and useful life, and died peacefully in her own bed. Small need to grieve for her!"

This was so clearly an allusion to Geoffrey Marsham's death that Elinor was not surprised when Priscilla uttered a gasp and pressed one hand to her breast. But worse was to come. Thomasine leaned forward, her thin hands clenched tightly on the arms of her chair. "Yes, Hannah died in her bed," she repeated. "I was with her at the end, and before she died she spoke of another passing, not peaceful like her own, but violent. Of a young man, her nursling, struck down before his appointed time." Her voice rose, and she flung out an accusing hand towards her sister-in-law. "Aye, you may blench, you Jezebel! She spoke of my brother, and how she saw him murdered on a winter's night six months ago!"

Priscilla cried out and cowered in her chair, flinging up an arm as though in dread of a physical as well as verbal attack. Elinor jumped up and went to her side, facing the older woman indignantly. "That is a terrible thing to say, Miss Marsham," she said sternly. "By what right do you make so dreadful an accusation, and against whom?"

"Against that wanton there," Thomasine retorted implacably, "and I have proof of what I say, madam, have no doubt of that. I was not alone at Hannah's death-bed. By her wish, the Vicar of our parish was there also, to hear what she had feared to tell before. Do you dare to question the words of a dying woman, spoken in the presence of a man of God?"

Priscilla was moaning softly, her face hidden in her hands. Elinor, feeling that she was in the grip of some lunatic nightmare from which in a moment or two she would awaken, put an arm about her and addressed Thomasine with a firmness she did not feel. "Your brother, Miss Marsham, died as the result of a tragic accident. No one questioned that at the time, and no one has done so since."

"Because we all believed what we were intended to believe, madam! Even I had no suspicion of the truth until I heard what Hannah had to tell."

"She is lying!" Priscilla exclaimed frantically, seizing Elinor's arm with both hands. "She, or that other wicked old woman! They both hated me, from the time I went to that house as Geoffrey's bride. They were always spying on me, and trying to make trouble for me. His death was an accident. You must believe me, Elinor, you must!"

"I do believe you, Priscilla," Elinor replied soothingly. "There is some terrible mistake here, of that I am convinced. Perhaps the old woman's mind was wandering in her last illness. Old folk have queer fancies at times—"

"Hannah's mind was as clear as your own, Mrs. Ashbourne," Thomasine broke in harshly. "She heard Geoffrey ride in late that night, and went down to see if there was anything he needed, because she knew the poor lad had been drinking heavily, driven to it as he was by his wife's wanton ways. But when she came to the hall she saw that another was before her."

She got up and advanced slowly towards Priscilla, her face livid now save for the spot of hectic colour which burned in either cheek, her eyes glittering so strangely that an involuntary shiver crept along Elinor's spine.

"It was so easy, was it not?" Thomasine went on. "You met him at the head of the stairs. He was drunk, and his boots wet and slippery with the snow that lay thick on the ground. One push was enough to make him lose his balance, to send him helplessly down the staircase on to the stone flags below. Enough to set you free, you and the Marsham fortune, for the lover who was even then sleeping beneath our roof. But he'll not have you, my fine lady! You thought your secret safe, but murder will out, and the tale that Hannah Pennan told will send you to the gallows."

"You are lying!" Priscilla sprang to her feet, dashing aside Elinor's protecting arm. Her white cheeks were flushed now with triumph, her words tumbled out headlong in her haste to refute her sister-in-law's accusations. "It is all a pack of lies! I did not expect Geoffrey to return that night, and I did not go down to meet him. He came to my bedchamber. 'Twas there that he—" she broke off with a gasp of dismay, her colour fading as quickly as it had risen, her eyes widening with horror as she realized the trap into which she had blundered.

"It was there that he was murdered!" Thomasine concluded for her in a terrible voice. "That is what you would say, is it not? Out of your own mouth you are convicted! I knew that we should come at the truth if you could be sufficiently frightened!"

"No," Priscilla whispered, "no!" All her defiance had vanished. She turned desperately towards Elinor. "It was an accident! I swear it!"

Elinor made no response. She stood with her hand still resting on the back of the chair from which Priscilla had risen, and it seemed to her that the smooth, hard shapes of the carving beneath her fingers were her only remaining contact with reality. Her mind felt numb with shock, and though she realized that there was some discrepancy between Priscilla's half-confession and the conclusion to which Thomasine had leapt, she could not for the moment identify it. She stared at Priscilla, trying to force that nebulous conviction into coherent shape, but meeting with no success.

Priscilla, reading into the younger girl's blank gaze and frowning brow the withdrawal of her only supporter, gave a little whimper of despair and cast a hunted glance about her. Miss Marsham put out a bony hand and gripped her by the arm.

"There's no escape for you, my girl," she told her in a tone of jeering triumph. "Run you never so fast nor far, the hangman will be awaiting you at the journey's end."

Priscilla jerked herself free from the elder woman's hold. Defiance was flashing again in her eyes, born not of triumph now but of despair, and with it the desire to strike back at the one who had trapped her; and strike back she did, in no uncertain fashion.

"You have been exceedingly clever, have you not," said said in a low, fierce voice, "tricking me with your lying tales into admitting that Geoffrey's death did not happen just as everyone supposed? Too clever, perhaps, as you will learn! He died in my bedchamber, so how came he to be found in the hall? Do you suppose that I carried him there? No, 'twas Lionel who did so, just as it was Lionel who killed him, and if you send me to the gallows, then as Heaven sees me, I'll not hang alone!"

Elinor, still staring at them both, saw an extraordinary change come over Thomasine Marsham. The last trace of colour fled from her face, and the glitter of triumph in her eyes gave way to a look of sheer horror.

She uttered a choking, incoherent sound of denial, and dropped down into the nearest chair as though her limbs refused to support her any longer. Priscilla stood over her, an expression of scornful comprehension in her pale face.

"That is a very different matter, is it not?" she said with biting contempt. "You old fool, do you think I do not know why you hate me so bitterly? Not because I took your place as mistress of your brother's house, or because in the early days of my marriage I could make him fulfil my lightest wish. That was only the beginning. It was when you realized that Lionel loved me that you really began to hate me, because you were jealous. Yes, mad with jealousy, because you want him yourself and have done so for years!" She laughed, an indescribable sound of malice and disdain. "Do you wonder how I know that, Thomasine? Why, your every word and look when he is present shrieks it loud! It has made you the laughing-stock of the parish these twenty years!"

Miss Marsham stared at her, flinching from each spiteful word as though it were a blow, and Elinor found that she could no longer bear to look at her ashen face. She caught Priscilla by the arm.

"In the name of pity, taunt her no more!" she said sharply. "Tell me instead what really happened on the night your husband died. By my faith, this is an unsavoury scandal you have stirred up between you!"

Priscilla looked resentful, but after a little hesitation obeyed the command. She freed herself petulantly from Elinor's grasp and went to fling herself down in another chair at some distance from her sister-in-law.

"There is little more to tell," she said sullenly.

"Geoffrey had told me that he would not be returning until the following day, and when he came back that night he found Lionel with me. Geoffrey was drunk, so drunk that for once in his life he forgot to be afraid. He flung himself upon Lionel, and in the struggle he fell, and struck his head against the stone fireplace. When we tried to rouse him we found that he was dead."

She paused, staring before her, her eyes wide and dark with the remembered horror of that discovery, and for a few moments there was silence. At length she resumed tonelessly: "I was terror-stricken. No one would have believed his death to be the accident it was if the true circumstances became known. I begged Lionel to find some way of protecting us both, and in the end he carried Geoffrey's body to the hall and laid it at the foot of the stairs as though he had slipped and fallen as he mounted them." She shuddered, pressing her hands against her white cheeks. "I had to go with him to light the way. It was dark and cold, and I lived through a lifetime of terror until I was safe in my room once more. It seemed as though the night would never end as I waited for the uproar which would tell me that the body had been discovered. I would not go through that again for ten thousand pounds!"

Thomasine had neither moved nor spoken since that last, inarticulate cry. She sat upright in her chair, her hands gripping the arms, her face pinched and grey and her eyes staring blindly before her. Priscilla cast a glance of loathing at her as she went on with her story.

"My vigil ended at last, and no one seemed to suspect that the accident had happened in any other way than it had been made to appear. For days I went in dread of discovery, but it did not come, and at last I thought we could account ourselves safe; and so we would have been but for this meddlesome fool with her suspicions and her jealousy. She thought she had found a way to be rid of me, and so she concocted this lying tale to trap me." She looked across at her sister-in-law, her face disfigured by a sneer which robbed it of all claim to prettiness. "What did you hope to gain, Thomasine? Did you think that with me gone, and yourself mistress of the Marsham fortune, you could bribe Lionel into marrying you even now? A bonny bride you would make, upon my soul!"

Miss Marsham stirred at last out of her frozen apathy. Her chin quivered, and slow, painful tears, the first, perhaps, that she had shed for many a day, gathered in her eyes. With a last, pathetic attempt to preserve her dignity she turned to Elinor. "I am not well," she said piteously. "If I could rest for a little while. . . ."

"Of course, Miss Marsham. Come with me." Elinor, devoutly thankful to set a term to this distressing scene, took her by the arm and helped her to her feet. As she led her to the door, she added briefly to Priscilla: "You had best wait here. I will come back directly."

She took Thomasine upstairs to her own bedchamber, and tried to persuade her to lie down upon the bed, but at first without success. Once out of Priscilla's presence the last shreds of Miss Marsham's self-control gave way, and she wept long and bitterly, with a wild abandon the more terrible by contrast with her normal rigid repression of feeling. For a long while all Elinor's efforts to soothe her were in vain, but at last she prevailed upon the elder woman to lie down, and presently had the satisfaction of seeing the reddened eyelids close and an expression of calm begin to creep into the tear-blotched face. She waited until she was certain that Thomasine had fallen asleep, and then she drew the curtains close about the bed and went softly out of the room.

As she made her way downstairs again she realized that she felt extraordinarily tired. The anxieties and conflicting emotions of the past week had been exhausting enough without the additional strain of the scene she had just witnessed, and she felt scarcely capable of dealing with this fresh problem alone. An almost overmastering desire to carry her troubles to Gervase was checked by the remembrance of all that Priscilla had been to him five years before, and might, for all she knew, be to him still. It was true that he had made no attempt to see her since his return to Fairwood, but that might be because he could not endure the reopening of the old wound. Cost her what it might, Elinor knew that she could not be the one to destroy his illusions concerning Priscilla, to rob him of them at a time when so much else had been taken from him.

There was no one, then, to whom she could turn for advice, for Hubert had not yet returned from his mission to Elias Ember, and she was reluctant to subject Sir William to the shock of such a disclosure. For the present, at least, she must somehow contrive to deal with the crisis unaided.

Priscilla was waiting for her in the West Parlour. She looked pale and drawn, but had apparently decided to adopt a defiant attitude, for as Elinor came in she said irritably: "What a time you have been! Did you contrive to quieten the old fool at last?"

Elinor dropped wearily into a chair. "She is resting now," she replied shortly, "but Thomasine Marsham is no fool, Priscilla, as you should know by now. She is shrewd enough, at all events, to have tricked you into admitting your guilt."

"She will not press the accusation now," Priscilla retorted confidently. "Not now that she knows 'twould mean accusing Lionel also. That will check her malice as would nothing else on earth."

"Perhaps, but do not provoke her too far," Elinor warned her. "Were I in your place I would do all in my power to placate her, instead of lashing her with cruel words as you did just now. Has it not occurred to you that her feelings for Colonel Venner may be changed by what she discovered today?"

"Why do you say that?" Priscilla's voice sharpened with sudden fear. "Did she say anything of the kind to you?"

Elinor shook her head, looking at her with cold distaste. "She was too distressed, poor soul, to say anything at all. Gracious Heaven, Priscilla! do you not realize the shock she suffered this afternoon? She doted on her brother, and you say—and I am prepared to believe it—that she has loved Colonel Venner since she was a girl. Yet now she learns that her brother died at Venner's hands, and that you were the cause of it. Try to imagine what that must mean to her, and then ask yourself how far you may depend upon her silence."

"You are trying to frighten me!" Priscilla exclaimed petulantly. "Why should you take her part against me? I know that we have never been friends, but I have done you no harm! I swear to you that Geoffrey's death was an accident! As for what came after, we did what we did to avoid a scandal which would have involved the Ashbournes along with the rest of us. You should be grateful to us for that."

"We should have been a deal more grateful if your anxiety to avoid scandal had extended to your subsequent behaviour," Elinor retorted tartly. "You might at least have had the decency to accord your husband's memory the outward tokens of respect."

"Oh, how your smug virtue sickens me!" Priscilla exclaimed passionately, springing to her feet with a swirl of black draperies. "What right have you to censure me? You do not know what my life in that house was like! You have always been made welcome at Fairwood. There was no other woman here to resent your coming, to spy on you and carry tales and stir up trouble. Yes, I took a lover, and I am not ashamed of it, no matter how scornfully you look down upon me from your own immaculate pedestal! What do you know of such matters, after all? I am free to wed Lionel now, but I would have gone with him any time these two years past had he asked it of me. Wife or mistress, it mattered not to me!"

"That I know!" Elinor, too, rose to her feet as she spoke. Her face was white and there was a world of bitterness in her voice. "Marriage vows have never meant a great deal to you, have they, Priscilla, whether they were your own or another's. That was made plain to me on my own wedding-day, five years ago!"

11

The Closing Snare

FOR the space of a dozen heartbeats there was silence in the room, a silence tense and charged with emotion. Priscilla's defiant self-justification was halted by that quiet challenge, and she stood staring at the speaker with wide-eyed dismay. One hand lifted in a fluttering gesture to her cheek, and she said in a strangled whisper: "What do you mean?"

"Surely you remember?" Elinor replied, cold irony in her voice. "How you and Gervase slipped away during that evening, and the tender love-scene that was played in a secluded chamber? How you pleaded with him to take you to London even though he was no longer free to wed you, and sneered at the merchant's daughter he had married for the sake of her father's gold."

Priscilla groped blindly for the nearest chair and sank down into it, still gazing disbelievingly at Elinor. "You knew?" she said incredulously. "All this while, you knew?"

"Yes, I knew," Elinor agreed bitterly. "I have lived with the knowledge for five years. Five empty years, Priscilla, while I waited in vain for my husband to come to me, knowing all the time what it was that kept him away. Yet you dare to say that you have done me no harm!"

"But that was all over long ago!" Priscilla protested. "Oh, it was real enough to both of us then, but it ended when Gervase went back to London. Not even a letter passed between us. You cannot condemn us for a few moments of madness which we have both forgotten long ago."

"You have forgotten—that I know," Elinor replied coldly, "but what of Gervase? How can you possibly answer for him? Not all hearts are as light and fickle as yours, Priscilla, and it may be that he loves you yet." Her voice was shaking, and she paused, struggling to control the emotion that threatened to overwhelm her. Her endurance had been strained to the uttermost, and now all the bitterness and jealousy, all the hopeless longing of the past years, surged up with a force that could no longer be denied and found expression in the words with which she lashed the other girl. "You say that Miss Marsham wished to be rid of you! Have I not as much cause, and more, to wish it as she has? I share your secret now, and I am not fettered by any fondness for you or for Colonel Venner."

"No!" Priscilla gasped piteously. "Elinor, you would not! Gervase cares nothing for me now, nor I for him! You do not have to take my word that it is so! Ask Gervase himself if you do not believe me!"

The hasty words ended in a gasp of dismay and she clapped a hand to her mouth as though just realizing what she had said. Then suddenly her face puckered and she began to cry. She buried her head in her hands and sobbed with hysterical abandon.

"I should not have done it!" The words came indistinctly, muffled by tears. "This is a judgment, a punishment for breaking so solemn an oath. He made me swear before God to keep the secret, but I meant no harm! No harm!"

"Priscilla!" With an awful clutching at her heart, Elinor sprang forward and gripped the bowed shoulder. "Try to control yourself, in Heaven's name! What have you done? Who made you swear an oath?"

Increasingly violent sobs were the only response. She transferred her grip to both shoulders and dragged Priscilla upright by main force.

"What have you done?" she repeated inexorably. "Tell me, Priscilla."

Mrs. Marsham looked up despairingly into the pale, resolute face bent above her. Her own face was streaked with tears and there was sheer terror in her eyes, but she was powerless to resist the force of a will stronger than her own.

"It was Gervase," she said incoherently. "I followed you to the cottage yesterday. While you were there I hid just inside the wood, because I was afraid to come near in case Duchess heard me and barked. When you had gone, I went in. Gervase was there. He made me swear to keep the secret before he would let me go."

Elinor released her and stood slowly upright, cold horror flooding over her. "And you have broken that promise," she said in a lifeless voice. "You have betrayed him to his enemies."

"No, no! You do not understand!" Priscilla clutched frantically at her arm. "He will come to no harm, I promise you! I have told no one but Lionel."

"Lionel Venner!" Elinor repeated brokenly. "Oh, God, Priscilla! Why?"

"That is what I am trying to tell you. Ever since I came back to Fairwood, I have corresponded with Lionel—it does not matter how. On the day the soldiers searched the house I received a message from him to say that he felt certain that Gervase was in hiding somewhere at Fairwood, and that if I could find out where, he could use the knowledge to force Sir William into letting us be married at once. I knew I should not have broken the promise I made to Gervase, but he will come to no harm. If I had not been certain of that I would have said nothing."

"You believe Colonel Venner honest in this?" Elinor asked bitterly. "You believe that he will make no other use of this knowledge, even though you know the grudge he bears us? How could you be so gullible?" She let her hands fall in a weary, despairing gesture to her sides. "God in Heaven! You have destroyed us all!"

Priscilla stared at her in white-faced horror, obviously unwilling to believe and yet with doubt beginning to stir in her mind. Elinor moved away from her and stood gazing with unseeing eyes from the window. Even now she could scarcely accept the hideous truth, or realize that all the perils faced and conquered, all the careful precautions and eager plans had been set at naught. Lionel Venner knew where Gervase was hidden, and would come with his soldiers to drag him to imprisonment and certain death; might, perhaps, have come already. Even as she stood here, Gervase might have been made prisoner and Venner be advancing upon the Priory to take those who would be accounted his accomplices. It was possible that they would never see each other again.

"I cannot believe that Lionel would trick me so," Priscilla was saying wretchedly, "but I wish I had never told him where Gervase is hiding. If only it were possible to recall the message, but I dare say it will have reached him by now!"

The last words pierced Elinor's apathy of despair, and she swung round to face her companion. "When did you send it?" she demanded.

"This forenoon," Priscilla confessed miserably. "It took me until then to resolve to break the promise I had made to Gervase. Oh, how I wish that I had not!"

"How soon would he have received it?"

Priscilla shook her head. "I cannot say with certainty. There is bound to be some delay, for the messenger would have to fetch my letter from its hiding-place, and then carry it to Lionel."

Elinor waited for no more. There was still a chance, however slight, of reaching the cottage ahead of Venner and his men, and warning Gervase of his danger. Without another word she ran from the room, across the wide, cool hall and down the steps, and so through the gardens to a gate giving on to the park. Careless now of any who might see her, she wrenched it open and sped on across the rough grass-land towards Hezekiah's cottage, now in the full blaze of summer sunshine, now in the shade of towering, indifferent trees. A herd of deer, startled by her flying figure, left their grazing and bounded away, the sound of their going seeming to her overwrought senses to be echoed by advancing hoofbeats.

She paused for a moment, straining her ears, but could hear nothing save the normal sounds of a summer day and the thudding of her own heart. Then on again, her long skirts clinging in hampering folds about her legs, a sharp pain tearing savagely at her side. The cottage seemed utterly deserted as she stumbled through the little garden and groped with shaking fingers for the latch, but before she could find it the door was opened from within and she reeled forward into Gervase's arms.

She clung to him, sobbing for breath, too spent even to utter the warning she had come to give, but her condition alone was enough to tell him at least a part of the truth. Without a word he thrust the door shut again and, picking her up, carried her across to the settle. Bending over her, he asked briefly: "Soldiers?" Then, as she nodded: "How far behind you?"

"I do not know!" The words came in a painful gasp. "They have been told you are here."

He stood erect again and she saw his face harden, but he did not immediately reply. Instead he moved away and filled a mug with water and brought it to her. She drank gratefully, her anxious gaze on his face.

"It was Priscilla, of course?" he said at last, and his tone made the words a statement rather than a question. "You know that she came here yesterday?"

"I learned of it just now." Her lips quivered. "I shall never forgive myself for leading her to your hiding-place."

He shook his head. "The blame is not yours, my dear, but mine. Priscilla never could keep a still tongue in her head, and I should have known better than to trust to a mere promise, however solemn, to keep her silent." He struck his clenched fist into the palm of his other hand. "Fool that I was to let her go! I should have guessed that she would babble the truth to Venner." He saw the startled look in Elinor's eyes and added in explanation: "Hubert told me the truth, and I realized that when we spoke of the matter you sought to protect her."

She could have replied that in evading the truth concerning Priscilla and Colonel Venner her care had been to spare him rather than his cousin, but it was impossible to say so. Instead she said quietly: "The Colonel led her to believe that he would use the certainty of your presence here merely to obtain Sir William's consent to their marriage. She would not have betrayed you, I am sure, had she not believed him."

He shot her a curious glance. "Did she tell you so?"

"Yes, when I had surprised her into disclosing what she had done." She moved her hands in a helpless gesture. "It is too long a tale to tell you now. Gervase, what are we to do?"

"Only one thing can be done. I must put as much distance as possible between myself and Fairwood. Unless they take me here they will have no proof save Priscilla's word that I ever received aid from any of you."

She realized that he had forgotten Captain Blake, who could identify him as the man who had posed as her servant, and she was glad of it, feeling that any danger to herself was now of small account. If Gervase were taken it would not matter very much what became of her; and how could he hope to evade capture? Forced to set out in broad daylight, unarmed and on foot, without resources of any kind and with Venner already informed of his whereabouts, it would be only a matter of time before he was apprehended.

"You must go back to the Priory," he resumed after

a moment, "and when Venner comes there, as come he will when he finds this place deserted, deny all knowledge of me. Keep to the pretence that we have not met these five years." He took the empty mug from her and put it on the table, and then took her hands to help her to her feet. "This must be farewell, Elinor! The longer we delay, the greater the danger."

She nodded silently, not trusting herself to speak, and so for a few moments they stood looking at each other, overwhelmed by the bitterness of parting. There was so much to say, so much that must now remain for ever unsaid, for the future in which she had dared to believe, and had taught him to believe in also, had by folly and by treachery been taken from them. So they stood, hands joined, each searching the other's face as though to imprint it indelibly upon the memory, and through the hush of the summer afternoon came the rapidly approaching beat of galloping hoofs.

As the sound intruded upon her consciousness Elinor caught her breath and involuntarily tightened her hold on Gervase's hands, but he, after listening for a second or two with a puzzled frown, said perplexedly: "That is but one rider, coming fast. Venner would have soldiers with him."

He went across to the door and opened it a crack, and then threw it wide as Hubert flung himself from his horse at the garden gate.

"Gervase," he gasped, hurrying forward, "I fear you are discovered. Venner——"

"I know!" Gervase broke in. "Elinor learned of it and came to warn me. You come in good time, brother! With a horse beneath me I may yet win clear of Fairwood and so avoid entangling you all in my danger."

"Wait!" Hubert caught his arm to detain him. There was hopelessness in his voice and eyes. "You do not know the extent of it! The whole place is surrounded. You have not a hope in hell of getting through!"

Gervase went white. "You are sure of this?"

"Absolutely. They make no secret of their presence and I saw them as I rode into the village. Then I spoke with some of our people, and they say it is the same on every side. The militia have already begun to search the outlying cottages. They mean to make no mistake this time."

Elinor had come to the door to join them, and when Hubert had concluded his grim tidings they stood in silence under the honeysuckle with which the porch was covered, three young people for whom the sands were all too quickly running out. Gervase stared across the park to the tree-dotted rise which hid the Priory from them, and tasted to the last dregs the cup of vain regret and self-reproach, for it was he, and he alone, who was responsible for the threatened tragedy. This day, he knew, would see the destruction of the Ashbourne family, for even if Sir William were spared, on the score of his great age and infirmity, from actual arrest, he could not survive the cruel shock of seeing those he loved rent from him. There would remain only Priscilla, who by her foolishness had destroyed her benefactor and her home, and who would not be harmed because it was she who had led the hunter to his quarry. Suddenly, with a flash of insight, Gervase perceived the truth, and knew why Lionel Venner was so determined to capture him at Fairwood. With Hubert and Elinor hopelessly involved, and so, in law, as guilty of treason as he was himself, there was no hope of escape for any of them. There would be only Priscilla to inherit Fairwood after Sir William's death.

Hubert was gazing distractedly at Elinor, unable to think of anything or anyone else. He would have given his life to ensure her safety, but he knew that he was as powerless to save her as he was to save himself, and the knowledge of his own helplessness was tearing at him like physical pain. Constantly in his memory echoed Venner's brutal words concerning the punishment prescribed by law for a woman found guilty of treason, and his whole being rebelled at the appalling picture they conjured up. That could not happen, not to Elinor! Yet with every moment that passed, the horror was drawing closer to her.

Elinor herself, standing between the brothers with closed eyes and clasped hands, was praying more urgently than she had ever done in her life, not for herself alone, but that she might be shown some way—any way—of saving them all. She would not give way to despair, would not admit defeat until the doors of prison finally closed upon them. She prayed for a miracle, and, miraculously, the prayer was answered, with a sudden blaze of inspiration as dazzling and uplifting as sunrise in a stormy sky.

"There is a way," she whispered. "Yes, I believe there is a way! Gervase, Hubert, listen to me! I believe I know how to check Colonel Venner's plans, but there is no time now to tell you how. You must trust me, and do as I say without argument, for if he finds us here, we are lost!"

"Tell us," Gervase said briefly. "We cannot be in worse case than we are at present."

"I will take Hubert's horse and ride back to the Priory, while you follow me on foot as fast as you can. Somehow you must reach Sir William's room unobserved, before Venner arrives with his men."

"But if Gervase is found there it will damn us all beyond hope of escape." Hubert protested, aghast. "My grandfather along with the rest of us."

"We are damned already, Hubert, unless we can find some means of thwarting Venner's malice," she retorted, and put out a hand towards each of them. "Will you not trust me, both of you? Oh, say that you will! There is so little time."

"I'll trust you," Gervase agreed recklessly. "I do not know what you hope to do, but anything is better than waiting here to be made prisoner. Let us at least make a fight for our freedom." He caught her hand in his, and looked across at his brother. "What say you, Hubert?"

"What can I say?" A weary smile flickered across Hubert's haggard face. "I'll do whatever you wish, Nell."

"Then there is no time to lose." Elinor led the way to the gate, and Gervase swung her up on to the back of the waiting horse. Settling herself as well as she could in the unaccustomed saddle, she looked down at the two young men. "Pray that this plan will work," she said simply, "for if it does not, then we are lost indeed."

She wheeled her mount round and urged it to a gallop across the park, leaving the brothers to follow her with what speed they might. A few minutes brought her to the door of the Priory, and sliding to the ground she ran into the house, calling to a startled servant to see that the horse was stabled.

She went straight to Sir William's room, and found him lying as he so often did, with his gaze fixed on the portrait of his wife, while Mercer busied himself quietly with some small duty on the other side of the room. Elinor caught the servant by the arm.

"Find Mrs. Marsham and bring her here at once," she commanded. "Tell her that Sir William desires to see her instantly, and pay no heed to any excuses she may make."

Mercer looked startled, but hurried off without question to carry out the order, while Elinor went across to the bed. Sir William was watching her with an expression of concern.

"What is wrong, my child?" he asked quietly.

Elinor dropped to her knees by the bed and took his hand between her own, meeting the shrewd glance with a frank and level gaze.

"We hover on the brink of disaster, sir," she said gravely, "but it may be that God has seen fit to place the means for our salvation in my hands. With your help I may be able to save us all, but first I must tell you what I have learned today."

When Mercer returned some minutes later with a reluctant and apprehensive Priscilla, Elinor was still kneeling at Sir William's side. She got up as they entered the room, and the old man beckoned both the newcomers forward.

"Bring me pen, ink and paper, Mercer, if you please," he said, and then as the servant bowed and moved away, his glance passed on to Mrs. Marsham. "Attend to me, Priscilla," he continued sternly. "You are to listen to what Elinor has to say, and do exactly as she tells you. Do you understand?"

"Yes, Sir William," Priscilla stammered, "but I do not see why—"

"You are not required to see anything," Sir William informed her curtly. "Merely to obey."

Mercer came back with the writing materials, and Elinor asked him to place them on the table near the window. Then she turned to Priscilla.

"It is very simple," she said. "All you have to do is to write a true account of your husband's death, as you described it just now to Miss Marsham and to me."

"To write—" Priscilla broke off, staring with an astonishment which rapidly gave way to horror. "No, I will not! You must be mad even to suggest it!"

"I promise you that it will be seen by no one outside this room," Elinor continued remorselessly, "but if you refuse, I shall accuse you before the Justices, and call upon Miss Marsham to confirm what I say. Once the accusation is made, I do not think it will be difficult to persuade her to give evidence against you."

"You would not!" Priscilla exclaimed, but her tone lacked conviction. She turned desperately towards the bed. "Sir William——!"

"Elinor has my support and authority in any action she may decide to take," he broke in sternly. "Do as she bids you. I command it."

Priscilla looked desperately from one to the other. The gaunt, predatory features and cold blue eyes of the old man held no hint of relenting, and she had felt the weight of his displeasure too often in the past to defy him easily now, but it was when she turned towards Elinor that her courage finally failed. The younger girl's face was white and drawn, the lips rigidly compressed, the gold-brown eyes cold and implacable.

She looked far older than her eighteen years, and capable at that moment of any ruthlessness.

The ready tears flooded into Priscilla's eyes and trickled down her cheeks, but she knew instinctively that weeping would be of no avail. She turned, and went with dragging steps to the table, and sat down. Mercer handed her the pen, and, with the tears dripping down to make small smudges on the paper, she began unwillingly to write.

12

Checkmate

LIONEL VENNER mounted his horse at the gate of Hezekiah's cottage, and looked back with cold fury across the trampled garden to the little house. The door stood wide, disclosing a scene of chaos within, for the men, enraged at finding their quarry's supposed hiding-place empty, had made of the search an excuse for plunder and destruction, and their Colonel had not attempted to restrain them. He realized now that Hubert Ashbourne must somehow have reached Fairwood ahead of him and warned his brother of the approaching danger, but though the knowledge angered him, Venner regarded the present failure merely as an irritating delay in his plans. Gervase Ashbourne could not escape; the trap this time had been too carefully set.

With a curt command to his men he urged his horse forward in the direction of the Priory itself, which a few minutes later came into view as they reached the crest of the rise. Riding down towards it, Venner studied the noble prospect before him and for the first time ventured to admit to himself the secret hope which had lurked at the back of his mind since the day he discovered that Gervase Ashbourne was an officer in Monmouth's army. Old Sir William, as everyone knew, was dying, and this day would see him lacking an heir. Very soon now, Fairwood would need a new master, and who more fitted for the part than the husband of the last surviving Ashbourne, an officer who had served his King with unswerving loyalty and devotion? The Colonel's anger began to subside in the light of that pleasing thought, and by the time he drew rein at the imposing doorway of the great house he was already picturing himself as its owner.

The afternoon sunshine was warm on the mellow stone, the still air sweet with the scent of flowers and herbs, and save for a gardener some distance away, who had paused in his work to stare open-mouthed at the soldiers, the whole place seemed as deserted as an enchanted palace in a fairy-tale. The men shifted their feet on the gravel, and the Colonel's horse snorted and pawed the ground, the small sounds seeming unnaturally loud in the silence. Venner dismounted and, ordering his men to remain where they were, went up the steps and into the house. As he crossed the threshold a man advanced from the far end of the hall to meet him.

"I am Sir William Ashbourne's personal servant, Colonel Venner," he announced with a bow. "My master desires that you grant him the favour of a few minutes in private before any further action is taken."

The Colonel was surprised, but dissembled it, and also the triumph with which the message inspired him. So the old autocrat was singing a different tune now, was he? No courteously-worded insults this time, but a humble request which was no doubt a mere preliminary to even more urgent entreaties. With a faint, sneering smile on his thin lips he turned to address the corporal at the foot of the steps.

"I go to speak with Sir William Ashbourne. Permit no one to leave the house."

He was still smiling as he followed Mercer across the hall and up the stairs, in grim anticipation of the coming interview. Where, he wondered, was Gervase, and his brother, and his impudent minx of a wife? Spirited away, no doubt, to some distant corner of the great house, to await apprehensively the outcome of their grandfather's attempt to divert their pursuer from his purpose. Well, they would wait in vain! He would listen to whatever Sir William had to say, would give himself the pleasure of seeing the old tyrant humbled and suing for mercy, and then he would summon his men and have them search the Priory from attic to cellar, and enjoy the further delight of seeing the three young Ashbournes in bonds before him.

With this amiable intention in mind he watched Mercer throw open the door of Sir William's bedchamber, and strode forward with a faint jingling of spurs, a conqueror entering a captured citadel. The old man was sitting up in bed, propped by many pillows, a rich bedgown about his shoulders and the flowing curls of a periwig framing his aquiline, bearded face with the disfiguring black patch over the empty eye-socket. He looked old and frail, but not at all humble; his air was rather that of a monarch giving audience to an importunate subject than of a supplicant for a conqueror's favour.

That was Colonel Venner's first surprise. The second was that there were several other people in the room. Elinor Ashbourne was seated in a chair close to the bed, and standing beside the chair, one hand resting upon its back, was a tall young man whose rough garments suggested the labourer, but whose proud features and challenging gaze proclaimed him unmistakably an Ashbourne. The rebel, Gervase, without a doubt.

Hubert Ashbourne was standing on the opposite side of the bed, and a little distance away, as though deliberately excluded from the family circle, sat Priscilla. She drooped miserably in her chair, her eyes red and swollen with weeping, and after one fleeting glance at Venner as he entered the room, did not look at him again.

Her presence there was something he had certainly not bargained for, though he had realized that sooner or later he would be obliged to disclose her as his informant. Surely, he thought, the old man was not foolish enough to imagine that she could be made use of as a hostage.

He halted at the foot of the bed and bowed with mock civility, first to Sir William and then to Elinor. Then he looked at the only man in the room who was a stranger to him.

"Mr. Gervase Ashbourne, I believe?" he said ironically. "Or should I say 'Captain Ashbourne'? That was the rank you held in Monmouth's army, was it not? You spare me the trouble of searching for you."

"I do not suppose that you would have needed to search far," Gervase replied in the same tone. "My new hiding-place, like the old, would have been betrayed."

"No!" The despairing cry came from Priscilla. "Oh, why will you not believe me? I told you yesterday that I would as soon betray my own brother." She looked wildly at Venner. "You told me that no harm should come to him. You promised me!"

"I am in the King's service, Priscilla," he replied impatiently. "I have my duty to do, and cannot afford to be influenced by sentiment."

Hubert laughed softly, a mirthless, bitter sound. "I'll warrant you cannot," he said, flinging back the words Venner had spoken to him earlier that day. "Does your enthusiasm spring from loyalty or self-interest, I wonder?"

A quick, hard glance from Venner told him the thrust had struck home, but that was the only betrayal. The Colonel's thin lips twisted in a sneer.

"Mock as much as you like, my young friends," he said ominously, "but today I think the last laugh will be mine. My men surround this place, and others wait below for my commands. Tonight you will find lodging in a prison cell." His glance shifted to rest on Elinor's pale face as he added softly: "All three of you."

She met the cold, malevolent stare composedly. "Perhaps," she said quietly, "and perhaps not. The game is not yet played out, Colonel Venner."

"I think it is," he retorted mockingly. "I am not

Captain Blake, Mrs. Ashbourne. From him you might have purchased your own immunity, but not from me."

Hubert uttered a strangled exclamation and took a pace forward, groping for his sword, and Gervase said in a voice tight with anger: "Blake paid for a similar suggestion with a broken head. He was fortunate to escape so lightly."

Venner laughed. "What, both of you to the lady's defence?" he jeered. "But in this, at least, the younger brother must yield place to the elder. He, as husband, has the lawful claim."

The insult implicit in the words was unmistakable. Gervase left his place to Elinor's chair and took two swift strides that brought him to Venner's side. His face was white and he was breathing hard. "That is the second time you have uttered such foulness in my hearing," he said between his teeth, "and you should answer for it, Venner, though you had a whole regiment within call. Hubert, lend me your sword!"

"Gervase!" Sir William's voice, commanding still for all its weakness, interrupted him. "Be good enough to leave this to me. Nothing will be achieved by brawling. As for you, Colonel Venner, I will bear with your presence but not your insolence. Is that understood?"

"You will bear——!" Venner broke off, apparently at a loss for words. Then he laughed, with a mixture of astonishment and anger. "Upon my soul, your effrontery passes all bounds!"

Sir William made no reply to this, but merely looked at him in silence. The Colonel endured the chill contempt of that piercing regard for a few seconds, but even he felt at a disadvantage before this imperious old man. He realized that mastery of the situation was passing from him, and was moved to fiercer anger than before.

"Enough of this tomfoolery!" he exclaimed furiously. "I did not come here to bandy words, but to arrest a rebel and those who have aided him. Prate you never so proudly, you will find the gallows as high for an Ashbourne as for humbler folk."

He turned, and was already half-way to the door when Sir William spoke again, as quietly as before but in a tone of even greater significance.

"Colonel Venner," he said, "how and where did Geoffrey Marsham die?"

The challenge halted Lionel Venner in his tracks. He spun round on his heel to stare at Ashbourne with an expression of blank, incredulous dismay. So for an instant, and then a mask of indifference, assumed just one fraction of time too late, seemed to descend upon his face. He directed one swift, suspicious glance at Priscilla, and then, looking again at Sir William, replied in a level voice: "By a fall on the stairs in the darkness of a winter's night, when his feet were made unsteady by wine. Why speak of that now?"

"Because," Sir William replied coldly, "it did not happen so. He died in the bedchamber of his faithless wife, at the hands of the kinsman with whom she had betrayed him. The kinsman who afterwards cast his body down the stairs to cloak murder in the guise of an accident."

This time Venner's silence was more prolonged. He looked from one to the other, and again his glance lingered longest of all upon Priscilla. At Sir William's words she had shuddered and covered her face with her hands, bowing her head so that the long black veil fell forward across her shoulders.

"An interesting theory," Venner said at last, and if there was the faintest trace of alarm in the sneering voice it was barely perceptible. "I repeat, however, why speak of it now? You do not, I trust, imagine that so wild an accusation can turn me from my purpose?"

"That is my hope," Sir William agreed mildly. "To be brief, sir, if you arrest my grandson or any member of my family, you will find yourself publicly accused of the murder of your kinsman. I have given you fair warning. Now the choice is yours."

"Is it by God?" Venner said harshly. "And who, may I ask, is to come forward as my accuser? You, Sir William? Your grandchildren? Your servant? Proven traitors, every one of you! You will all be too busy trying to save your own necks to have the opportunity to cast a rope about mine."

Sir William's brows lifted. "There is your cousin, Thomasine Marsham," he said softly. "It was she who first brought the truth to light, and you cannot silence her, Colonel Venner, with a charge of treason."

"Thomasine?" Venner stared blankly, but made a quick recovery. "Her wild fancies are notorious! No one would give credence to such a story unless she could offer proof of it."

"The proof exists, Colonel Venner." It was Elinor who spoke, breaking her long silence. There was a note of scornful amusement in her voice. "A true account of the events of that night, set down by Priscilla and bearing her signature, written in the presence of Sir William, his servant and myself. Does that influence your decision, sir?"

He stared at her, dismay and disbelief struggling for mastery in his face, and then he strode across to Priscilla and gripped her by the shoulder, forcing her erect.

"She is lying, is she not?" he demanded harshly. "My God! you were not mad enough to——"

"I had no choice," Priscilla sobbed. "Thomasine tricked me into admitting it, and then Sir William and Elinor made me write it all down and sign it. They said that if I did, no one outside this room would ever see it, but if I refused, they and Thomasine would inform the Justices." She clutched frantically at his sleeve. "Lionel, do not look at me like that! I did it to save us both."

He dashed aside the pleading hand. " 'To save us both!' " he mimicked furiously. "How? By placing the means to destroy us in the hands of those who wish us ill?" He swung round again to face the bed. "Show me this so-called confession!"

"So that you may attempt its destruction?" Elinor retorted coolly. "We are not so easily duped, sir! The confession is securely bestowed in a safe place, and there it will remain until my husband is safely across the sea, or until Miss Marsham lays it before the Justices. I do not think that you will find it."

"I see!" Venner came slowly back to his former position at the foot of the bed. His face was white and vicious with fury, but he was making a superhuman effort to keep his temper under control. "You are clever, Mrs. Ashbourne, and ruthless as only a woman can be in defence of her own. I am right, am I not, in supposing this situation to be of your devising?"

Elinor inclined her head. "You are, sir. I give thanks that the means to thwart you were granted to me."

"Do not give thanks too soon, madam," he warned her. "I am not beaten yet. What is to prevent me from searching the house until this incriminating document comes to light?"

She raised her brows. "Fairwood is a very large house, sir, and the object you seek is very small. There are a thousand places where it might be concealed."

He shrugged. "I have men enough to make the task less formidable. Better still"—he glanced over his shoulder at Mrs. Marsham's huddled figure—"I can enlist the aid of one who has known this house since her childhood. Tell me, Priscilla, where are objects of value generally concealed?"

Priscilla made no response to this; Sir William said sharply: "In my strong-room, sir, but you would seek the paper there in vain. Priscilla has no more notion of where it is hidden than you have yourself."

"A pity!" Venner's voice was still controlled, but there was a murderous anger in his eyes. "It seems, then, that I must seek the information I need elsewhere. From the instigator of this ingenious scheme, for example." He looked again towards Elinor. "Well, Mrs. Ashbourne? There are a number of ways in which I might persuade you to confide in me, and none of them are pleasant. What is to prevent me from using them?"

The tone of his voice, and the cold, pitiless glance which accompanied the words, seemed to threaten unspeakable things. Elinor's eyes widened with shock and dismay, and Sir William's gnarled hand clenched suddenly upon the coverlet. He opened his lips to speak, but was forestalled by Gervase, who was standing now in his former position by his wife's chair.

"This, Venner," he said quietly, and levelled the pistol he had taken from his pocket at the Colonel's heart. "Both my brother and myself are armed. Take one step to put your threat into execution, and as God sees me, you will not live to take a second."

"You young fool!" There was a ragged edge of fury to the other's voice. "Do you not realize that the sound of a shot would bring my men upon you?"

"I know it," Gervase agreed calmly, "but you would be dead before they could reach you, and I do not think your devotion to duty is so great that you will make yourself a martyr in its name. You will find small satisfaction in delivering us up to the law if you cannot see in the deed some profit to yourself."

"Wait!" The interruption came, unexpectedly from Priscilla. She rose to her feet, tossing back her veil, and faced them all, pale but resolute. "I have a word to say! Lionel, when you urged me to discover where Gervase was hiding, you promised me that you would use the knowledge only to obtain Sir William's consent to our immediate marriage. Because I love you, I did as you asked, even to the extent of breaking an oath sworn in the name of God Himself. But you deceived me, and have come with soldiers at your back to arrest Gervase and those who aided him. So be it! Take them if you must, but know that if you do, I will take my own life sooner than wed with you. I mean it, Lionel! If they perish, their blood will be upon my hands, but, God aiding me, I will not join those hands with others even more foully stained!"

For a second or two after she had finished speaking there was utter silence in the room. Venner was staring at her in the most complete stupefaction, for whatever opposition he had expected and prepared to meet, he had certainly looked for none from this quarter. So for a moment; then, recovering himself, he went across to her and sought to take her hand in his.

"My dear, you are overwrought," he said with an attempt at solicitude, "I did deceive you, and I admit my fault, but in this matter both you and I are but the instruments of a greater power—the power of the Law. Your kinsman has plotted rebellion and borne arms against his lawful King. The others have aided him and so become as guilty as he. I have no more power to pardon than I have to condemn. I am but the instrument of Justice."

She pulled her hand away. There was anguish and terror in her face, and a stubbornness that transcended both. "Then prove it!" she retorted. "Call your men, and risk a bullet in your heart, or a rope about your neck when the truth of Geoffrey's death is made known. Why do you hesitate? If Justice be satisfied, what matter if its instruments be destroyed?"

"Priscilla, this is not like you!" Venner protested. "You do not mean the things you are saying——"

"I do mean them," she broke in desperately. "I have sinned, I know! I have been weak and selfish, but there are some things I will not do. Fairwood is my home. When the plague left me an orphan, Sir William took me and brought me up as though I were his own child. Gervase and Hubert were as brothers to me. By my folly and wickedness I have placed them all in mortal danger, and it may be beyond my power to save them, but one thing I will have you know. If you take them forth from here as prisoners I will never see you again as long as I live!"

Lionel Venner looked at her and knew that he was defeated. Even in her present distress she was very fair, and he still desired her. He desired her fortune even more. It was not as rich a prize as he had hoped for, but compared with his own meagre, younger son's portion, even his cousin's snug estate promised extreme affluence. There was, he knew, no hope that Priscilla did not mean what she said. Easily influenced though she generally was, there was a hard core of obstinacy to her nature with which he had had more than one previous encounter. If she said she would not see him again, she meant it, and he might wait until doomsday for her to change her mind.

So, although it was one of the hardest things he had ever done in his life, he choked back the fury that threatened to overmaster him, and put as bold a face on the matter as he could. Gervase had judged him accurately when he said that empty glory and a martyr's death were things he did not covet. Better to accept defeat with as good a grace as possible and be certain of the smaller profit, than to lose all by trying to grasp too much.

"You leave me no choice," he said with a shrug. "For your sake then, Priscilla, and for no other reason, I will do this thing—if I can! It will not be easy. My men know what quarry they seek, and that I was informed of his presence here. How can I send them away empty-handed?"

"Let them search the house," Sir William advised him. "This room they need not enter, since you are already here. Tell them your informant was mistaken. They expected to find Gervase at the cottage, and did not. They will not suspect."

"You have overlooked nothing, have you?" Venner remarked bitterly. "What of this document you made Priscilla sign? I shall feel easier in my mind when I have seen it destroyed."

"Priscilla herself shall bring it to you," Sir William replied, "as soon as we receive word from my grandson that he is safely across the Channel. Until then, it must remain hidden here. I give you my word that it shall be seen by no one outside this room."

"One thing more, Colonel Venner," Elinor put in as the old man paused. "As long as that paper exists, your anxiety for Gervase's safety will well-nigh equal ours. Help us then, to set a term to it. Furnish him with a safe-conduct so that he may travel to the coast."

He shot her a glance charged with hatred. " 'Sdeath, madam, you ask too much! I have no authority to issue a safe-conduct, and if it were discovered that I had done so to enable a known rebel to escape, my own life would be forfeit."

"Your life hangs in the balance already, sir," she pointed out calmly. "If you cannot provide an official safe-conduct, there is nothing to prevent you from giving Gervase a letter stating that he is traveling to the coast on your behalf, on some matter of private business."

"So entangling myself even deeper in this treasonable affair," Venner said bitterly. "You have bound me fast with your scheming have you not? So be it, then! You shall have the letter tomorrow. Now, in God's name, let us make an end of this mockery."

He turned again towards the door. Hubert said swiftly: "I will come with you. Mercer, do you remain outside the door of this room. Colonel Venner will order his men not to enter."

The Colonel looked at him with furious comprehension but made no protest, and they went out of the room together. Mercer followed them and closed the door, and for the space of several moments no one moved or spoke, so great was the reaction from intolerable tension. Then Gervase uncocked the pistol and returned it to his pocket, and as though the small movement had released them all from a spell, the others moved also. Sir William relaxed wearily against his pillows; Elinor, after one searching glance at him, got up and went to the cupboard where cordials and medicines were kept; and Priscilla, still standing rigidly beside her chair, passed a trembling hand across her brow and turned towards Gervase.

"I dare not ask your forgiveness," she said in a low voice, "but I beg you to believe that I meant you no harm. Had I guessed what Lionel would do, nothing would have made me divulge your hiding-place. And I have done what I could to make amends."

"I believe you, Priscilla," he said wearily, "and if my forgiveness means anything to you, know that you have that also. Venner betrayed the trust you had in him. There is no more to be said."

For a moment longer she continued to regard him, and then her eyes turned timidly towards Sir William. The old man stared back implacably.

"Do not look to me for forgiveness," he said harshly. "You are a fool, Priscilla, and I find it harder to bear with fools than with rogues. I will house you here until your cousin is safely across the sea, and then you may make this marriage for which you are so eager, but which I fancy you will regret before all is done. Meanwhile, do not come into my presence again."

"Hush, Sir William!" Elinor came back to the bedside, a glass of cordial in her hand. "You agitate yourself needlessly, and today's events have already taxed your strength to the uttermost. Drink this, and try to sleep."

"Sleep? How can I sleep while those damned red-coated louts are ransacking my house?" he demanded fiercely, but he swallowed the draught nevertheless, and patted her hand as she took the empty glass from him. "You look to be in need of rest yourself, my child."

"I am well enough," she replied with a faint smile. "I must leave you for a little now and go to Miss Marsham, for it is best that I should be with her while the soldiers are in the house, but Gervase and Priscilla will stay here, and Mercer is outside the door should you need anything."

He nodded, and it was a sufficient indication of the exhaustion he denied that he made no attempt to detain her. It was left to Gervase to do that, and, following Elinor as she moved away from the bed, he said in a low voice: "Must you go? You have already suffered too much discourtesy from King James's men, and only in this room will you be safe from further indignities."

She shook her head, though her heart warmed at this evidence of his concern for her. She would have given much to do as he asked, to send Priscilla to reassure Miss Marsham and spend these few precious minutes with Gervase, for who could tell when such an opportunity would occur again? Sir William was already nodding against his pillows, and to all intents they would be alone. For a moment she almost yielded to temptation, but she knew that though Lionel Venner had been forced into striking a bargain with them, the danger would not be over until he had marched his men away from Fairwood.

"I dare not stay," she said softly. "Remember, Miss Marsham shares a dangerous secret, and if she were brought before Colonel Venner, or even learned of his presence in the house, she might in her present state of mind say something which would bring all our schemes to ruin."

He realized the truth of what she said and nodded resignedly. The men searching the house might be rough in their manners, and fail to use a woman with the respect which was her due, but here in the Priory Elinor could come to no real harm, while the peril in which she would stand if by Thomasine Marsham's intervention their plans went awry was too appalling to contemplate.

"Yes, you are right," he agreed reluctantly. "Go to her, then, but be sure that you have servants within call lest you need protection. I do not think that Venner will exert himself to restrain his men."

"I am quite sure that he will not," she replied dryly. "He will hate us all more bitterly than ever for this day's work, though as long as he lacks the means to gratify his hatred it need not trouble us." She hesitated, and then added, so softly that even he could scarcely catch the words: "It was Priscilla who turned the balance in our favour, Gervase. Without her ultimatum to Venner I do not think we could have prevailed."

He looked curiously at her, and then glanced at Priscilla, who had dropped into her chair again and was not looking at them, Gervase smiled slightly.

"I know it," he said quietly, "and I am grateful to her, but do not regard her action in too noble a light. She intervened to save herself and Venner, and had no danger threatened them I do not think she would have exerted herself to save us. In short, my dear, Priscilla has never done a wholly unselfish deed in her life, nor do I think she ever will."

Elinor stared at him. The words had been spoken without bitterness, even with a certain wry humour, and for the first time she was able to believe that Priscilla had spoken the truth when she declared that Gervase no longer cared any more for her than she did for him. It was as though an unbearable weight had been lifted from her, and her spirits rose in a warm flood of hopeful joy which swept away both weariness and the consciousness of lingering peril, and filled her with a glad certainty of the future. The rapture lasted only a moment, like a passing gleam of sunshine from a lowering sky, but the memory of it stayed warmly in her heart as she turned from him and hastened out of the room and through the house to the chamber where Thomasine Marsham lay.

13

The Conscience of Thomasine

WHEN she reached the room, however, she found that the elder woman was no longer lying upon the bed, but standing by the window and looking out into the garden below. She turned at the sound of the opening door, and Elinor saw that she had restored her appearance to its customary severe neatness. Only her face, haggard and swollen with weeping, betrayed the emotional crisis through which she had passed; she seemed to have aged immeasurably since her arrival at the Priory.

"There are soldiers in the garden, Mrs. Ashbourne," she said without preamble. "What do they want here?"

Elinor closed the door and came further into the room, hoping devoutly that Colonel Venner himself would not come within his cousin's range of vision.

"They have come to search the house," she replied in as indifferent a tone as she could command. "Some say that my husband was out with Monmouth, and the authorities cannot rid themselves of the suspicion that he sought refuge here after the rebel defeat. This is the second time within the week that they have descended upon us. I came to warn you of their presence."

Thomasine nodded, and to Elinor's relief moved

away from the window. "We live in troublous times," she remarked grimly, "though I would have supposed that Sir William Ashbourne's known loyalty would be sufficient to protect his household from such intrusion as this."

"Few people in the West are above suspicion today," Elinor replied sadly. "This summer has brought tragedy to many a home, both proud and humble."

"Not the summer alone," Thomasine corrected her harshly. "Mrs. Ashbourne, we have today been put in possession of a dreadful secret, and I cannot yet see for what purpose that knowledge has been granted to us."

Fear stabbed sharply at Elinor's heart, for if Thomasine felt it to be her duty to disclose her discovery to the Law, the bonds so cunningly forged about Lionel Venner would count for nothing. In a voice which not all her efforts could keep entirely steady, she said: "One thing at least is clear to me. We must do nothing without first giving it deep and careful consideration. Action taken under the stress of any powerful emotion will sometimes prove mistaken in the light of calmer reflection."

Miss Marsham inclined her head. "That is very true. Perhaps in prayer the answer may be found." Her mask of cold composure gave way suddenly and she turned aside, twisting her bony hands together in anguish. "God help me! how could I accuse him? How take the risk of bringing him to his death?"

Elinor's alarm was turned to pity by that despairing cry. She went quickly forward and took the writhing fingers in her own warm clasp. "Do not distress yourself so, my dear Miss Marsham," she said earnestly. "Your brother's death was no less an accident because it happened as it did rather than as everyone supposed. Surely you believe, as I do, that neither Priscilla nor Colonel Venner sought Mr. Marsham's death?"

"How can I believe it? They may not have planned to kill him, but they must have wished him dead, both of them, time and again. She never cared anything for Geoffrey, and Lionel is ambitious, greedy for wealth and influence. He was always so, even as a boy."

She moved again, and sank down on the cushioned chest at the foot of the bed. Her voice had grown reflective, her thoughts turned back toward the past, and Elinor deemed it best to let her talk as she chose, without interruptions. Thus, perhaps, some clue to her intentions might come to light.

"I remember how he used to visit my father's house." Thomasine went on musingly. "He was a lad in his early teens when he first came there, but even then there lurked behind his courtesy a bitter resentment of all that we had, and he lacked, for his family was poor and he had three elder brothers. We became friends, for there is but two years between us, and he used to talk to me of a world greater than that which we knew, and of the career he meant to make in it. He wanted to be a soldier, and when he was old enough I persuaded my father to purchase a commission for him, since his own father had not the means to do so. He swore then that he would never forget what I had done for him, that whatever he achieved of worldly success he would owe to me."

She paused, and Elinor went quietly to sit beside her, but though Thomasine glanced at her as she did so, Elinor felt that she did not really see her. It was as though the other woman were speaking her thoughts aloud, living again the hopes and dreams of her girl-hood.

"It was some years before we met again," she resumed after a moment, "and then he came to visit us, soon after my father died. In my sorrow and loneliness I turned to him for comfort, and so learned to love him. He let me believe that he returned my love."

She fell silent again for a space, staring straight before her, while Elinor looked at her and tried to picture her as a young woman dreaming of romance. It was not easy. Thomasine Marsham was one of those who give the impression of never having known youth.

"You cannot be expected to understand my feelings at that time," Thomasine said abruptly, and the words so exactly echoed Elinor's thoughts that it startled her. "You are beautiful and beloved, and were wed straight from your schoolroom. I was twenty-four when my father died, already well past marriageable age, and resigned to a life of spinsterhood under my brother's roof; and I was plain, plainer than any of my younger sisters, who had all made good marriages. Yet now, it seemed, my turn had come, and for a month I lived in a fool's paradise." Her mouth twisted with self-contempt and there was indescribable bitterness in her voice. "Then Lionel told me of the lady in London to whom he was already betrothed. She was young and well-dowered, and her father possessed influence of a kind invaluable to a soldier seeking advancement."

Elinor was surprised into speech. "I did not know that Colonel Venner had been married!"

"Nor has he," Thomasine replied dryly. "The girl died a few weeks before the wedding-day, and Lionel's hopes of advancement died with her. So it has been throughout his life. Always when a prize has seemed within his grasp, something has happened to snatch it from him."

So it had happened today, Elinor reflected. Venner must have accounted Fairwood as good as his when he rode up to its door, and the stratagem which had robbed him of it must have been as cruel a blow as any he had ever suffered. Yet it left him still the bride he desired, and the comfortable fortune she had inherited from his kinsman. Or was that, too, to be dashed from his grasp by the woman he had deceived and deserted years before? Compelled by her own fears and the need for certainty, even certainty of the worst kind, Elinor said slowly: "It lies within your power to shatter his present hopes, to rob him of life itself. Do you mean to do so?"

Thomasine started, stared at her as though she had forgotten her presence there, and then covered her eyes with her hand.

"I do not know," she confessed in a stifled voice. "How can I bear to have his death upon my conscience? Yet my brother died at his hands! It may be that the truth has been revealed to me in order that justice may be done, and the burden laid upon me as punishment for my sins."

"For your sins?" Elinor repeated blankly. "I do not understand."

Miss Marsham's face quivered. "The fault was mine," she said wretchedly. "I hated Priscilla, for her youth and her beauty and the way in which Geoffrey doted on her when they were first wed. It is true that I tried to stir up trouble between them, for it seemed that she had everything that I had been denied. In the end I was to learn that she had won, too, the thing I had desired above all others on earth."

She paused, but Elinor did not venture to speak. She guessed that this must be the first time in her life that Thomasine had spoken so frankly of her feelings to anyone, and because so much might depend upon her own clear understanding of the other woman's tortured mind she dared not take the risk of halting the flow of confidences.

"Lionel had been bidden to their wedding," Thomasine resumed after a little, "but after that we did not see him for close upon two years. Then he left the army and came home to Wiltshire, and began to visit us frequently. I guessed what lure it was that brought him, and it was plain that she was drawn to him as he was to her. I had thought I hated her before, but it was as nothing to the hatred I felt now. I began to hint to Geoffrey at an intrigue between them, and they were together enough to lend colour to my words, but they were more discreet than I supposed. So discreet that even I never guessed that the tales I carried to my brother were true." She broke off, pressing her hand-kerchief to her lips, staring above it into Elinor's startled eyes. "You perceive the irony of that, do you not? Until today I believe that Priscilla killed Geoffrey, in the manner that I pretended Hannah had de-scribed to me. I did not know that Lionel was her lover in very truth!"

Astonishment deprived Elinor of speech, but as all the implications of Thomasine's words dawned upon her, understanding came, and with it a swift flood of compassion. This unhappy, embittered woman, having fabricated a malicious story to gratify her jealousy, had found it recoil upon her as proven truth more terrible than anything she had invented. It was small wonder that she was so distraught.

"Geoffrey was my only brother," Thomasine continued drearily after a pause. "Our mother died to give him birth, and 'twas I who brought him up. He was like my own child! I loved him more than any being in this world save one, and that one took my brother's life. But the blame was mine! Had I not sown the seed of suspicion in Geoffrey's mind, he would not have returned that night, nor surprised them together, nor lost his life!" She buried her face in her hands, and though her next words were muffled, a passionate earnestness sounded in them. "God pity me! What am I to do? I would sooner face death itself than that decision!"

Elinor laid a hand comfortingly on the thin, bowed shoulder, and tried to find words which would convey the profound pity she felt for Miss Marsham and at the same time convince her that only one decision was possible. Then, before she could frame the reply she sought, the door was flung rudely open and a militiaman clanked into the room.

He checked for an instant on finding it occupied, and behind him in the doorway Elinor saw Hezekiah and the footman whom she had told to stay within call. Her hand tightened warningly on Thomasine's shoulder, and she said coldly: "That you have your duty to do I know, but pray be quick about it. This lady is unwell."

Miss Marsham's drawn and tear-stained face confirmed these words, and the soldier, somewhat abashed by the obvious distress of the one lady and the icy disdain of the other, set about his search hastily, almost apologetically. He was a young countryman, a very different type from the swaggering dragoons of the Tangier Regiment who had come to Fairwood with Captain Blake, and he seemed overawed by the grandeur of his present surroundings, the obviously feminine character of the room, and the hostile stares of the two servants in the doorway. Elinor surmised that this was the first time in his life that he had been either so far away from his native village, or inside such a house as the Priory.

Nevertheless he was thorough in his search, and any fugitive endeavouring to conceal himself in the room would have had little hope of evading discovery. Elinor thought of Gervase, waiting tensely in the one room in the house which would remain inviolate, and again gave thanks that the means to thwart Lionel Venner's malice had been granted to her. Unlike Miss Marsham, she had no doubt of the purpose for which the secret had so providentially been revealed.

When at last the soldier had completed his task and left the room, Elinor waved the servants away and turned again to Thomasine.

"We must talk of this matter again," she said, "when you have had time to consider it more calmly. You will spend the night here, will you not? I doubt whether the soldiers would permit you to leave until they had completed their search, and in any event it is too late for you to reach home again before dark."

"You are very kind," Thomasine replied stiffly, making an obvious effort to be courteous. "I shall be very glad to avail myself of your hospitality, if you will hold me excused from joining you below. I feel the need to be alone this evening."

"I understand," Elinor assured her, "and as soon as we are rid of these intruders I will have a room prepared for you. Meanwhile, rest quietly here. I do not think you will be disturbed again."

With that she left her, and pausing only to give orders for the preparation of a bedchamber for Miss Marsham, made her way back to Sir William's room, where, in addition to the impassive Mercer, a militiaman stood guard outside the door. Obviously Colonel Venner was intent upon keeping his side of the bargain.

She found the old man asleep, Priscilla still huddled in her chair, and Gervase sitting beside his grandfather's bed. He got up as she entered, but she laid a warning finger to her lips and went softly across to join him.

"There is a soldier at the door," she whispered. "Do not say anything that may be overheard."

He nodded.

"What of Miss Marsham?"

"All is well, for the present," Elinor replied, for she did not wish Priscilla to discover Thomasine's state of mind. "She does not know that the militia here are under the command of her cousin."

He nodded again, but the presence of the soldier outside the door rendered any prolonged conversation dangerous. They sat silent, straining their ears for any sound which might reach them from other parts of the house, or from the garden below, but it seemed that the search was being conducted in a reasonably orderly manner. At last, after what seemed an eternity of waiting, Hubert came into the room with Mercer at his heels. He looked tired but triumphant.

"They have gone," he announced in a tone of relief, "and I do not think that they will trouble us again." He dropped into the nearest chair and rubbed his hand across his brow " 'Slife, I'm weary! God grant we never have to live through another such day as this."

"Amen to that!" Gervase agreed. "Though good has come to us out of it, when all is said and done. And remember, Hubert, that 'tis few enough days of any kind we should have left but for Elinor's quick wits."

Elinor looked up at him with a weary smile. "Wit would have been of small use without knowledge, Gervase." she reminded him gravely. "It is by God's mercy that we have won through to safety, and beside that, all else is naught."

The few remaining hours of that momentous day passed for Elinor in a kind of dream. As soon as the militia had marched away, Hezekiah hastened to the cottage, and returned appalled by the chaos he found there, so that Elinor had to marshal servants and send them back with him to set things to rights. Only when this had been done, and darkness had fallen, did Gervase venture out of the sanctuary of Sir William's room and make his way back to his former hiding-place, there to await the letter from Lionel Venner which was to take him unscathed through his enemies to the coast and safety.

When he had gone, and Hubert, who had accompanied him, returned with the news that the cottage had been safely reached, Elinor at last permitted herself to give way to her overwhelming weariness. She felt that she had lived through a whole lifetime in one endless day, and that she had reached the uttermost limit of endurance. Only one duty was still to be performed.

On the way to her own bedchamber, dazed with fatigue though she was, she paused at the room allotted to Miss Marsham, and went in to assure herself that her guest had everything needful for her comfort.

A single candle faintly illuminated the lofty room, lessening the darkness rather than affording light, but the window framed a luminous vista of moonlit countryside, and there Thomasine was standing, looking out. She turned her head as Elinor went across to join her.

"The answer is not easy to find," she said in a hopeless voice. "All the evening I have prayed for guidance, but none has been granted to me."

Elinor did not reply at once, but stood looking from the window and trying to shape a sensible reply from thoughts made unruly by fatigue. Perhaps it would be best to tell Miss Marsham the whole truth, to show her that there was a purpose in all that happened, and that other lives besides Venner's depended on her silence. Was the risk too great? She did not know. She was too tired to make so grave a decision tonight.

Below her, on the edge of the gardens, the moonlight was caught and reflected by water between the trees. This was the fish-pond, a survival of monastic days, fed by the stream which flowed into and out of it and still kept stocked against the needs of the house. The bright gleam of it seemed to mesmerise her and she could not tear her gaze away. Her eyelids felt leaden, weighted with sleep. Nothing more could be done tonight. As long as Thomasine was beneath the Priory roof she could do nothing to overset their plans, and in the morning they could discuss the matter again.

"Forgive me," she said huskily. "I am very tired. So much has happened today, and neither of us is in a fit state to come to a decision now. Try to sleep, and to-morrow we will talk of it again."

Thomasine uttered a harsh, mirthless laugh. "Sleep?" she repeated. "Shall I ever sleep peacefully again? But you are right, Mrs. Ashbourne. Perhaps the night may bring good counsel and a clearer perception of right and wrong."

She returned to her contemplation of the peaceful scene without, and Elinor went quietly away, carrying with her the memory of a gaunt, haggard face and haunted, tormented eyes. It stayed with her as she made her preparations for the night, and even when the deep sleep of exhaustion claimed her, recurred uneasily in her dreams. It was still vivid in her mind when she awoke, so vivid that as soon as she was dressed she made her way to Miss Marsham's room, for in the clear light of morning she realized that so vital a matter could be set aside no longer.

Even so, she was prepared, if she found the other woman asleep, to leave her undisturbed, and so she entered the room very softly, to halt again immediately in sudden, uneasy surprise. Miss Marsham was not there. The candle had burned down to the socket, the bed was smooth and unruffled, and there was nothing to indicate whether the room had been empty for minutes or for hours.

Alarmed now, and filled with a nameless dread, Elinor left the bedchamber and made her way downstairs, where, dissembling the uneasiness she felt, she inquired of the servants whether any of them had seen Miss Marsham that morning. None had, and, thoroughly frightened now, Elinor hastened in search of Hubert.

He listened gravely to her hurried tale, but shook his head when in conclusion she asked anxiously: "Do you suppose she felt it her duty to accuse Colonel Venner, and has gone to lay the facts before the Justices?"

"I should not think so. Had she reached that decision she would have told you, for your testimony would be needed in support of her own."

Elinor made a hopeless gesture. "Hubert, she was in no state to consider that! I tell you, she was almost beside herself."

He stood for a moment or two in frowning thought, then, bidding her await his return, he hurried away. Elinor endured ten frantic minutes of anxiety and then he came back into the room, looking more perplexed than before.

"She cannot have gone far, at all events. Her servants are still here, her coach and horses in the stables. Wherever she went, it was alone and on foot."

They looked at each other, their relief tempered with anxiety, for though this seemed to dispose of their worst fears it merely deepened the mystery, and whatever Thomasine Marsham was, she carried with her the power to destroy them all.

"We must find her," Elinor said at length, and Hubert nodded his agreement.

"I will send the servants about it without delay. You had best find Priscilla and tell her what has happened. She knows Miss Marsham better than any of us, and may be able to throw some light on the matter."

This hope, however, proved to be unjustified, for Priscilla was as puzzled as they were by her sister-in-law's disappearance. She and Elinor sat together in the West Parlour, discussing the matter in low voices and racking their brains to recall anything in the events of the previous day which would offer some clue, however slight, to the whereabouts of the missing woman. In this they met with no success, but persisted because they could think of nothing else to do, until, midway through the morning, Hubert came into the room. One glance at his white, shocked face told them that he brought news, and that the news was bad.

"We have found her," he said in a shaken voice. "She is dead!"

Priscilla uttered a little cry, and Elinor said in a horrified voice: "In God's name, Hubert, how?"

"The pond!" he replied disjointedly. "We found her in the shallows by the reed-bed. She had taken her own life."

Elinor sank back in her chair, staring at him in horror, but seeing instead a gaunt, tormented face against a background of moon-silvered water. What agonies Thomasine must have endured, what desperate conflict of emotion, to drive her into taking her own life rather than make the choice which circumstances had forced upon her.

"This is my fault!" she said in a deadened voice. "I should have realized how desperate she was. I should not have left her alone."

"That is absurd, Nell," Hubert said sternly. "No one could have foreseen this tragedy. When you recover from the shock of what has happened, you will realize that."

"She was mad!" Priscilla said with conviction. "She has been half-crazed for years, and the shock she sustained yesterday must have dealt the final blow to her reason."

"Priscilla is right," Hubert said firmly, and went forward to grasp Elinor's hands in his own. "She was unwell when she came here yesterday—everyone remarked the strangeness of her aspect. Nell, you must believe it, for all our sakes! For Miss Marsham's most of all!"

Elinor stared at him, and slowly the truth and meaning of his words dawned upon her. Only if a suicide's insanity was proved could he be afforded Christian burial; the alternative was an unhallowed grave at some lonely cross-roads, with a stake driven through the body to imprison the unquiet spirit. If they wished to save the unfortunate Thomasine from that ultimate horror, they must believe her mad, and persuade others to believe it also.

"Yes, you are right," she said slowly. "We must believe it. She was mad, poor, lonely, unhappy soul, and we are all, perhaps, a little to blame for that. God grant that she has found peace at last!"

14

Parting at Daybreak

HUBERT and Elinor were walking across the park to Hezekiah's cottage. It was early morning, so early that the sun had not yet risen to dispel the white mist which lay thickly upon the fields and beneath the trees, or to dry the dew-wet grass. They walked in silence, each engrossed in thought, for this was the day on which Gervase was to venture forth from hiding in his attempt to reach the coast. They were on their way now to bid him Godspeed.

Lionel Venner had kept his word. On the previous day a messenger had come to Fairwood, bearing, under cover to Sir William, the letter which Gervase was to carry with him. It represented him as Giles Allen, in the service of Colonel Venner, bound for Brixham to settle, on his master's behalf, a matter of family business with the Colonel's kinsman there. Some papers purporting to deal with this imaginary business were also enclosed.

As soon as the letter arrived, Hezekiah had been sent off to Elias Ember to explain this new development and seek the promised guide without further delay. His mission had been successful, for now that Gervase could travel openly, fewer precautions were necessary. The guide, a cheerful young man for whom Master Ember himself was prepared to vouch, had returned with Hezekiah and spent the night at the cottage.

Preparations for the journey had been hasty but thorough. Money, a horse, fresh clothes more in keeping with the new part Gervase was to play, had all been conveyed secretly to the cottage, and by now, no doubt, he was ready to depart. Elinor's heart was heavy at the thought. His safety meant more to her than anything in the world, but he was going into exile and there was no way of knowing when they would meet again.

Hubert, walking silently beside her, looked at her

from time to time with some concern. The dangers and anxieties of the past week had taken their toll; the faint, healthy colour had faded from her face, leaving it pale and drawn, and there were dark shadows like bruises beneath her eyes. The shock of Thomasine Marsham's death had stricken her hard, and he feared that she was still secretly blaming herself for the tragedy even though she pretended otherwise, but he knew that that was only a small part of the trouble. It was his brother's imminent departure which had stolen the light from her eyes.

They came at length to the cottage, and Elinor's little spaniel pranced ahead of them along the narrow garden path, on either side of which flowers and vegetables lay bruised and withering where the heavy boots of the militia had trampled them into the ground. Hezekiah opened the door as they approached and Elinor passed through, but Hubert paused to speak quietly to the old man. Hezekiah nodded, beckoned to Elias Ember's man to join them, and all three walked round to the shed at the rear of house where the horses were concealed.

In the cottage kitchen, Gervase and Elinor were left facing each other. They had not met since his stealthy departure from the Priory, and now only a few brief minutes were left to them, for he must be beyond the boundaries of Fairwood before the activity of the day began in farm and hamlet. Elinor was poignantly aware of the passing of time; so acute was her awareness of it that it seemed as though she could feel it flowing round her like a swift, strong current which no power on earth could check. A kind of desperation seized upon her, and though she had lain awake rehearsing in her

mind the things she meant to say to Gervase when she
bade him farewell she could not now remember one of
them.

Gervase seemed to be equally tongue-tied. He took
her hand and lifted it to his lips, and then stood for a
moment or two looking down at it as it lay passively in
his grasp. At length he said slowly: "Hubert told me of
Miss Marsham's death. He is concerned because he
fears you are still blaming yourself for not watching
her more closely."

"How can I not blame myself?" Elinor's voice
trembled in spite of her efforts to keep it steady. "She
had talked to me, confided in me more, I think, than
she had ever confided in anyone in her life. I knew
how she was suffering, torturing herself with the bitter
choice before her. I should have stayed with her, tried
to help her, but because I was weary I left her alone.
And she killed herself."

"You could not have helped her, Elinor," Gervase
said quietly. "It was a decision she had to make alone.
Do not torment yourself with needless regrets which
can profit you no more than they can benefit you."

"I will try," she promised wearily. "Perhaps Hubert
is right, and when the shock of this dreadful thing has
passed I shall be able to regard it more calmly. That is
not easy at present. The whole parish is chattering of
it."

"Another burden laid on your shoulders," Gervase
said with bitter self-reproach. "God! what a craven
wretch I am to be skulking here, and creeping away
merely to save my own miserable skin while you bear
responsibilities which are rightly mine."

Had he spoken with the intention of rallying her

spirits, he could have found no more certain way to do it. Her fingers tightened on his, and she said gently: "That is folly, Gervase, and you know it. 'Tis the safety of all of us you carry with you, and that is a burden heavy enough for any man. As for the rest, we shall contrive, Hubert and I. We have weathered storms before."

Gervase stood silent, staring at her, feeling himself shaken by a jealousy so fierce and sudden that for a moment he was incapable of speech. Into his memory flashed a picture of Elinor and Hubert as he had seen them on the night of his first visit to the Priory, talking intimately together in the candle-light, while he stood like an intruder upon the threshold. A burning resentment against his brother took possession of him, resentment of the past during which Hubert had watched Elinor grow from a timid child into lovely womanhood, and of the future which they would spend together at Fairwood, while he lived an exile's lonely life in foreign cities. She was his wife, and he knew now that there was nothing in the world he wanted so much as to take her with him out of England, and never be parted from her again.

Would she go with him, if he asked it of her? The question shaped itself unbidden in his mind, but sudden doubts stifled it on the brink of utterance, for he knew, as surely as though the words had already been spoken, what answer she would make. She would say that any delay would be dangerous, that fresh plans would have to be made, since Mrs. Gervase Ashbourne could not travel in company with Colonel Venner's supposed servant; that she could not leave Fairwood while Sir William still had need of her. All undeniably true, but could he ever be sure that the truth was not being used merely as an excuse, when the real reason was that she did not wish to leave England, or Fairwood, or—Hubert?

No blame could be laid upon her if it were so, he reflected bitterly; the fault was his alone. Though she had borne his name for five years, they had been strangers until a week ago, while Hubert had become part of her life. With a stab of shame Gervase recalled how she had come to Fairwood at the time of their marriage, a shy, lonely child desperately in need of reassurance. He had been too resentful then, too selfishly absorbed in his hopeless passion for Priscilla, to treat his bride with anything but polite indifference. It was his brother who had given her kindness and friendship, who had helped her then, and through the years that followed, and it was little wonder if the bond forged then had endured and strengthened, while his own neglect of her bore its inevitable and well-deserved harvest.

So because he feared the answer, the question that he would have given the world to ask, and she to hear, was never spoken. Instead he loosed her hand and turned away, saying quietly over his shoulder, "Yes, you will contrive. You are well-loved here, both you and Hubert, and though folk may chatter they would stand by you to the death. The only aid that I can give is to take myself out of England as speedily and secretly as may be, and that, God aiding me, I will do. Too many have been endangered for too long by my presence."

Elinor stood silent, with bowed head and clasped hands, fighting to check the tears which had risen blindingly to her eyes. She was determined not to betray her unhappiness, or to lure him by any show of emotion into avowals which he did not mean and might later come to regret. The swift passage of time was her ally now, and not her enemy; if she could remain outwardly calm and composed for just a few minutes longer, he need never guess the turmoil of despair and longing within her.

She blinked back her tears and looked at him as he stood by the hearth, a long, steady look which endeavoured to imprint upon her memory every detail of his appearance. The tall, spare, active figure, clad now in a suit of sober grey homespun befitting the new part he was to play; the arrogant profile with aquiline nose and firm, imperious lips, the dark head, uncovered at present, held with that inherent, unconscious pride which was as natural to him as breathing. How could any ordinarily perceptive person be deceived by his disguise, or fail to realize that in spite of humble garb and misleading papers this was a man accustomed to command rather than to serve? She sighed, and as once before reminded him of the identity he had assumed.

"Gervase, you are posing as Colonel Venner's servant. 'Tis so he describes you in the letter you carry, but none will believe it unless you remember to bear yourself more humbly, and not to look at every man you meet as though you would challenge him to stay you."

He roused from his preoccupation with a start, and looked at her with the faint, impatient frown which the past week had taught her to know so well. She went closer to him and laid a hand on his arm.

"I know that you would infinitely prefer to fight your way to the coast, sword in hand," she added gently, "but that is not possible, my dear! This way alone holds out some hope of success."

He smiled faintly and covered her fingers with his own. "I know it," he said ruefully, "and you are too shrewd in your judgment of me. I have small liking for the shifts to which I am put, but I will play the part as best I may, for your sake if not for my own."

The door of the cottage opened. Hubert stood on the threshold, not looking at them, and behind him the misty landscape was slowly brightening.

"Forgive me," he said in an odd, abrupt voice, "but the sun is rising and it is time Gervase was away. The horses are at the gate."

Elinor uttered a little gasp of protest and of pain, a sound so faint and fleeting that even an instant afterwards Gervase could not be certain that he had heard it at all. Her hand was cold and unresisting in his as he led her across to the door, taking his hat from the table in passing, and in a moment they were all three standing again in the porch beneath the honeysuckle, as they had stood two days before when Venner's soldiers were closing inexorably in upon them. Gervase released Elinor's hand and held his own out to Hubert.

"There are no words for a moment such as this," he said quietly. "I thank you, brother, for all you have done, and all that is yet to do."

Hubert's face was working, and he made no response save to grip his brother's hand. Gervase turned to Elinor, and set his hands lightly on her shoulders, and bent to kiss her cheek. She stood motionless, resisting the impulse which prompted her to turn her lips to his.

"God keep you both!" he said in a low voice, and turned sharp on his heel and went quickly along the path to the gate where Hezekiah was holding his horse, and the guide was already mounted. Elinor's little dog went scampering after him, but Hubert followed and caught it while Gervase paused to take leave of the old servant. He rejoined Elinor in the porch, putting her pet into her arms. She looked at him with tragic, tear-filled eyes, and with an instinctive desire to support and comfort her he flung an arm about her shoulders.

Gervase swung up into the saddle and looked back across the little garden to the couple in the porch. For an infinitesimal fraction of time he was still, and then he raised his hand in farewell and set spur to his mount, urging it to a canter along the narrow track bordering the wood. The other man followed him, and in a moment or two both riders were lost to sight in the pearly mist, and only the lessening sound of hoofbeats rang faintly through the still morning air.

Gervase spurred his horse to a gallop and, maintained the reckless pace until his companion drew alongside to utter a warning against the folly of drawing attention upon themselves by such headlong speed. He nodded then, and slowed to a brisk trot, but continued to ride in tight-lipped silence which the other man made no further attempt to break.

He assumed that Mr. Ashbourne was distressed at bidding farewell to his home and family, with no certainty of when if ever he would see them again, but this assumption was only partially correct. Before Gervase's eyes hovered with tormenting clarity the memory of his last glimpse of Elinor, standing in the flower-hung porch with her little dog clasped to her breast, and Hubert's arm about her shoulders. His wife and his brother, standing together in that close comradeship which his own coming had briefly interrupted, and which with his departure could now be resumed. That memory was to remain with him for many a day, a rankling source of jealousy and uncertainty to make him realize to the full how much he had cast away, and come to value only when it was beyond his reach.

Had he but turned his horse about during those first few minutes of his journey into exile, and returned to the cottage, he would have learned beyond all doubt how mistaken he was. The sound of his going had barely faded into silence before Elinor was huddled on the bench by the kitchen table, her head buried in her arms as she gave way to a storm of weeping, while Hubert and Hezekiah looked on helplessly, and Duchess pawed her dress and thrust at her with anxious, inquiring nose. At length Hubert signed to Hezekiah to leave them, and the old man tucked the spaniel under his arm and went out, shaking his head in perplexity and distress.

Hubert moved slowly forward until he stood close beside the weeping girl, but for a moment or two he did not speak. He stood looking down at her, his face drawn with concern, and at last laid a hand diffidently on her shoulder.

"Nell!" he said wretchedly. "Don't cry so, my dear! He will win safely through to France, I am sure of it."

She raised her head and looked at him, the tears streaming unheeded down her cheeks. It was some seconds before she could force her trembling lips to shape the words she desired to utter, but at last she whispered incoherently: "God grant he may, but oh, Hubert, he is gone, and I do not know how to bear it! Who knows when I shall see him again? He said nothing of it, nothing!"

Hubert's face contracted with sudden pain, but he set his own feelings aside in the need to comfort her. He sat down beside her on the bench and drew her into his arms, and she turned her face against his shoulder, sobbing uncontrollably. He was conscious of a curious sensation compounded of bitterness and gladness; to spare Gervase she had imposed upon herself a rigid self-control, but with him she felt no need of subterfuge or pretence. He was at once more to her, and infinitely less.

"There has never been anyone else for you, has there, Nell?" he said ruefully when the violence of her grief had subsided a little. "No one but Gervase."

She shook her head. "No one in the world," she said simply. "Child as I was, I knew that from the very first, and nothing that followed had the power to change it. I am his, and will be until the end of time." Her voice broke again. "There were moments during this past week when I dared to hope—but he said nothing, and now I am alone again."

"What did you expect him to say, Nell?" Hubert chided her gently. "It is a dangerous enterprise on which he was embarked, and will be until he is safely across the Channel. Did you look for him to take you with him? To ask you to leave my grandfather when your presence means so much to him? Gervase is proud, and it has not been easy for him to accept our protection, and know that we were facing peril on his behalf. I thought you realized that. You spoke of it to me only a few days ago."

Elinor sighed, pushing the dishevelled hair back

from her brow. "My mind accepts the truth of what you say, but my heart yearns for some sign, however small, that I may one day mean to him one tiny part of all that he means to me. I would have been content with a single word, if it had held out to me some hope for the future."

"Perhaps women regard these matters in a different light," Hubert said thoughtfully, "but I, at least, can understand something of what Gervase must feel. To his mind, he has failed. He is a hunted fugitive in his own land, and an exile in any other. Even if there were no ties to hold you here, he would not ask you to leave the shelter and security of Fairwood to share such a life with him. I know that I would not do so, in his place."

"How eloquently you plead his cause," Elinor said quietly. "You have done so much, Hubert, for him and for me, with no thought of self."

"No!" Hubert said in a strangled voice. "Nell, you must not say that! You do not know the truth!"

He got up from the bench and began to move about the room in such obvious distress that concern for him drove her own sorrow to the back of her mind. It occurred to her that for several days he had seemed to be labouring under the burden of some grave trouble, but so many other things had happened that she had had neither the time nor the opportunity to discover what it was. Now remorse for that neglect seized upon her, and she put out her hand towards him.

"What is wrong, Hubert?" she asked gently. "What is troubling you?"

He paused in front of her, looking at her with an-

guished eyes, but made no attempt to take the proffered hand.

"I never meant to tell you," he said miserably. "I
never meant to tell anyone, but I cannot live with such
a secret and not go mad! It happened two days ago,
when Venner's men stopped me on my way home from
Master Ember's house. They were at that little tavern
where the road forks—you know the place—and he
made me go in and drink with him. He was in a vicious
mood. 'Twas before Priscilla's message reached him,
and perhaps he thought that she had failed him, or
could not discover what he wished to know. Whatever
the reason, he sought to persuade me to betray my
brother's hiding-place, and promised secrecy for me,
and immunity for all at Fairwood, if I would do as he
asked."

Elinor had listened with widening eyes to this disclosure, and as he paused she said indignantly: "Oh,
he is vile, and sees only vileness in others! How dare
he say such a thing, to you of all men!"

Hubert shook his head; his face was white, and there
was naked agony in his eyes.

"Nell, do you not understand what I am trying to
tell you? He asked me where Gervase was hiding, and
reminded me of all I stood to gain if he were taken,
and I—God forgive me, I was tempted! For a few moments I actually contemplated betraying my own
brother to a traitor's death!"

Again he paused, but this time Elinor made no reply, merely staring at him with wide eyes in which he
thought to read horror and revulsion. He flung out his
hands in a despairing gesture.

"Well, you may look at me like that!" he said with

passionate self-reproach. "If he were vile to ask such a thing of me, how much worse am I who was tempted to agree! The devil spoke to me that day through Venner's lips, dangling before my eyes the chance to possess myself of everything in this world I most desire to have, and to my shame I was prepared to listen. 'Your brother's title and inheritance can be yours,' he said to me, 'and, above all, your brother's wife.' " He dropped to one knee beside her, flinging his arms around her and burying his head in her lap. "Nell, I love you! 'Twas there that temptation lay! I love you, and because of it I came near to taking my brother's life and breaking your heart."

There was silence for a moment or two after the pitiful confession ended, and then Elinor spoke, very gently and lovingly, laying her hand on his bowed head.

"To have met temptation and conquered it is cause for thanksgiving rather than remorse. You must not reproach yourself, Hubert! There is no need."

He lifted his head to look wonderingly at her. "You will forgive me?"

"What is there to forgive? You did no wrong, to Gervase or to me, save perhaps for a moment or two in your thoughts. What is that when set beside all the good we have received at your hands? No, I think the only one unwilling to forgive you is yourself."

"There is so much more now that I will find hard to forgive in myself," he replied wretchedly. "I should at least have refrained from burdening you with a confession merely to ease my own mind. Nell, believe me, it was not my intention to speak of my love for you! I should have guarded that secret from you above all others."

"Do you think I did not know?" she questioned gently. "I knew, and it grieved me, for I am not worthy, Hubert, that you should go lonely for my sake. You are my dear friend and brother, but I can offer you no more than that. I would have you find a woman with whom you might know complete happiness."

He shook his head, his gaze resting adoringly upon her face.

"Where could I find one to take your place? You are nonpareil, my dear." She made a little gesture of protest, and he smiled without mirth. "Rest easy, Nell! I shall not importune you with unwanted protestations of love. You must forget what I have been weak enough to confess to you today."

"We shall not speak of it again, but I shall not forget. I shall remember it with humility and pride." She set her hands on his shoulders, her troubled compassionate gaze searching the tired young face and unhappy eyes. Then she leaned forward and kissed him gently on the forehead. "God grant you find happiness one day, Hubert! No one ever deserved it more."

The Epilogue

September, 1685

A CHILL autumn dusk was falling over the old city of Amsterdam, and a wind that carried with it the threat of rain sighed through the lime-trees bordering many of the streets. The withering leaves floated down from them, drifting into courtyards and doorways to the exasperation of meticulous Dutch housewives, or settling on the calm waters of canals busy with shipping. The streets were busy, too, even on this inclement evening, but those abroad went briskly about their various errands and showed little inclination to loiter, for there was that in the air which spoke of approaching winter, and the prospect of fireside and candle-light called strongly.

Yet some there were in the bustling throng who walked idly and aimlessly, and among the latter was Gervase Ashbourne. He was alone, for though he had many acquaintances and some close friends in the city, both among the native Dutch and the many English exiles who dwelt there, he was that evening in a mood which desired solitude rather than companionship.

The truth was that he was profoundly uneasy. He had made his escape from England with little difficulty, for his guide had led him south-westwards by unfrequented ways, and when they did meet with any challenge, the papers which Lionel Venner had supplied stood them in good stead. They had come at length to a tiny fishing village on the Devon coast, and there, after another two days in hiding, he had embarked on an innocent-looking little craft from which he passed, under cover of darkness, to the deck of a larger vessel. This had in due course set him ashore while taking aboard a contraband cargo from a lonely stretch of the French coast.

The French counterparts of the English smugglers had guided him to the nearest town, where he wrote a letter to Sir William telling, in carefully-worded phrases which would convey little to any hostile eye, of his safe arrival and his intention to travel on to Amsterdam. When it had been despatched, he hired a horse and set forth on the first stage of his journey northward through France and into Holland.

He came at last, during the first week of August, to Amsterdam, one of the very few of all those who had left it to follow Monmouth ever to see the city again. He had established himself in his former lodging, and waited, with as much patience as he could command, for news to come to him from Fairwood.

Now, in late September, he was still waiting, with an anxiety which grew as his patience diminished. News of a general sort there was in plenty, and none of it was reassuring. Monmouth was dead, executed on Tower Hill just one week after his capture, but on the scene of the rebellion itself the work of retribution was still in progress. The brutalities of the Tangier Regiment had been succeeded, towards the end of August, by butchery of a more formal kind, under the expert guidance of Baron Jeffreys, Lord Chief Justice of England. In the course of an Assize the purpose of which was vengeance rather than justice, his lordship was engaged in disposing of the hundreds of rebel prisoners crowding the gaols of the West Country. Many of these had already died of their neglected wounds or of diseases resulting from the hideous conditions of their imprisonment, and the survivors Lord Jeffreys was condemning wholesale, since to give each an individual trial would occupy too much time, to execution or to that slavery in the West Indian plantations which was a living death.

Every ship from England brought news of fresh barbarities, but the story which aroused the greatest indignation was that concerning Dame Alice Lisle. This aged lady had in all innocence given a night's shelter to two fugitives from Sedgemoor, and as a result was hauled before Lord Jeffreys on a charge of treason. His lordship then terrorised the reluctant jury into giving a verdict of guilty, and sentenced Dame Alice to be burned alive according to the law, but under pressure from the cathedral clergy of Winchester, where the trial was held, agreed to suspend execution until the matter had been laid before the King. This was duly done; influential people pleaded for her life; but the only concession which could be wrung from King James was that she should be beheaded instead of burned, and the poor old lady paid with her life for showing mercy to a hunted man.

That story haunted Gervase from the first time he heard it, for if a woman could be condemned merely for giving food and shelter to Monmouth's men, what hope would there be for one who had repeatedly tricked the Royal soldiers and contrived the escape of a rebel officer? What had happened at Fairwood after his own departure? If Venner had not kept his word, if Priscilla's tongue had betrayed her as it had done so often in the past, or even if discovery had come by chance from some entirely different source, the result would be the same. Even as he walked here under the lime-trees, Elinor might be imprisoned in some noisome gaol, suffering untold indignities and brutality before being dragged off to a trial which was a mere travesty of justice.

There were times, of course, when his black mood lightened a little, and he could assure himself that the lack of news from Fairwood was in itself reassuring, an indication that life there was continuing its pleasant, placid course. Then would come uncertainties of a different kind, and he would recall again that closeness and understanding which he had sensed between Elinor and Hubert, and picture them happy together at the Priory, with so little thought for the exile across the sea that they did not even trouble themselves to send him a word of reassurance.

It was the uncertainty of it all which had brought him to the brink of desperation, the awful sense of being completely cut off from all contact with his home and family. In the days before the rebellion this had never troubled him. He had been too long away, grown too accustomed to the independent life of Court and camp, flung himself too wholeheartedly into plans for the liberation of his country and the establishment on its throne of a Protestant king. Now all that was lost, and in the losing of it he had been granted a glimpse of another kind of life, less ambitious perhaps, but infinitely richer, before that, too, was taken from him by the harsh force of circumstance.

Walking there in the September twilight beside the canal, Gervase came at length to a decision. He would risk one more letter to Sir William, as carefully-phrased as the first, so that if it fell into hostile hands no evidence against his family could be gleaned from it. He would wait a reasonable time for a reply, and if none came he would return to England. It would mean chancing his life again to do so, but if any of the fears which now tormented him were justified, life would be of very little value after all.

He halted, and stood staring down into the dark water, a tall, richly-dressed young man whose lean, arrogant face gave no hint of the turmoil in his mind. One or two passers-by glanced curiously at him, and in the eyes of one of them at least, a young girl tripping by on her father's arm, curiosity was tinged with admiration, but he was unaware of this fleeting interest. So absorbed was he in his thoughts that he might have been standing solitary upon a mountain-top rather than in a busy street, for he was making, not without a struggle, the final surrender of self, and realizing that if Elinor's happiness lay with Hubert rather than with him, he must find the means to set her free. That, he reflected with a flash of wry humour, should not be difficult for a known rebel in England today.

The resolve taken, he turned on his heel and went, walking briskly now, in the direction of his lodging, with the intention of writing to his grandfather without delay. It was nearly dark by the time he reached home, and the number of people in the streets was noticeably diminishing, while lights shone from nearly every house. Gervase stepped into the hall, pulling off his gloves as he went, and began to mount the broad, shallow staircase towards his rooms on the first floor. He was halfway up to the top when a movement above caused him to glance up, and then he stopped dead in his tracks, wondering if he were the victim of some strange hallucination.

From the topmost stair of the flight, and so level with his astonished gaze, a little, glossy-coated spaniel was regarding him with bright, inquiring eyes. Its pink tongue lolled from its mouth, and its absurd tail moved slowly from side to side in uncertain welcome.

"Duchess!" Gervase breathed incredulously. "Duchess!"

At the sound of its name the dog made a prancing movement, and the action of its tail accelerated furiously. Then it uttered a sharp yelp of delight, and scampered off along the upper hall towards the half-open door at the farther end.

Gervase mounted the remaining stairs two at a time and raced after it, and as he burst into his own parlour the slim, dark girl in black who had been sitting beside the fire rose to her feet and turned towards him. In that moment of reunion there was no room for doubt, he did not even pause to wonder at the miracle of her presence there, but strode forward and caught her in an embrace to which she responded as naturally as a flower to sunlight.

For a few timeless moments they clung together, but then as his hold slackened and he looked down at her, the significance of her sombre attire dawned upon him. He said in a low voice: "My grandfather?"

Elinor nodded. "He died a little less than a month

ago, Gervase," she replied gently. "Hubert and I were with him at the end, and the last words he spoke were of you. 'Tell him,' he said, 'that I die happy in the knowledge that all that is dearest to me I leave in worthy hands.'"

A spasm of pain crossed Gervase's face. "Worthy!" he repeated bitterly. "How can I ever be that?"

"He deemed you so," she reminded him softly. "It is for you to prove his faith justified."

They were silent for a space, Gervase staring into the fire and Elinor watching him with loving compassionate eyes. The news of his grandfather's death had moved him deeply, even though he had known it must come soon, and he was pierced with sharp regret for all the pain he had caused the good old man. Sir William had been a stern guardian, often autocratic, sometimes intolerant, but unfailingly kind and wise. When he had been harsh, demanding from others a degree of self-discipline and self-denial to match his own, it was always with good cause and he was usually proved right in the end. Now he was dead, and through sorrow, and self-reproach Gervase was conscious of a profound thankfulness that Elinor had persuaded him to make peace with Sir William while the opportunity still offered.

His gaze, returning to her face, found grief there, and weariness, and he felt himself filled with an overwhelming tenderness. He said gently: "We both loved him, my dear, and as long as loving memory endures, he is not lost to us. Try to find comfort in that."

Her eyes filled with tears and she hid her face against his chest. Sir William's death had left an aching void in her life, and a greater sense of loss than she had known even when her father died, and nothing, it seemed, had been able to pierce the frozen desolation she felt. Hubert's anxious, affectionate concern, the well-meant comforting words of friends, the honest grief of the country-folk for the man they had trusted and respected, had touched her mind but not her heart. Dry-eyed, she had sat by his death-bed, and knelt to pray for him in the chapel, and all the while the tears had waited somewhere deep within her, deep as the sorrow which could find no relief in outward expression. Now Gervase's simple words had somehow reached her where all else had failed, and she could weep at last, not bitterly, but with a blessed feeling of relief.

Gervase guessed something of this and at first made no attempt to soothe her, but merely held her close, his cheek against her hair, conscious of a profound gratitude that she was here in his arms, and all his dread fears proved groundless. Remembering the decision made such a short while since under the lime-trees, he had the sudden odd fancy that had he not made it, he would not have found her waiting for him on his return. Not until he could bring himself to set her free could she come to him.

Yet how had she come, and why? Slowly the more practical aspects of her arrival asserted themselves in his mind, shaping a score of questions which only she could answer. He tilted her face up towards his and smiled into her still tearful eyes.

"I am so overcome by your presence here that it has only just occurred to me to ask how it comes about," he said. "Is Hubert with you?" She shook her head, and he added incredulously: "You did not make the journey from England alone?"

"No, Hezekiah and Martha came with me. Your servant has taken them under his care."

Gervase looked surprised. "Were they not unwilling to leave their home and go travelling at their time of life?"

"They refused to be left behind," Elinor replied with a faint smile. "I would have chosen younger attendants, deeming them, as you do, too old to uproot themselves from their native land, but they would not hear of it. I think it would have broken their hearts had I not agreed to bring them, and what could I do in the face of such devotion?"

"Then you did leave Fairwood from choice? You were not obliged to take flight?"

Elinor looked puzzled. "No, all is well at home. As I told you in my letter, we were not troubled again by the authorities after Colonel Venner's visit ended."

"I had no letter," Gervase said quietly. "No word at all from Fairwood since the day I left. I have been near frantic with anxiety."

"Oh, my dear!" Elinor's hand lifted in an impulsive gesture to touch his cheek. "When we received the news that you were safe in France, I wrote to tell you that all had fallen out as we had planned, and the letter should have been waiting for you here. Of Sir William's death I did not write. I felt that such news as that I must break to you myself."

Gervase looked at her for a moment in silence. Then he led her back to the chair from which she had risen to greet him, and, drawing forward a stool, sat down at her side and took her hands in his.

"In these uncertain times it is not rare for a letter to go astray," he said, "so tell me now, since I know nothing of it, what followed my departure from Fairwood. I have been picturing all manner of disasters befalling you."

Her fingers tightened upon his.

"And all the while there was not the least need for anxiety," she said contritely. "Master Ember's man came back by way of Fairwood, and told us that he had left you with trustworthy folk in a village on the Devon coast, so we knew that you had gone so far in safety. Then, after what seemed an eternity of anxiety, Sir William received the letter you wrote to him from France. As he had promised, he sent word at once to Colonel Venner, who, as you may depend, had kept in close touch with us meanwhile, and he came to the Priory as soon as he was able. When he came, Sir William sent for Priscilla—it was the first time she had been admitted to his presence since the Colonel's previous visit—and gave her the confession she had signed that day, bidding her hand it to Venner.

" 'I gave you my word,' he told him, 'and no one outside this room is aware of the existence of that document, so destroy it, and your secret will be safe. I also withdraw my objection to your marriage. Take your mistress and go. I desire to see neither of you again.'

"There was black fury in Venner's face, but he contrived to subdue it. He just bowed very coldly to Sir William, and took Priscilla's hand and led her out of the room. All was in readiness, they were married in the chapel, and left Fairwood again that same day."

There was silence for a little while after she had finished speaking. She was afraid to look at his face for fear of what she might read there, and fixed her gaze instead upon their joined hands, drawing comfort from the sight, and from the warm, strong clasp of his fingers upon hers.

After what seemed a very long time, Gervase said slowly: "That, after all, was what Priscilla desired, and I suppose none of us have the right to blame her for the means she used to gain her own way. She did what she could to mend matters, when she realized how Venner had tricked her. The only wonder is that she was still willing to marry him after that."

"I do not blame her now," Elinor replied in a low voice, "for I believe that she loves Colonel Venner more deeply than he deserves. I hope that he will make her happy, though I would place no dependence upon it."

"No more would I," Gervase agreed soberly, "but at least she follows now the path of her own choosing, and can blame no one but herself if it does not lead to happiness."

Neither words nor tone suggested that he was mourning a twice-lost love, and Elinor plucked up courage to lift her eyes to his face. What she saw there caused her heart to leap joyfully, but at the same time filled her with unwonted shyness. Her gaze dropped again, and she said breathlessly: "I have something for you. Loose my hand, and I will give it to you."

He did as she asked, and she took something from her pocket and held it out to him. It was the gold signet ring he had taken from his finger and given into her keeping on the day he assumed the identity of Jacob Hunt.

"You may safely wear it now," she said softly, "and never lay it aside again. I have guarded it carefully against this day."

He thanked her and took the ring from her outstretched hand, but as he slipped it on to his finger he said with a touch of bitterness: "I may wear it as long as I remain in exile. If I return to England it must needs be under an assumed name."

The sorrow and anger in his voice did not escape her, and she laid her hand over his again.

"Perhaps your exile will not be of long duration, Gervase. Before Sir William died, he had us write to every person of his acquaintance who has the least influence at Court, in the hope of enlisting their aid to obtain a pardon for you. If his efforts on your behalf bear fruit, we may be back at Fairwood before the year is out."

Gervase shook his head. "Do not place any dependence upon it, Elinor! My grandfather had been long away from Court, and the past services of our family to the Crown are not likely to outweigh, in the eyes of King James, my present rebellion against it. It is his intention to make of the West Country an example of the dire consequences befalling any who rebel against his authority, and so to discourage others from attempting it. You, who have come straight from Somerset, must know that even better than I."

She was too level-headed not to perceive the truth of what he said, and honest enough to admit that she had put too much dependence on a slender chance. She refused to be cast down, however, and said after only a moment's pause: "Well, perhaps a pardon cannot be obtained from King James, but he is not a young man, and when he dies there will be a Protestant on the throne again. Then we may return to England."

"Perhaps," Gervase agreed cautiously, "though Prince William is not likely to look with kindness upon those who supported one who would have usurped his future crown." He rose to his feet with a restless, impatient movement, while Elinor watched him with troubled eyes. "The Duke should never have heeded those who urged him to proclaim himself King! That was the greatest blunder of the whole campaign! Had it not been committed, who can tell how the venture might have ended?"

He rested one hand against the mantel and stood looking down into the fire, the leaping flames casting a flickering light across his face. For a while there was silence in the room, and then Gervase roused himself from his thoughts and looked again towards Elinor.

"What use to speak of that now?" he said with a sigh. "It is easy to be wise when all is done. The Duke is dead, and many of his followers with him, and we few who escaped the holocaust must give thanks that we are left with life and freedom, even though we must enjoy them in a foreign land."

"Perhaps," Elinor suggested diffidently, "when the Prince and Princess of Orange succeed to the throne, those old enmities will be forgotten. Sufficiently, at least, for you to return to England, as long as you live quietly at Fairwood and take no part in public life. Could you be content with that?"

"Content?" he repeated. "I would ask no more of life! I have had my fill of the great world, the intrigues and the battles, the petty jealousies, and the high adventures wherein one gambles with the lives of men. It is the small world of home and family I covet now. When it was mine for the taking I looked on it with contempt, but now it is beyond my reach I can see that it is worth more than all the rest."

Elinor could feel her heart beating fast, and realized that her hands were trembling. She clasped them tightly together in her lap, and looking steadfastly down at them, said in a low voice: "Not wholly beyond your reach, Gervase. We are all happiest in a place we know and love, but home can be anywhere in the world. It is not merely a certain house or a certain country, but is built from shared joys and shared sorrows, from laughter and tears, kindness and contentment," she hesitated, and then added very softly, "and most of all from love."

There was another, longer silence. On the hearth a log fell apart, sending up a shower of sparks, and Duchess, sleeping before the fire, half roused, stretched luxuriously and sank back into slumber. Elinor waited breathlessly wondering if she had been mistaken, if his words and the warmth with which he had greeted her had tricked her into saying too much.

It seemed a very long time before Gervase spoke again, and when at length he did, it was merely to ask, with seeming irrelevance: "What of Hubert? You have not spoken of him at all."

"Hubert?" She looked up at him in hurt surprise, shocked by the unexpectedness of the question. "I left him well. He sends you his affectionate duty, and assures you that he will care faithfully for Fairwood until you return."

"He has my gratitude. And when I return, what then?"

She looked at him with puzzled, anxious eyes. "I believe he wishes to try his fortune in London. That has long been his desire, but in the past it was not possible of fulfilment."

"He has confided his hopes to you, of course?"

"Of course," she agreed hesitantly. "Why should he not? He is ambitious and the great world of which you say you have had a surfeit calls strongly to him. Given the opportunity, I think he will one day make in it no mean place for himself. Sir William thought so, too. Before he died, he urged Hubert to leave Fairwood when it became possible for him to do so, and to fashion his own life to his own ideals and hopes."

She broke off, remembering the last occasion on which she and Hubert had spoken of the future, on the day before her departure. He had told her then of the decision he had reached, to leave Fairwood when she and Gervase returned.

"For I could not stay here, Nell," he had said with quiet finality. "My grandfather knew that when he urged this course upon me, but even if he had not done so, I think I must have reached such a decision alone. I cannot live for ever in the shadow of my grandfather and my brother. I must justify myself, in my own eyes if in no one else's."

"And he will do so," she said reflectively now, more to herself than to Gervase. "Whatever difficulties stand in his way, I believe he will conquer them in the end."

"So Hubert is to conquer all!" There was bitter irony in Gervase's voice. "Your opinion of him is high indeed!"

"I speak only what I believe to be true," she protested. "What else would you have me say?"

"I would have you tell me why you came to Holland," he said with sudden intensity. "Why you left the home where you are so beloved, to journey to a strange land. Was it because you felt it your duty, or because it was my grandfather's command that you should do so when he died? It cannot be by Hubert's advice! He would not wish you to leave Fairwood."

"I do not understand!" Tears of bewilderment and dismay welled up in Elinor's eyes. "Are you displeased that I came? Why do you speak so strangely of Hubert?"

Gervase turned abruptly back to the fireplace, gripping the carved beam above it with both hands, his head bowed so that she could not see his face. When he spoke again his voice was rough with emotion.

"Because since the day I left Fairwood I have suffered the tortures of the damned, picturing you together there. He loves you! I realized that the first time I saw you together, and it would not be surprising if you loved him in return. God knows he deserves it more than I!"

Understanding flooded over her, and with it a joy so overwhelming that for several moments she could not trust herself to speak. Then, because she was human, she took a small revenge for the shock he had dealt her a few minutes earlier.

"I do love him," she said quietly, and knew, by the sudden stiffening of his tall figure, and the tightening of his hands upon the beam, that her own shocked dismay was repaid in full. She went on quietly: "I love him deeply and truly, as a sister should. He has been my friend and adviser, a staunch support and comfort in time of trouble, and he will always hold a special place in my heart. But love of the kind you speak of I have given to one man only, and he is my husband."

"Elinor!" He swung round to face her, his eyes alight with hope. "Do you mean it? Is it possible, after the way I have neglected you since our marriage?"

"Oh, my love!" She put out her hand to him, laughing a little although there were still tears in her eyes. "I was lost from the moment of our first meeting, and nothing that followed could change that. Why else do you suppose I came here?"

He took the outstretched hand and drew her up out of the chair and into his arms.

"I deserve nothing, and am given the whole world," he said softly. "My dear one, I have caused you much sorrow in the past, but I will never, God aiding me, do so again." He took her left hand, and looked down at the plain gold band encircling the third finger. "It is five years since I placed this ring here, but the vows I made with my lips that day I make again now, with all my heart."

"I, too," she whispered. "This is our true marriage, Gervase, and what does exile matter as long as we can be together? Our home is in each other's heart."

The chill autumn wind sighed round the house, and the first rain from the darkening sky drove in a flurry of drops against the window-panes, but Gervase and Elinor paid no heed. The dark summer was ending, and, lit by the bright blaze of love and faith, the prospect of winter could not daunt them.

Sylvia Thorpe

Sparkling novels of love and conquest set against the colorful background of historic England. Here are stories you will savor word by word, page by spellbinding page into the wee hours of the night.

☐	BEGGAR ON HORSEBACK	23091-0	1.50
☐	CAPTAIN GALLANT	Q2709	1.50
☐	FAIR SHINE THE DAY	23229-8	1.75
☐	THE GOLDEN PANTHER	23006-6	1.50
☐	THE RELUCTANT ADVENTURESS	23426-6	1.50
☐	ROGUES' COVENANT	23041-4	1.50
☐	ROMANTIC LADY	Q2910	1.50
☐	THE SCANDALOUS LADY ROBIN	23622-6	1.75
☐	THE SCAPEGRACE	23478-9	1.50
☐	THE SCARLET DOMINO	23220-4	1.50
☐	THE SILVER NIGHTINGALE	23379-9	1.50
☐	THE SWORD AND THE SHADOW	22945-9	1.50
☐	SWORD OF VENGEANCE	23136 4	1.50
☐	TARRINGTON CHASE	23520-3	1.75

Buy them at your local bookstores or use this handy coupon for ordering:

Mary Stewart

In 1960, Mary Stewart won the British Crime Writers Association Award, and in 1964 she won the Mystery Writers of America "Edgar" Award. Her bestselling novels continue to captivate her many readers.

☐	AIRS ABOVE THE GROUND	23077-5	1.75
☐	THE CRYSTAL CAVE	23315-4	1.95
☐	THE GABRIEL HOUNDS	22971-8	1.75
☐	THE HOLLOW HILLS	23316-2	1.95
☐	THE IVY TREE	23251-4	1.75
☐	MADAM, WILL YOU TALK?	23250-6	1.75
☐	THE MOON-SPINNERS	23073-2	1.75
☐	MY BROTHER MICHAEL	22974-2	1.75
☐	NINE COACHES WAITING	23121-6	1.75
☐	THIS ROUGH MAGIC	22846-0	1.75
☐	THUNDER ON THE RIGHT	23100-3	1.75
☐	WILDFIRE AT MIDNIGHT	23317-0	1.75